AF421207

KNOCKED UP BY THE ROCKSTAR

A Mile High Rocked Novel, Book 2

CHRISTINA HOVLAND

For rights information, please contact:
Prospect Agency
551 Valley Road, PMB 377
Upper Montclair, NJ 07043
(718) 788-3217

Holly Ingraham, Development Editor
Shasta Schafer, Proofreader

<del>For Gretchen—
Because she'll get a "kick" out of it. Also, she totally deserves a book
dedicated to her awesomeness.</del>

This book is now dedicated to this picture of my cat licking her nose:

Author's Note

All of my books are standalone and can be read in any order, and the Mile High Rocked books are no different. However, there is some overlap between the events in these books. You'll notice two of the scenes in this book were also included in *Played by the Rockstar*, but now you're going to see them from the perspective of Courtney and Bax.

It is my hope that this opportunity allows for a rich reader experience.

Enjoy the story!

Christina

Chapter One
COURTNEY

COURTNEY LINCOLN WAS NEVER one to point fingers. Never one to be supremely philosophical either. But even she couldn't deny that the enemy of her enemy was a mega jerk-face.

She might not care for rock star Brennan Baxter—Bax—or his perpetual asshat rocker attitude, but she never wanted him to get run over by the tour bus or anything. Though a little nudge from the fender wouldn't hurt to deflate his ego a tad.

All that aside, she really didn't want him to get run over by the bus of life.

Unfortunately, that's pretty much what his ex-fiancée did to him. Figuratively, at least. According to the band manager, Hans, Bax's heart was well and truly crushed. This was not a fender bump. Nope. His ex had crushed him like a Valentine's Day lollipop under the heel of her Louboutin boots.

So, yeah, Bax's ex-fiancée was a mega jerk-face. Because even Bax didn't deserve that kind of betrayal.

"Explain to me why *I* have to go to save him. Don't we have people for that?" Courtney balanced the cell between her ear and her shoulder and scooted to the side so a gaggle of girls could hit up the ladies' room.

Taking her note from the Lizzo song, she flipped her brown hair over her shoulder and checked her nails.

Friday night was club night for Courtney and her friends. Thanks to her position as publicity manager for the band Dimefront—Bax's band—and being bassist Linx Lincoln's little sister, she'd dropped names like confetti in the ocean breeze and scored a VIP table at Pew, the latest and greatest nightclub in Los Angeles. The place where everyone who was anyone wanted to be seen.

Courtney was everyone who was anyone. Thus, here she was.

"He's almost to the Beverly Hills Hotel," Hans said, his deep voice clear—she was off the clubbing circuit for the night. The club and hotel were only a block apart, now the call made all kinds of sense. Blah, this stunk.

"C'mon, Court." Her best friend, Irina, strutted toward her in three-inch high heels and a little black sheath dress that accented her curves in all the right ways. Irina gestured toward the dance floor and did a little shimmy shake. "You're off duty tonight."

Oh, if only that were true. The teeny tiny nerve endings in Courtney's feet tickled, willing her forward toward Irina. Toward the dance floor and fun. Unfortunately, Hans continued yammering instructions, so she was very much on duty. That duty did not include getting her boogie on with Irina.

Courtney readjusted the phone to hear Hans better, but Irina rallied with hands on her hips and a mouth in a full pout.

"Did I lose you?" Hans asked.

"Uh-huh," Courtney said, making big eyes at her friend and then pointing toward the phone. "I mean, nuh-uh, I'm listening." Sort of anyway.

"You're not off duty, are you?" Irina's defeat was evident in the words as she folded her arms across her cleavage, bumping it up higher. Irina shook her head, so her shoulder-length blonde hair flicked against her chin. "Nope. You're totally working tonight."

Irina was 100 percent correct and about to be mega-disappointed, since they'd been planning this night for months.

"Hans? How did you even know where I am?" Courtney paused and glanced around the dark room where bodies on the dance floor squirmed and grooved. She shook her head. Nope, didn't need to know how Hans found her, because it would probably only serve to piss her off. "Never mind, don't answer that."

The Dimefront band manager seemed to know everything about everyone in the band and those who worked with the band.

Their location, latest medical checkup, preferred brand of snack food, and beverage choice.

"Beverly Hills Hotel," he said, since that's all he needed to say.

"Fine." Courtney huffed, looking longingly at the leather booth with the sleek black table that her friends would get to enjoy and she would not. Hans's marching instructions in place, she wrapped up the call and sighed.

"Which one this time?" Irina asked, her Taylor Swift red lips pinched to the side.

Courtney didn't answer, because her nonanswer told the story for her.

"Bax?" Irina lifted her eyebrows. "Seriously?"

Courtney sighed, nodded, and shoved her phone into her purse.

"But you got dressed up." Irina dove into full pout mode. "You cannot waste it on Bax. I forbid this."

She wasn't wrong that Courtney had gotten dressed up. In

her own stilettos and an adorably short red dress that stopped mid-thigh, Courtney had even gotten a blowout on her hair, fresh all-over waxing, and new fingernails.

"One drink first?" Irina asked, using her best impression of a sad basset hound.

"I really can't." But man, she wanted to.

Irina thought on that for two beats. "Half a drink?"

Courtney went in for a *sorry I have to leave, best friend* hug and squeezed before Irina could make it to the tequila shot suggestion that would be coming next. "Rain check. Tell the girls?"

Resignation etched on her face, Irina nodded. "This sucks."

Yes, indeed it did.

The grudge against Bax built with each footstep as Courtney hoofed it to the Beverly Hills Hotel. *Click. Tap.* Why couldn't he have picked a location closer to Hans? *Click. Tap.* Why did he always ruin things for her? *Click. Tap.* This didn't need to be her problem. *Click. Tap.* She had a life. A life where she made plans. *Click. Tap.* To finally embrace being single again and maybe bring a guy home. *Click. Tap.* A guy who wasn't looking to insert himself into her forever and ever.

She and the last guy, Levar, lasted about six months before it became clear he wanted more, while she wanted less. That got sticky quick, and she ended things with Levar. Then she took a break to think about what it was she wanted out of life.

Fun was what she wanted out of life. Nothing serious so she could embrace her free spirit and run with it.

Striding to stand near the valet, she did a quick check to see if Hans had sent any other details other than his request that she ensure Bax not check into the hotel, where he was sure to be seen.

Courtney's job was simply to ensure he was *not* seen.

Hans worked to make other arrangements at another hotel

where Bax could enter through the back, and they would book the room under a pseudonym. Courtney just needed to get him there, and then she could (maybe) get back to her night.

Maybe get back to having that fun she'd been searching for.

Depending on how long this took.

And how intense the Bax-induced headache was at the end.

Her cell chimed with an incoming message.

Hans: Bax ETA 3 Minutes

Courtney leaned against a pillar to fiddle with her phone. She texted her mom, then her brother.

This was literally the antithesis of having a good time.

Just then, Bax's Aston Martin slid into the pristine circular asphalt drive, heading for the valet stand.

Courtney stepped away from the pillar, shifted the thin strap of the Gucci purse on her shoulder, and placed her hand on the passenger door handle before Mr. Valet could even consider coming to check Bax in.

She pulled open the door. Thankfully, it wasn't locked. She slipped inside, right onto the leather, letting her skirt ride up just a touch on her legs. Not so much that it was indecent, just enough to make her point that she did not give two fucks what Bax thought of her or her clothing choices. Also, she'd gotten a spray tan earlier, since her skin was way pale and she had spent no time at the beach lately. Might as well show off that spray tan.

Bax had dirty-blond hair—some might call it brown. Really, it depended on the lighting. Gorgeous blue eyes that he did not deserve, and either he'd gotten a spray tan, too, or he'd hit the beach. Because he was also rocking a California tan. He'd probably hit the beach, knowing Bax.

He didn't even flick a look at her legs as he growled, "Fucking Hans."

Why did all the excessively hot guys have to be assholes?

"I believe the words you are searching for are 'Hey, Courtney!'" She settled into the leather, pulling the seat belt across her lap. "'Thanks for saving my ass.'"

Bax gripped the steering wheel and didn't move forward.

"I believe the words I am looking for are 'I need a hotel room for the night.'" This he said with a teensy bit of sadness that actually tugged on the little strings around her heart because he sounded like his old self. Brennan. The guy who grew up on the same street. The guy who started a band with her big brother.

The guy who eventually morphed into the asshole who was Bax.

"Hans has me on damage control." She balanced her purse on her knees and aimed for chipper. "Which means no one will see you going into this hotel the day before the tabloids trash your engagement."

Well, in truth, his ex had done the trashing.

The tabloids were just going to finish it tomorrow. So said Hans and her contact at *Raglan*—the most offensive and therefore most popular of the online tabloids.

The short version of the story? His ex-fiancée lived in his house, took his cash, enjoyed the trappings of his fame... while cheating on him with one of his Bel Air neighbors—an investment broker who wore suits.

"Where am I supposed to go?" he asked. And dammit again with the lack of Bax in his tone and a lot of Brennan. "Em's still at the house. I told her she could stay until she found somewhere else."

Courtney's eyebrows seemed to lift right up of their own accord. This was not normal Bax, because Bax was badass. This guy—the one with a voice crack—was not badass.

Brennan was the guy who used to be nice to Courtney

and shared his after-dinner Andes chocolate mints when their families went to supper together. He was the guy who assured her there was nothing wrong with her when Tommy Rigby broke her heart at sixteen. He was the one who made her feel seen when everyone was all eyes on her musical savant of a brother.

"Do you want to talk about it?" Courtney asked, dropping her tone into neutral territory and not you-have-me-up-against-a-wall-so-I'm-gonna-spit-in-your-eye territory. That's where they spent most of their time these days.

He shook his head, opening and closing his hands on the steering wheel.

"Do you want me to drive?" she asked—and not just because she'd never driven his Aston Martin before and would actually really enjoy it. The circumstances notwithstanding.

Instead of answering with words, Bax revved the engine and headed toward the road, winding around the tropical flowers and palm trees lit from the bottom with spotlights like they were the genuine celebrities on the property.

"How are your mom and dad?" Courtney asked, chirpy. She already knew how they were—her mom reported in on them often. They were presently on a world cruise they'd planned to stay on up until Bax's wedding—the wedding that wasn't happening anymore.

"They're fine. Currently in paradise or playing the slots on some ship. Right or left?" he asked, terse, without emotion.

Brennan was well and truly gone… again.

Yay.

Not.

"Gotta choose," he said with a growl. "Before the light turns green."

Yup, total Bax, which made her stomach hurt a little, since she hadn't seen the hope of Brennan like that in years. She sort of missed that guy. Missed who he had been back then.

Missed who *she* had been back then.

"Serious, Court. Right or left? Where to?" he asked, terse as hell.

She scowled and glanced at her cell to find a serious lack of instruction from Hans.

"Right," she said on a whim.

He turned. "Where are we going?"

"My condo."

"Court," Bax said. No… he didn't say it. His voice cracked a little as he whispered her name. Huh, maybe Brennan was back for more than a brief stay. "It's Friday night. Tell me you don't have plans?"

"Of course I *had* plans." She rolled her eyes dramatically and did a Vanna White air-swipe along her red dress. "Those plans, however, have been wrecked. So now I have new plans. You plans." She made sure the point came across that she didn't like those plans.

"Me," he said like a grunt.

"Ding, ding, ding." She twirled her index finger in his direction. "You."

"I can stay at Hans's place." He scowled. "If he won't let me check in at the hotel, I'll just stay with him. Then you can get back to your *plans*."

If only it were that simple, right? Alas, no. Simplicity was missing from the evening.

She shook her head, that blown-out brown hair tumbling.

"Hans stopped responding for right now, *which means* I don't know where he is or what magic he's whipping up. *Which means* I do not want to drive across town to find out that he's not home." She paused. Patted the dash of the truly impressive Aston Martin. "Besides, this is currently my ride. You can take me home. Then you can go wherever Hans directs."

"Fine." Bax's shoulders dropped. "Your place."

"My place."

He scratched his neck. "Where exactly is your place?"

"You don't know where I live?" she asked, a spicy little ache nestling in the center of her chest.

Unlike Hans, who knew everything about everyone, Bax was more of an "all about himself" kind of guy.

"Never needed to know until right this moment," he said, and the truth of those words stung.

So she relayed the address to Bax.

Brennan wasn't coming back, and that sort of tore a little more hurt into her heart.

Chapter Two
COURTNEY

HER CONDO WASN'T anything super special, though it was in one of the nicer buildings in this part of Los Angeles. Given that she traveled with the band or visited her parents where they lived in Tennessee and hung around there, she wasn't at her place very often. Irina lived across the hall and kept her eye on things when Courtney wasn't around.

When she bought furniture, she'd gone with white because it was easier to match. And the carpet in the apartment was already white. And she didn't really spill things on the regular, since she wasn't home often. So, yeah, she'd gone with fifty shades of white.

It worked for her, because as luck would have it, there were actually around fifty (or more) shades of white.

"Huh," Bax said upon entering her space. His not-really-a-question and not-really-a-grunt made no sense.

Whatever, this was her space, not his. The kitchen and living room were one big room with a small patio. There was no dining room, just an eat-in kitchen island with barstools. Her bedroom—the bigger of the two other rooms—was to the right, while the other room served as her office and shoe closet. She had a bit of a thing for collecting shoes.

Beside the kitchen, not the side near her bedroom, was the one and only bathroom.

This setup worked for her, since she rarely had guests, and when she… ahem… did, she didn't mind if they hopped in the shower with her.

It's not like she entertained like that often.

"Come on in." She tossed her keys in the bowl beside the front door, slipped off her shoes, and left her purse on the counter. "Home sweet home."

He paused at the wall of photos she kept. There were photos of her and Linx on the Dimefront Penny Pincher tour. One with her parents in their backyard by the tulips. Another with her and Irina—Irina decked out in doctor scrubs had just come from an audition for Emergency Blues.

"Huh," he said again.

That was grating on her nerves. Truly. The building was really nice. Perfect for what she needed. There was even a pool because… this was California. The workout area was nice too. Though she didn't use it often.

Ever. She didn't use it ever.

Still, she'd been in there, and they seemed to have lots of things that people who worked out would want. Machines and those weight rack thingies, and the big exercise balls that she liked to bounce on when she was a kid.

"Help yourself to the kitchen," Courtney said, heading to her bedroom to take off her big-ass hoop earrings and put on something made of cotton and comfy. "If you're hungry."

By the time she reemerged in jogger pants and a tank top, Bax was digging through her small pantry.

"What else you got?" Bax glanced up as he stuffed the cinnamon crunchy yumminess back on the shelf, next to the marshmallow puffies.

Courtney had a bit of an addiction to sugary breakfast cereal. Sue her. Actually, don't. She didn't really like lawyers and courthouses and… ugh.

Not that she subsisted entirely on cold cereal—she also had an entire freezer full of prepackaged lunches and dinners that only required a trip through the microwave to become delicious sustenance.

She pulled open the freezer door to offer her stash up to Bax.

"Frozen dinners?" He sounded appalled. Why did he think he had any right to be appalled?

Blah, he didn't have to sound so judgy about it.

Bax's body was his temple. He wasn't the rocker who required specific kinds of candy in his dressing room. No, he required some green juice stuff that looked disgusting and probably tasted like cucumbers and beets.

Courtney preferred frozen dinners and cereal and the occasional can of SpaghettiOs.

She crossed her arms over her chest. "You're always so critical. Have you considered… not?"

He scowled, grabbing another box of cereal to peruse the ingredient label. "I was checking into a hotel when I got told I couldn't. Now I'm here, I'm hungry, and there's no food."

"There's food." She gestured to the menagerie of cereal and frozen options.

"That's not food." He put the box back on the shelf.

Technically…

"They sell it at the store, people put it in their bodies, it keeps them alive, thus that makes it food," she countered.

He pinched his lips to the side.

Yeah, she felt that same way.

"I don't eat in much," she said in defense of herself. "When I do, I keep what I like on hand."

"I'll order something." He reached for his cell and thumbed open the screen. "Something edible."

She grabbed it from his hand. Really, she didn't expect he'd let her take it, but his reflexes must've been off because of the whole breakup thing.

"You can't order as *you*, because then someone will know you're here." No one could know he was there. Which was why she'd moved her car out of the one-car garage that came with the place, and he'd pulled his car inside to be tucked in safely where no roving paparazzi could happen upon it.

She wasn't that altruistic, but she was the one who would deal with the fallout once the photographers found Bax and started weaving stories together that were entirely untrue.

"Okay, then you order in." He pointed to his phone.

The club would've been so much more fun.

"What do you want me to order?" Because actually she'd been looking forward to dinner out with her girls and not eating frozen dinner either.

"I don't know. You stole my phone. I can't search to see what's open." Now he was just being difficult.

"I don't trust you with your phone right now. You'll probably just call the paparazzi and tell them you're here to spite me and make my job harder." That was the God's honest truth, she would not put it past him.

"Yeah. Probably," he conceded, rolling his tongue over his bottom lip.

"Bax." She squinted her eyelids into slits. "Don't be difficult about this."

He didn't respond.

"Please," she added for good measure.

"I decided something today."

"Oh?" She didn't like the sound of that one teeny tiny bit.

"I'm ready to be done with the whole fame thing," he said, shoving his hands in the pockets of his jeans and looking like a puppy she'd just kicked.

She had not kicked him. For the record.

"If they want to know where I am, tell 'em," he said.

"No." She shook her head and channeled that tone her mom used when she was insistent on something she thought was important. "Maybe Bax of yesterday was done with fame. But Bax of today needs to seriously reconsider his options." This was her professional opinion and she was sticking to it.

Huh. That seemed to get his attention.

"Brennan Baxter, you built this." She waved a hand up and down in front of him. "You're a big deal. Stop trying to downplay what that means." Also, one did not just extract himself from the empire he'd built with the band Dimefront. Not without a lot of forethought and planning and consulting his freaking publicist. Otherwise, it hurt the people who relied on the band for their income.

She for one.

But also the sound guys and the roadies and the drivers and the producers and the list went on and on.

"I want to be," he said, again. "Done."

"You don't."

"I. Do."

"Okay." She held up her hands, but still kept her grip on his phone—just in case he wanted to make a swipe at it. "Maybe right now you want to be. Maybe yesterday you wanted to be. Things changed. Your life plans changed. You've got bills, people who rely on you for their paychecks. Are you really going to screw everyone over on a whim because a bad thing happened to you?"

"You know nothing about me," he said, the words ice. "This has been coming for a long time."

"I know everything about you," she replied. "We know everything about each other." That was 99 percent of the issue between them. They knew each other too well. Maybe he didn't know her address, but it couldn't have been a shock to walk into her condo and find a pantry of cereal and a freezer of premade meals.

Just like she knew that if she walked into his kitchen, she'd find tofu and cucumbers.

That was what came from growing up across the street

from one another. Growing up together. From finding their way to Hollywood as a team with Knox and Linx. They knew each other.

They didn't like each other, sure—but they knew each other.

"If you stopped for more than two seconds," her voice wobbled. That wasn't good, no voice wobbling allowed. No feelings around this guy. "If you let yourself heal from this bullshit that Em is dragging you through, then maybe you'll come out on the other side and realize you've got many people who care about you."

"Like you?" he asked. He didn't sound hopeful, he sounded like this was an accusation.

"No." She shook her head. "I got over caring for you a long time ago."

Things in her life got easier when she didn't care about Brennan Baxter or what he thought of her life choices.

The light in his eyes dimmed a smidge.

Perhaps that was too low a blow for the current circumstance. He deserved to be off-kilter, but... "Bax, I need you to let Hans and me deal with the media and whatever Em's going to say. We figure out the planning, because this is our gig. When you're onstage, that's your gig. We don't tell you how to do it."

"You did." He glanced up from where he'd been staring laser daggers into the carpeting of her floor.

One time. One stupid time early in the game she caught him feeling up a groupie behind the speakers and she'd thought Brennan was better than that. Thought that he wanted to be better than the cliché of a rocker he'd apparently become. She seriously thought he was the kind of guy who wouldn't take advantage of his celebrity to get a few rocks off. She'd said that, out loud, and it hadn't gone well.

The parting shot was when the woman he felt up told

Courtney she was jealous because she wasn't a girl who got the rock star.

It stung because Bax didn't correct her, so maybe it was true. From that moment forward it was game on between Courtney and Bax.

Hating him and sparring was easier than missing Brennan.

"Can we puh-lease move forward from *one* thing I said years ago? I made a suggestion." She thought her opinion mattered to him. Thought he appreciated her thoughts. Turned out, he *really* didn't. "You didn't like my suggestion. We survived. I learned my lesson."

Don't talk to Bax. Or care about him. Or wonder why you're not the kind of girl Bax would give a bracelet to.

He grunted.

"I'm ordering Mendochetti's." She made a spur-of-the-moment choice.

He raised his eyebrows at that. "Thin crust. Veggie and Canadian bacon. No pepperoni or sausage."

"Thin crust. Pepperoni on half."

She didn't like pepperoni, but she would not give him exactly what he wanted either.

"As long as your pepperoni doesn't touch my half."

"For once, we agree on something," she said.

"At least we agree on the important stuff," he said under his breath.

She wasn't totally in agreement with that assertion, but she'd hit her quota of arguing with Bax for the decade, so she figured she'd let that one go.

The pizza was delivered quickly, and they settled in front of the television. She turned on her favorite girl-meets-boy reality show du jour, the one she was currently bingeing on Hulu.

"What the hell is this?" he asked, gesturing to the TV with his pizza.

"It's television." She picked off a pepperoni from her slice.

"That's like the sugary cereal of television." He made a gagging nose.

"Someone really jacked your logic up if you think that's a bad thing."

Not that she could really defend hers as she was picking off the make-a-point pepperonis.

They didn't talk for a while after that. Which, to be clear, was a good thing.

"Thank you for this," he said finally, eyes still riveted on the television like he actually might be interested in the show—he wasn't, she was sure.

"You're welcome for this," she replied, ripping off another slice of pepperoni.

Her phone finally—thank hell, finally—chimed with a message from Hans.

Hans: Problem. He needs to sit tight at your place. Photogs everywhere. He gets your couch, yeah?

Uh. No. No. No. No.

Courtney lifted her phone and dialed Hans.

"Are you serious right now?" Truly, Courtney didn't mean to sound shrill. This, however, was not good news.

Bad news.

This was bad news.

"We've got to keep him low," Hans said. For the first time since she'd known him, he actually sounded tired.

Generally, Hans had an unlimited amount of energy.

Hans was a big guy. Big in the bodybuilding sense. When he wasn't managing the band, he was hitting the gym. Brown skin, brown eyes, and a kick-ass smile that made up for the fact that he'd probably planted a microchip tracker somewhere in her shoes. Because how else did he know where she was every second?

"A few hours? A few days? What are we talking?" Courtney specifically didn't look at Bax as he moved to the kitchen and… huh, he washed his plate. That was nice of him. Very un-Bax-like.

"A few days? Nah. More like weeks," Hans corrected. "Em preempted. She went to TMZ. She's looking to spill every drop of tea about their relationship. This is bad."

Courtney gasped. Bax stilled.

"Em went to TMZ," Courtney said to his back.

Okay. Right. Weeks. Shit.

Her mind began working out which angle she would play as publicist. Where Bax could go in the interim—because her house was very temporary. They'd probably kill each other in the literal sense if forced to live together for any extended period.

Em had not waited for *Raglan*'s exposé—an exposé Courtney was pretty certain she had tempered to nearly nothing.

But if Em went straight to TMZ…

"She made some choices to get the press on her side so she could nudge along a Dimefront documentary deal," Hans said, filling in Courtney.

Em's side of the story painted Bax as a womanizer— which he was. Or he used to be. He hadn't been since Em came into the picture.

Her side of the story painted Bax as an absent partner— which, when he was on tour, he was. But he hadn't been on tour in over a year. Not since he'd proposed to her.

Her side of the story made Em look like she was a saint, while Bax was the devil. Which, while Bax might be part-devil, Em didn't exactly have angel wings. Her past was rockier than Bax's.

"We spill it. We spill Em's tea," Courtney decided in the

moment. That was the angle they'd have to take. "Bags, coffee beans, anything and everything."

Hans had been filling the teakettle on Em for a while. They both had a bad feeling about her from the beginning.

Usually, Courtney wasn't one for fighting fire with fire. She preferred water for flames. Stay above that little line that etched markings onto one's soul.

But this wasn't about her.

This was about the band.

Saving a lot of terrible publicity.

"No," Bax said. Firm. He set the plate down in the dish rack and leaned into the edge of the counter, his back still to Courtney. "We stay out of it. It'll go away."

"Did you catch that?" Courtney asked Hans, already knowing he totally caught that.

"Let me talk to him," Hans said.

Courtney had no issue handing over the phone and letting Hans talk some actual sense into her houseguest.

Judging by the scowl, Bax was not impressed with what Hans had to say. Still, he listened. Because that was what a person did when Hans spoke.

"Fine, yeah." Bax glanced up and clocked her with his gaze, perma-frown plastered in place. "I'll stay here. But we don't go after Em. Agreed?" He lowered his voice a little. "She's still Em."

Right. On that note, she'd just go grab him a towel and some bedding for the couch.

———————————————

Chapter Three

BAX

———————————————

LAST NIGHT, Bax decided he might as well embrace his fucked-up life. He also stopped fighting Hans about staying with Courtney while Hans figured out a longer-term plan. Unfortunately, Hans made good points, Courtney's couch did not suck, and her shower was amazing. He might as well live in this shower.

Arm against the tile, he dropped his head to his forearm, letting the water flow over his back.

His band was totally fucked.

His relationship was totally fucked.

He didn't even have a dog.

He'd always wanted a dog, but Em didn't like dogs. Apparently, what Em enjoyed was stepping out on him, so he was questioning a lot of her likes and dislikes. He resolved right then that her name was off-limits—the woman had no name as far as he was concerned.

More than the anger at her was the anger at him. He fucking knew better than to get in a tangle with her. Not when he knew her history, knew he was not what she wanted, but he was a damn fine plaything while it lasted. A perpetual ATM and credit card with unlimited cash back bonus rewards.

He shook the water from the hair he'd allowed to grow longer than usual, since his not-to-be-named ex preferred the length.

A haircut was in order.

Yeah, that was what he needed.

First, a dog, then a haircut.

Except a haircut would relieve none of the pent-up anxious stress brewing inside.

The thing he needed?

Fuck it. The thing he needed was a release from this stress. Something that didn't matter. Goddamn, just something to take the edge off of this… anger mixed with a heavy dose of pain.

Make no mistake, it fuckin' hurt. His heart hurt. His soul hurt. His head hurt.

Thanks to Courtney's outstanding couch, his back didn't hurt though. He should probably tell her that she picked good furniture. They hadn't attempted to say nice things to each other for quite some time until last night.

Resolved to make things right, he let the water in Courtney's shower beat into his skin, washing away the night before, Em's betrayal, and what he had to face today.

Courtney said she had his public relations challenges in hand. He didn't doubt it, she was excellent at her job.

The only thing he had in hand was his dick.

His life was fucked beyond all recognition, and his dick still wanted an early morning release. Given that he'd lived in this body for, oh, going on thirty-some years, he knew that if he didn't handle this situation, then he'd be more of an asshole than usual later in the day.

Everybody around him deserved better than that.

He closed his eyes, gave himself a stroke, and squeezed the tip with just the right amount of pressure, letting nothingness take over any space in his brain with a shiver.

Given that most of his spank bank currently comprised a

woman he did not want to think about and who wouldn't be named, he scrolled back through his mind. Unfortunately, or fortunately, depending on how a guy looked at it, Courtney's face when she climbed into his car came to the forefront. The way her dress crept up high on her thigh.

The sass and attitude she tossed at him.

He stroked again and groaned.

Okay, let's just see where this went.

He moved his hand up and down on his shaft, his whole body shivering and clenching along with his fist.

Courtney's legs with just the little gap between her thighs, sitting in his Aston Martin. She could just take a finger or two and slide it up along her inner thigh.

His balls tightened in response. He gripped harder.

Fuck it, she was off-limits, but this was a fantasy and no one else had to know.

He stroked. He moaned. The water sluiced over his shoulders.

"Oh my God," Courtney of his fantasy said, more than a little breathy.

"That's right, baby," he murmured, pressing his eyelids shut so he wouldn't ruin the fantasy that was giving him the best erection he'd experienced in forever.

"Holy crap, you're... Oh my God," Fantasy Courtney whispered, her voice pitching higher at the end so it wasn't really a whisper anymore.

His dick hardened further in his palm and damn. Fuck. Shit. He was playing with fire.

"Enjoy the ride, Court," he murmured to Fantasy Courtney.

His forehead clunked against the clear glass of her shower, and breathing heavy, he opened his eyes and—

Shit. Damn. Fuck.

"Are you seriously thinking of me? While you—" Courtney gestured to his hand and what it held.

Uh-huh. Courtney was standing there in her robe, her mouth a perfect little circle, her eyes fastened right on what his hand was doing to himself.

He blinked away a whole slew of water.

This wasn't Fantasy Courtney. This was the real deal.

She was breathing faster as she said, "You've been in here forever…"

Her abundance of brown hair piled high on the crown of her head. Her perfectly pink lips still in that adorable little O. Her eyes fastened on his dick while her pupils dilated.

Now, he wasn't entirely sure of the protocol here.

She continued on. "I got worried. You didn't answer when I knocked."

Yeah, he'd been fucking his hand right about then.

Annnd, she kept talking. "I thought maybe something happened…"

Given that he was the naked one, he figured she should be the one to turn around and leave.

Given that this was her shower, maybe it should be him?

In any case, somebody should leave.

Yet his hand moved once more on his shaft to ease just a smidge of the ache.

That cute little tongue of hers darted out to lick at her bottom lip, wetting it there.

"In or out," he said, instead of telling her how absolutely gorgeous she looked like that—first thing in the morning, her hair a mess, her face fresh from sleep. Instead of telling her how comfortable her couch was for sleep.

The least he could do was give her a compliment after he'd jacked her hot water and also jacked…

"Your call," he continued, instead of apologizing for giving himself a hand job with her coconut-scented conditioner.

"My call?" Her eyes flared dangerously.

He was fucked. She would kick his ass out on the sidewalk

and have every reason to do it. Then what would the tabloids think? Everyone was looking for his car. Looking to see where Bax went to lick his wounds.

He dropped his hand from his dick, ready to turn off the water and take his walking papers. Willing his erection to chill for a while.

But Courtney? Giving him a demand to get the hell out? *That* is not what she did.

No. She did *not* kick his ass out on the sidewalk.

Courtney Lincoln untied her robe and let it fall to the floor. "I'm in."

Uh, fuck him to Florida. The water should've been a cold wake-up call instead of hot steam.

But she kicked the robe aside, and he held her with his gaze, eye fucking her as she slipped black cotton panties over her thighs, and stepped out of them.

Was this some kind of test? Probably a test.

Seeing as he started the exam, he should probably have a better idea of what was going down.

Though, given that she opened the shower door and her eyes fell on his hand and what it was doing, he might be the one going down.

"Don't say a word," she said, low, with a note of sultry he didn't know she possessed. "And please, don't stop on my account."

More of his blood pooled south, which was the only reason he took her command and said nothing. Because, really, he should've told her not to be bossy. That was what he should've done.

"Hands to the wall." She said this like she was in charge of everything and had it under control.

Good. Fuck. He needed someone to just take over for a while.

He turned to put his hands on the wall as her palm ran up his back to the muscles of his shoulders, massaging there.

The groan that slipped from his lips? Totally not his fault.

Not his fault, because she gave up on his shoulders and trailed her hand along his abs to his twitching dick standing at attention in front of him.

With one hand, she gripped the shaft and let the conditioner and water combination do their thing.

Her tits pressed against his back, and the scent of her surrounded him. This was better than any deposit he'd ever made in his spank bank, that was for damn sure.

On that thought, he nearly came all over her fingers. But he caught himself, regained control when he rinsed the rest of the conditioner from himself and turned around, so his dick slipped between her legs.

Not inside her body, just saying hello to prove a very thick point.

Opening his mouth to say something—what? He did not know. But something. Probably something that would come out wrong, since that was usually how it went with Courtney. Best of intentions were slaughtered as soon as his trap flapped with her sharing his space.

"Don't you say anything," she gritted out as he pushed her against the tile wall. She lifted her leg to wrap around his outer thigh and give him better access. In that moment, it appeared every argument, every pissed off word they'd spoken to each other, had led them right to this moment.

A moment where there were no words. Oh, there were loads of sounds. Mostly grunts. A few moans, but nothing coherent.

The water continued to pelt them when he gave her a boost. She wrapped her legs around him, and he drove home. Drove home while ensuring he gave plenty of attention to the bundle of nerves at her center.

Her nails bit into his back as she bucked against him, murmuring, "Yes."

Over and over, it was yes.

"Don't stop." She pressed those talons of hers into his back, and, honest as fuck, her body squeezed and her orgasm brought him straight to the edge with her.

All that time they'd spent arguing about bullshit and they could've been doing this instead? They should've been doing this instead.

Her internal muscles between her legs wrung him dry while her legs gripped his waist harder.

The water stopped being so hot and turned lukewarm right about the same time the expression in her eyes shifted.

He didn't dare move. Not only because he'd just fucked his friend's sister against the shower wall. Not because he'd just fucked his publicist against the shower wall. And not because he was pretty sure that in doing both things, he'd fucked himself.

"Did I hurt you?" he asked, careful as he helped her feet to the floor. He should've gone slower. Paid more attention that he didn't hurt her when he pushed inside.

She was wobbly. Hell, he was wobbly too.

One did not come like the FedEx delivery man during the holiday rush without being wobbly.

"No." She stepped back. He didn't touch her, given that didn't seem to be what she wanted. "You didn't hurt me."

"Good." He wasn't entirely sure where to look. They were both there. Naked. Spent.

"Let's, uh…" She gestured between them. "This didn't…"

"Happen." He finished her thought for her, knowing exactly what she wanted to say.

"Right. It didn't." She pulled open the door and scrambled to grab her robe. He'd never seen a woman cover herself with terry cloth so quickly.

He didn't move, didn't know where he'd go if he moved. But the water was getting cooler by the second, so he probably should grab a towel and see himself out.

Which was precisely what he did because he was an asshole.

And what had happened?

Like she said, it never happened.

Chapter Four
BAX

Five Weeks Later

HANGING with Knox sucked because Knox had a lot of opinions about how things should be and didn't mind sharing those. But also did not suck, because they were on a beach.

The way things went down after Bax had fucked up in Courtney's shower was straightforward.

He left, went to Hans, spilled the whole can of beans in Hans's office because Hans would've figured it out anyway.

Then he did what Hans said to do—which was hop on a flight to Bermuda with Knox.

This was one of the few plans Hans had come up with that Bax did not hate. He understood Knox a helluva lot more than he understood Courtney. Understood why others didn't get who Knox was. Why he wasn't the favorite.

The guy had preferences.

Preferences and no problem telling the entire world what those were.

Which made him not the best guy to go on an extended vacation with, to go on a multi-country world tour with, or to even have dinner with.

Yet here they were in Bermuda.

Knox. Bax. And Courtney Lincoln in his brain.

Oh yeah, she took up permanent residence in Bax's skull. Even the waves of the ocean couldn't knock her, or that didn't-happen-shower, out of his mind.

Hans had sent Knox to keep track of Bax and ensure he did nothing stupid—like sleep with another friend's little sister. Knox didn't know about the shower sex. He just wanted a trip to the islands and asked no questions when Hans said, "Go."

"Know what the problem is with this beer?" Knox asked. One beach towel over, he tipped his Bermuda Triangle Stout so he could apparently read the label better.

"Bet you're gonna tell me," Bax said, closing his eyes.

"The problem is that it's two swallows from being empty," Knox said with a flash of white in his smile. "Need another."

Bax didn't reply, because he'd rather just wallow in his Courtney thoughts than think about Knox's beer situation.

"Still thinking about her?" Knox asked, clearly oblivious to Bax's plight and the stirring of brain matter around a particularly invasive species of brunette female.

Bax grunted. This time in a sort-of reply.

Here's the way it worked with the band—Knox played keyboards and sang backup for Dimefront. Linx played bass —and every other instrument imaginable—and sang backup. Sometimes Linx took the front-man spot, but most of the time, he preferred to play bass versus sing vocals. Drummers came and went, none of them sticky enough to hang around long.

Bax was a vocals guy, he played nothing and sang front man. When Linx took lead, Bax sang backup.

He liked his job well enough, was good at it, and stuck with it because it was what everyone expected. What kind of a guy walked away from a career like this one?

Still, he'd been ready to give it up for a dose of normal

with Em. Normal outside of rock 'n' roll chaos. At least, he'd thought it was normal, real, perfect… at the time.

"You didn't fuck it up, man." Knox had that know-it-all tone going on, the one that usually came with sage advice. "This isn't on you."

If they were talking about how things ended with Em? Knox was correct.

If they were talking about how things ended with Courtney? Knox was not so accurate.

"It is on me. I brought her into my life. I turned my head because I didn't want to see what was in front of my face." Bax lay spread eagle on his towel, the sand warm beneath the fabric, the sun pelting him with vitamin D.

With Bax off the radar, Hans and Courtney handled the fallout of the Em near-scandal.

Apparently, and Bax did not care for this one iota, Hans paid her off, acting as her new ATM so she'd keep things hush-hush. That thought made Bax's stomach cramp.

Hopefully there was a limit to Hans's line of credit.

While Hans handled Em, Courtney handled the media. She'd done some public relations magic, coordinated with another publicist for a huge record announcement drop for Tucker McKay, and, in the sleight-of-hand publicity shift, turned the attention the other direction. Em and the media were no longer a problem.

Done and done.

Much to his mother's dismay, wedding plans were untangled, invitations unsent, reservations canceled, and tuxedos returned.

Through everything, he didn't miss Em. Maybe she'd been right when she said they'd moved on from each other already, and this was only the last step.

Bax didn't know how much she'd cost him, but he figured it wasn't a little, since she'd left his house within days.

Within a couple more days, he'd listed the house with a real estate agent that Hans assured wouldn't fuck him over.

Now, the house was in escrow, and he'd never have to return to the place he shared with the woman he'd been sure he loved. The woman he'd been sure was his normal, his forever, the one he'd been sure was *it* for him.

"That woman wiggled right into your brain," Knox said, like that hadn't just confirmed that very thing.

"Yeah," Bax said. This was not a lie. He hadn't clarified which woman he was thinking about. Em should've been top of mind, since his heart was supposed to be crushed. Devastation and a post-breakup bender seemed like a great idea.

Except he couldn't get his mind off of Courtney… not just what they'd done in the shower. He spent his time checking her social media—which she rarely updated. Checking his texts and email—which she didn't reach out to.

"Can I ask you something?" Bax asked.

Knox took a fresh beer from the beach cocktail server as he nodded. "Ask away."

"What if it's not Em I'm thinking about?" *Would that be the worst thing?*

Knox stilled mid-swallow. He looked at Bax, pulling his sunglasses down to the tip of his nose. "You fucked around on Em?"

Bax shook his head. "Never. But after…"

"Ahh… the infamous *after*." Knox grinned, a flash of wolfish white teeth on display. "Afternoon delight breakup sex is sick. Anyone I know?" Knox studied Bax in that creepy way of his. Like he could see straight through the facade.

Bax squirmed.

"Shit." Knox sat up, shit-eating grin in place. "I know her. Spill."

"I can't." He really couldn't.

"Spill."

He should've kept his trap shut. "I seriously can't."

"That actress lady you dated before Em?" Knox flashed another smile. "She was hot. Though, I don't do actresses"—he shivered—"too much drama." He made a *ba-dum-bum* sound with his hands on his thighs.

Bax shook his head. "Wow. We're at the awful jokes portion of our vacation, huh?"

"It's not a joke if it's true." Knox rolled back down, staring straight up at the blue island sky. "Have you considered a tropical fling? I think a tropical fling is exactly what you need."

"I'm not doing that."

"A tropical fling?"

"Stop calling it that."

"That's what it would be though…"

Bax's stomach soured like that time he'd eaten an entire bag of chocolate-covered gummy bears. He didn't want a tropical anything. He didn't want to be celibate, but nothing had gotten his juices flowing since he'd left Courtney.

He hadn't even gotten himself off in the shower this whole time because all that did was bring up memories of her. Bringing up memories of her made him wonder what she was doing, where she was going, how she was feeling about life… about him.

"Was it Sharon? I bet it was Sharon." Knox seemed to be deep in thought, squinting against the sunshine. "No judgment, man. She knows what she's doing."

How the hell did Knox know—

Bax shook his head. "What happened was an accident. Onetime thing."

"There's no way you can know that." Knox was slipping into his all-wise Knox mode.

Bax hated when he did that because usually that was when he was right about things. In this case, Bax couldn't afford to be incorrect.

"*Courtney* was clear, that's all it was." There. He let it out. Out there, right in the wild for Knox.

Knox didn't appear to be breathing, however, as he'd stopped moving and his jaw fell open.

The itchy silence that descended between the two of them felt like Bax had dumped sand into his wool socks.

Then a look of appalled horror sketched across Knox's face. "Fuck no, you and Courtney?"

"Yeah," Bax admitted. Look at that, it felt better to admit it.

"I gather that you've decided you actually want Linx to murder you with a toilet plunger?" Knox asked, still clearly appalled. "Because it seems like you want Linx to murder you with a toilet plunger."

"Not particularly." Though he probably deserved it.

Knox leaned back against his towel, balancing his beer bottle on his sternum. "I'd like to point out that this is fucked up."

To put it mildly. Bax swallowed the lump lodged in his throat. "I know."

Knox did not quit talking, nor did he give any sage advice. "But it's also the best news I've had in forever. Do you even know how excited your moms are going to be? They've been so disappointed since you two decided to hate each other."

Bax refused to think of his mother and how much she loved Courtney and wished they'd just get married so she and Courtney's mom could be official family.

"I'm not sure Courtney likes me any better now, after…"

"Well, then this really is so fucked up."

"Again, I know."

Bax sort of hoped that Knox's thoughts would hold more wisdom than this.

"You had your chance with her and you blew it? I don't think you know the ramifications of how fucked up this is." Knox was losing his easygoing charm.

And, yes, actually Bax had a pretty solid idea of how fucked up this was.

Knox continued, "More fucked up than the time I let Sharon take me home and have her way with me as long as she made garlic bread afterward."

"I don't want to hear about you and Sharon and her garlic bread." Bax wished he'd snagged a beer too, but he hadn't. He continued to live his life as a fuckup who made poor decisions and didn't ask for a beer when he had the opportunity.

"Can't say it was my finest moment." Knox shrugged. "Damn good night though. Damn good garlic bread."

Bax sat up, brushing the sand off of his shoulders. He'd experienced enough of the beach for the day. "There's something very wrong with you, you know that?"

"I didn't have sex with my buddy's sister, so I think the pot just met the kettle." Knox pointed to himself, then to Bax, but did not appear to be ready to get up.

Bax reached for his sandals.

"Did you at least give her a bracelet after?" Knox asked, because apparently he wanted to get the shit beat out of him with a bag of pasta.

"No." Bax had not given Courtney a bracelet. Was that even something she would've wanted? That was what the women on the road wanted, but Courtney wasn't like that.

He'd offered one to Em after their first night, and she'd taken it, but she took everything, so that wasn't a surprise. At the time he'd figured sentimental reasons were her game. Nostalgia, even. Courtney's immediate declaration that what happened had not happened did not seem like a woman who would've appreciated if he'd have sent a thanks-for-the-good-time, here's-to-the-memories bracelet.

"Bet that pissed her off," Knox said. "You two communicated since the *boiiing*?"

"Uh. No. And don't call it that."

"You should send her a bracelet. Maybe she'll still speak to you."

"Shut it." Bax shouldn't have told Knox. That would've been good data to have five minutes ago.

"I'm just saying, if I were her and knew your history and still found it in my soul to give you a pity fuck, I'd be pretty pissed that I didn't get a diamond out of it."

"Courtney isn't like that." And it wasn't a damn pity fuck. If anyone was pitying anyone, it was her to him, and he absolutely rejected that. No one pity fucked anyone, and that was the end of that.

"It's the thought that didn't count, man." Knox sat up and held his knuckles out for a bump.

Reluctantly, Bax tapped them with his own, only because he couldn't leave a guy hanging like that. "I hate you."

"Tell yourself what you need to tell yourself." Knox settled back against his towel, the fresh beer hanging from two fingertips. "Doesn't make it true."

"You two are having a chummy time," Hans's unenthused voice came from behind.

Bax turned. Knox sat up.

Hans strode toward them—full suit, not even caring that he was probably getting sand in his shoes.

"Well, look who came to have tropical time." Knox stood and did a handshake-slap-the-back maneuver with Hans.

"What brings you to paradise?" Bax asked. "Decided you finally need a break?"

Hans was not one to take a time-out.

"We've got a problem," Hans said, sitting on the edge of a wicker-and-fabric lounger near the two of them. His white dress shirt contrasted with his brown skin as he ran his hand over his close-cropped hair.

"We've always got a problem." Knox sat back down. This time he went for crisscross applesauce instead of lying down completely.

"You two need to decide about the band," Hans said, sounding a little defeated.

"What's there to decide?" Knox asked. "We're on break. Maybe we'll play again. Maybe we won't."

Bax had insisted on the break when he and Em set their wedding date. He figured the break would become an extended absence and eventually they'd do their own things with their own lives.

Knox was all in on the time off—he'd been moaning about needing a breather since the last tour.

Linx loved the studio and the music, always seemed to have energy for more. But the same energy that fed him zapped the life out of Bax. Linx lived to create, Bax did not.

Playing for a stadium full of people? Uh-huh, Bax loved it. But time in the studio only left him weary as overwhelming, soul-sucking fatigue took over.

"Linx is ready to make a move to get on with his career." Hans scratched his temple. "With or without the rest of Dimefront."

Wait.

Bax stilled, the weight of the words "without Dimefront" settling over him. This was what he thought he'd wanted, so why did he feel like puking all over the beach? "Seriously?"

The three of them came together as teenagers with a dream of hitting the big time.

They'd hit the big time.

They'd gone through multiple drummers—no one had enough glue to stick around long—but the core of the band remained together.

"Linx wants to go solo?" Knox asked solemnly, apparently now taking this conversation to heart.

"Linx met some new guys in Denver. Musicians ready to get started." Hans said this slowly, like he was trying to prepare them for a blow.

"Fuck," Knox said.

Yeah. That. Bax's world started to spin quicker, ready to throw him off the ride.

"If he decides he's going to go that route," Hans continued, "I'll be going with him."

Hold up.

"The hell?" Knox asked.

Yeah. Again, that.

"You two can't make a call like that without talking it through with all of us," Bax said.

They were giving him his out, the one he'd craved only weeks ago. Hell, hours ago. So why did it feel so wrong? Why did he want to fight it?

And why did it feel like he'd just been punched in the gut, worse than finding Em with the neighbor guy?

"I haven't talked about this with anyone yet," Hans said. "You're my first stop, and you've got to decide now what angle you're gonna play this. Retirement is on the table, since you've both mentioned that frequently. We'll support that if you choose."

"I say shit all the time. Once I told my mom I liked her broccoli salad," Knox said. "I definitely don't want it shoved down my gullet."

"Did you just compare your career to broccoli salad?" Hans asked.

Bax's entire life seemed to flash before him—from the garage band beginnings, to the Grammys, to his decision to marry Em.

Of all of that? The only thing he had to be proud of was this band—a band he hadn't even fucking honored.

Instead, he tapped out whenever shit got hard, or he got tired.

"I'm not ready to retire," Bax said, suddenly certain that he couldn't—wouldn't—give up the crowds and the stadiums.

"Why isn't Linx here?" Knox asked.

"Because Linx already made his choice, even if he hasn't

fully realized that yet. If you two are going to be in, we've got to convince him that he made the wrong one," Hans said, full of sage wisdom like they'd gotten used to from him. He was better at this than Knox, that was certain. "No more threats. No more complaining."

"Let's not get loopy here." Knox held up his hands. "No more threats to retire, sure, I get that. But the other?"

"Linx is seriously leaving?" Bax asked, ignoring the sarcasm in Knox's words.

Hans nodded, shrugging off his suit coat, because only Hans would wear a suit coat to the beach. "You know Linx, know what makes him tick. It's the vibe. It's the song. It's the tune."

For Knox and Bax, it'd been about the touring. About the fans cheering. About the result. Then the fatigue after would make them want to quit all over again.

Linx was the heart, Bax was the brains, Knox was the asshole.

They'd had that figured out long ago.

"This day continues to be a wonder of infinitesimal shit." Knox unfolded his legs and set his beer aside. He reached for his flip-flops as though he was ready to roll out.

"What are you doin'?" Hans asked, clearly not ready to roll.

Knox didn't miss a beat. "I'm gonna go get our boy so we can keep making music. What are *you* doing?"

"Hold up." Hans held up his hands. "You two don't get it. Sit your ass down."

To his credit, Knox sat his ass down. Likely because Hans was as serious as the sauce on a bowl of Buffalo Wild Wings, and when he got serious, they listened.

"Then explain it," Bax said. He had to fight not to grit his teeth. Not because Linx was ready to move on with his career and his life—Bax got that, he did. No, Bax gritted his teeth because he'd spent so much time not knowing what he wanted until it was ready to walk away.

"The new guys have great sound." The way Hans said "great" should not have made Bax green-eyed jealous. And yet...

"That good, huh?" Bax asked, curious now as to Hans's angle.

His stomach cramped, not because of the oysters he'd eaten last night, or the thought of chocolate-covered gummy bears, but because his safety net was walking away. He'd always had the band as a backup. Things didn't work out? Need to buy a new pad? Call up the band and run a tour because Dimefront was bigger than any of them individually.

"Better than good." Hans steepled his fingers. "I think they could be something big."

"What does that mean for Dimefront?" Bax asked, already knowing the answer.

He and Knox could make a band together. Could find a new bass player. But without Linx, Dimefront would not be Dimefront.

Bax might have been the lead, he understood his importance, but Linx was the reason things worked. The reason they pulled together and made the music that provided the soundtrack of a generation.

A person couldn't walk through any mall in America and not catch a few bars of one of Dimefront's hits.

"We either go get Linx in Denver, convince him you're in —and you better fuckin' be in if that's the route you want to go. Or we cut loose. I go make a new band with Linx and these guys, and we live happily ever after," Hans said.

"Happily ever after is overrated." Bax knew this firsthand.

"I get it." Knox was standing now, hands on his hips. "I'll probably still complain. I'm still me. But I won't threaten to leave. I'm in."

I'm in... Courtney's words floated through Bax's mind.

"You can't just be in," Hans said. "You spend all your time telling us how bad you want to be out."

Knox leaned forward. "That's when I thought I had a choice. No choice? I'm in."

Funny, but Bax could relate to that logic. That he related to Knox's logic was concerning on many levels.

"You?" Hans pointed to Bax.

Bax paused for a solid three seconds. "Not letting my band go without some CPR."

"Then let's go get Linx." Hans stood, brushed some nonexistent sand from his slacks, and strode toward the resort hotel.

Fuck it, they would go get Linx.

He might have made a mess out of everything else, but he'd still have Dimefront.

Chapter Five
COURTNEY

IF THERE WEREN'T tequila shots and loud music, then having fun was probably not happening.

The worst part of an annual doctor visit wasn't actually the exam, in Courtney's estimation. Yeah, that was no fun because… speculum and no tequila. She shivered.

While not a trip to Dairy Queen for an Oreo Blizzard—royal-style, because, duh—the exam was not the worst part.

No. The worst part was wearing an open-backed gown while sitting bare-assed on the crunchy sanitary paper thing covering the exam table, while trying not to move too much and rip said paper.

She squirmed. Not too much. Not so she'd rip the paper.

Because that was the only thing that made this exam worse—sitting on torn paper.

Which was sort of a metaphor for her life recently.

The job security was iffy, since the band was imploding. Though, Courtney had hope that Linx would hire her as publicist for his new band, and she figured she could always bribe him. Like Hans did with Em—he paid her right off.

Linx was seriously ready to leave the band. For real this time. And sending Bax and Knox to the tropics as part of the say-nothing-don't-be-seen PR plan was not helping the band bonding situation.

Linx, meanwhile, was in Denver taking a much-needed Dimefront respite and apparently forming a new band.

The Dimefront guys were tired, tired of each other and tired of the business. Which gave Courtney a lot of time to focus on herself.

As part of her focus-on-Courtney plan, she'd been getting caught up on her appointments. Namely, this one.

She glanced at the pamphlet she'd snagged from the rack behind her. The one about uterine fibroids, since she'd already read through the one on endometriosis three times.

Her cell buzzed from her purse hanging on the wall across the room, like it was challenging her to get it while not tearing the damn paper.

Whatever, she was totally getting her phone. It'd already been over fifteen minutes of waiting in the little claustrophobia-inducing exam room with only the table, the rolling stool, a chair, a teeny tiny sink, and some of the terrifying speculums to keep her company.

Her phone continued to ring.

Maybe this was her contact with *Rolling Stone?* She'd been working to pitch a feature article and going with the assumption that she still had a band to pitch.

Phone still ringing, she gnawed at her bottom lip. She didn't want to be rude and take a call when the doctor came in.

As a general rule, she didn't keep her phone in hand during a doctor visit, because she'd get totally caught up in work, and then she'd take a call, and then she either had to be rude to the doctor and finish the call, or be rude to the caller and cut them off. Or even worse—pause reading an interesting article mid-sentence.

Except the clock ticked slowly on, edging toward twenty minutes past her appointment time, and she knew everything the brochures had to say about endometriosis and uterine fibroids.

The only other brochures were about conception via IVF, and one titled *All About Your Pregnant Body*.

Those brochures were definitely unnecessary, since she was never having kids. There was no way she could handle a baby and still keep up her clubbing and work routines.

Her phone stopped ringing.

Good. Phew. Okay. She could just sit here a little longer.

It rang again.

Screw it. She'd risk ripping the paper and being rude for *Rolling Stone*. Carefully, she stood. Good. No tearing.

But… not *Rolling Stone*.

"Mom, hey. Everything okay?" she asked. Because while they talked all the time, usually Mom didn't call right back—unless maybe something was super wrong.

There'd probably been a car accident. Or a boating accident. Though they didn't own a boat, so that probably wasn't it. Still… she gripped the phone and tried to shake off boating accident vibes.

Besides, what the hell? She wasn't one to jump to the worst-case scenario. That was specifically her mother's job.

"Just needed to hear my baby girl's voice." Mom was chipper and chirpy as ever and didn't sound at all like she'd just been maimed in an accident.

Courtney released a breath slowly, so she got good use of all that oxygen.

"Here's my voice for you." Courtney tried to ignore the wobble in her words. Seriously? What was up with her?

The light knock on the door of the exam room signaled the end of this call.

"Uh, Mom. Now's not a great time. Can I call you back?" Courtney asked, then called out, "Come on in."

"Is everything okay?" The chipper disappeared from Mom's voice.

Courtney smiled at her doctor as the woman entered the room and washed her hands. "Annual girl checkup. Gotta go."

Mom said a quick goodbye, as she would, because she'd never been exceptionally great at talking about the girl stuff. When it'd been time for Courtney's first period, Mom stumbled through the birds and the bees talk. Thankfully, that talk had been quick and to the point. She'd covered the basics. Conversations with her high school friends filled in the gaps.

Dr. Carol did the obligatory check-in. "Hey, how are you today?" Then she dove right in, glancing at the clipboard. "Sorry I'm a little behind. I was taking a second look at your labs," Dr. Carol said in that way that made a person's blood pressure spike. Sort of like Dr. Google saying you're about to die when you have a slight earache. Same feeling, but from an actual doctor.

"That interesting, huh?" Courtney tried for light, but really she had the feeling like she might be about to go boating… without a boat… on ripped paper.

Dr. Carol took a deep breath then steadied her gaze on Courtney. "Is there a reason you asked for a full panel this time?"

Full panel meaning an *entire* STD panel. Yes, she'd asked for one because she'd had her encounter with Bax.

"I had a… I had sex with a guy." Hoo boy, the mind-blowing, holy-crap, earth-moving kind, which was why, "We didn't use protection." Courtney held up her hands. "You know that I always insist. This time…" It just happened.

The thing was, as a human being, things happened to her often. Things that didn't involve finding Bax naked and moaning her name in the shower. Normal things happened that didn't cause worry of STDs—like the time she found a whole Oreo in her cookies 'n cream milkshake from Shake Shack, or two weeks ago when she discovered an extra twenty in the pocket of a pair of old jeans.

But *this* happened, and then he left, and he didn't even have Hans send her a damn thanks-for-the-good-time bracelet. His other hookups got bracelets because that was Bax's calling card on the road.

Bag the lead singer? Grab yourself some bling.

Not that Courtney *needed* a bracelet or would wear a Bax bracelet. Still, that wasn't the point. She would've appreciated the opportunity to send the bracelet back, that was all.

"Okay." Dr. Carol definitely didn't look like the labs were good. Which meant Courtney might not be STD-free, which was not awesome.

At least there were antibiotics and ointments. Most everything was treatable, right? While this might not be whole-Oreo goodness, thanks to science, it wouldn't be untreatable.

Only a few things weren't, and this *couldn't* be that. Unless...

Blurgh, her mind would not stop with the worst case. Probably because she'd never played with this brand of fire before and had always exercised extreme caution in the bedroom, shower, or on the kitchen counter.

"Something's wrong." Courtney stated what did not need to be stated with the vibe rolling off of Dr. Carol.

"Not *wrong*." Dr. Carol leaned against the counter where they kept the cylinder of cotton balls and stick depressor things. "Courtney, you're pregnant."

Ha. No.

If she had anything, it was something that would require *antibiotics*, not diapers.

Of this, she was sure—totally sure—as sure as any woman could be.

"That's impossible." Courtney shook her head.

Pregnant? The word was just wrong. She'd know it if she was *pregnant*. Would know it if the words were the truth, because if they were? She'd be numb, processing, and panicking.

Also, she wouldn't have had her period on time.

She wasn't numb, felt everything just fine, and had nothing to process.

Thus, this was impossible. She gestured to the clipboard held in her doctor's grip. "Those aren't my results, then. I got my period after the whole… you know… I probably just need some antibiotics and a lecture."

Dr. Carol gave Courtney a look that didn't seem to imply that antibiotics and a talking-to would help.

"They're your results, and you've had unprotected sex." Dr. Carol let that little nugget hang right on out there. She pulled up the rolling stool and sat down as though this was a conversation that would take longer than a few moments.

It wouldn't, because these were not her labs.

"The only way to not be pregnant is to abstain from sex," Dr. Carol said, matter-of-fact.

Maybe if she gave Courtney a lecture on STDs and condoms and a small demo on how to put a condom on the wooden banana thing, then this wouldn't be so weird. But Dr. Carol didn't judge or lecture. Up until today, that was Courtney's favorite thing about her. That and she'd always been right about Courtney's pelvic health concerns.

"You had sex?" Dr. Carol confirmed. "That's what you'd said, unprotected sex."

Okay, well, first, yes. But also, no.

After Bax, Courtney decided to abstain.

"I'm not pregnant." Sixth grade health and wellness for the win here: period equals not pregnant.

"Your other labs are clear. But this one? This one clearly shows pregnancy." Dr. Carol kept her tone in the whole neutral doctor category. "Are you experiencing any nausea? Sore nipples?"

"Run it again," Courtney said through gritted teeth, since they would not be discussing her nipples. They weren't sore, and she wasn't puking.

Because she was not pregnant.

"You left a urine sample today?" Dr. Carol asked, still in full not-panicked doctor mode. Maybe it'd be better if she was a little panicked? She should be panicked because somewhere in this office was a pregnant woman who didn't have the right labs.

"I left you a whole Dixie cup of *not-pregnant* urine." Courtney nodded toward the door.

"Let me see if the nurse has run a strip on it yet." Dr. Carol stood. She didn't look like Courtney's mom, but she had that mom vibe to her. That one like she genuinely cared, but she would also kick you in the ass if you needed her to. Or inadvertently asked for it.

Things that Courtney *was* included the following: preparing to go visit her parents, putting the down payment on a cute little Mustang because she'd decided she wanted a fun car, and doing some side-gig consulting work with rocker Tucker McKay while Dimefront figured out if the implosion was permanent this time.

Things that she was not included primarily one thing: pregnant.

Dr. Carol left.

Courtney waited.

She should probably just start reading an article on her phone. Even if she got cut off mid-sentence, it'd be better than being left in her own brain right now.

A light knock and the door opened.

"Courtney." Dr. Carol did not have the look of a woman with not-pregnant news. "The urine test is positive. The blood work is positive. *You* are definitely pregnant."

Courtney stared at the doctor for a long beat. Could she be? If she was, the only guy she'd been with remotely in the time frame was…

Fucking hell.

She was having Bax's baby because apparently she'd been very naughty in a previous life and this was her penance.

Oh hey, there was that numb. That was nice, she didn't like to feel things right now.

"You should know that you have options here." Dr. Carol pulled up the stool again, this time her face much more serious. "There are choices you can make. It's still very early."

Courtney said nothing because her lips didn't seem to want to move.

"If you're going to continue with the pregnancy, then we need to start you on prenatal vitamins and book your next appointment. If you decide not to continue, we can start that process too."

Courtney lay back on the exam table, the paper crumpling and tearing into pieces behind her back.

She tried to breathe, but suddenly even that was hard. Her nipples were fine, but breathing hurt.

Okay.

This was fine.

She pressed the palms of her hands to her eyes.

"If you're right..." She wasn't totally on board with that theory yet. "I'm keeping the baby." She said this so softly she wasn't entirely sure that Dr. Carol heard her. "If you're right about this, what do I need to do?"

Surely there was a test or something she needed to take. Like a driving test but for mothers.

That was a thing, right? They couldn't just send her out of here pregnant and then home with a baby once they got to that part. She was the younger sibling, so she'd never even changed a diaper. What did it say that Linx would make a better parent than she would at this point?

Holy. Holy. Holy. Shit.

"Take a breath," Dr. Carol instructed, illustrating deep inhales and slow exhales. "You have to breathe."

Courtney breathed like Dr. Carol said because otherwise

she'd pass out, and while that sounded fun to her at the moment, it probably wasn't good for the baby.

"What does it mean that I'm not sick? That my boobs are totally fine?" she asked, eyes pressed closed. She resisted the urge to pinch her nipples and see if maybe it hurt more than usual? Then again, she didn't make a habit of pinching the girls, so she wouldn't really know if it was worse than before.

"Some women don't get nauseated. For many women, symptoms don't appear until well into the second trimester. By my calculations, based on your intake, you'd be six weeks along."

Oh, well. Courtney sat up. "Then it's not Bax's baby."

"Sorry?" Dr. Carol raised her eyebrows.

"It can't be Bax's baby. We had sex five weeks ago." Thank. Hell. She held up her five counting fingers to clarify. "I didn't have sex six weeks ago."

"We count from the beginning of your last period," Dr. Carol said, pulling out a little round card thing that looked like it belonged to a board game.

"My last period was two weeks ago." Again, Courtney held up two fingers to illustrate her point.

"The period before that. My guess is that what you had was breakthrough bleeding or the like." Dr. Carol turned the wheel of the card thing and held it out for Courtney to see. "This would be your due date."

Oh. God. Courtney hadn't had a due date since she was in high school algebra with assignments that she forgot to turn in. She was shit when it came to due dates.

She pressed her eyes closed again. Then opened them, sat up, and asked the wall, "Why is this so complicated?"

"Babies are complicated." Dr. Carol moved to hold Courtney's hand. "But you've got this."

That was nice. She didn't feel so alone right then. A little light-headed, but not alone.

You know who would have a good idea about what came next? Irina. She should call Irina.

"I think I'd like to pass out now," she said, lying back down, ripping the paper more and not even really caring.

"Deep breaths. In through the nose, out through the mouth." Dr. Carol illustrated like Courtney was in labor on a television sitcom. But Courtney didn't follow.

"I have to do that, don't I?" Courtney asked, still holding her breath.

"Breathe?" Dr. Carol gave her hand a squeeze. "Yes. You have to breathe."

Courtney did. She breathed because apparently it was important for the baby. "No. The other thing."

"What other thing?"

"Give birth." She pointed to her girly bits, totally tearing the rest of the paper with the movement. "I'm going with that option, so this baby has to come out of me."

Her blood pressure spiked, and this must be hyperventilating.

She breathed faster, her head getting heavier as the room got tilty. How was she going to get a whole kid out of her? And then raise it? And hope that somewhere along the way, it didn't end up being a serial killer because it had a crappy mom who fed it sugary cereal and didn't go to the gym?

Pressing her head against the exam table, she paused and utterly missed her life of five minutes ago when her biggest worry was being rude to *Rolling Stone*.

Also, yes, so far (as far as she was concerned), motherhood sucked.

But.

She was great at figuring things out.

This was just another thing to figure out. Right?

"Courtney." Dr. Carol was using her mom voice. It cut right through the spinning.

Courtney fixed her eyes on the doctor.

"The baby will come out of you. You'll do great. Women do this every day."

"I don't." Women might, but Courtney didn't.

"I promise, you will do amazing." Dr. Carol squeezed her hand. Again, that was nice. But—

"You can't promise that."

She couldn't. No one could.

But this was Courtney's disaster to deal with. "Women do this every day."

They figured out how to make it happen.

Dr. Carol nodded. "They do. You will."

All right. So she was in. She could admit that she was now responsible for a living being.

She could do this.

Maybe.

Chapter Six
COURTNEY

A Week Later

COURTNEY ADJUSTED her phone against her cheek as she headed toward the kitchen in Linx's house in Denver. "Linx's new girlfriend is really great."

"I didn't call to talk about your brother's new girlfriend. I called to check in on *you*," Irina said.

Funny, things happened pretty quickly after the *hey, you're pregnant* appointment. Especially when she had a best friend antsy to plan a baby shower and put on notice that she couldn't quite yet. Not until Bax was informed of his upcoming parental opportunity.

That was how she planned to spin it, at least. This was her job—to take something potentially negative and spin it into the positive. *Oops, I'm pregnant?* Oh no, that wasn't it. It was an upcoming parental opportunity.

Had she told him yet? No. No, she had not.

Would she tell him? Yes. Yes, she would.

Soon.

Seriously, she understood that he deserved to know. Understood that he had his own decisions to make about his involvement—even if she bet that he'd choose to walk away, leaving her with the opportunity to make decisions herself.

She got it. This whole thing was a super-complicated parental opportunity that she'd decided to embrace.

So, she'd tell him. First, she'd practice by spilling the beans to her family. Then, once things were a little more settled with the pregnancy, she'd mention it to him. Maybe she'd take Irina's path and send him a postcard in Bermuda. Decisions like that didn't need to be made right now.

"You still haven't answered how you are," Irina pointed out.

Courtney squared her shoulders like the motherly badass she aspired to be. "I am fine."

Mostly fine. She'd decided to be fine, and thus she made it so. Did she have a new aversion to pork, poultry products, and her formerly favorite cereals? She did. Suddenly, she also really craved kale and beets. That part was the worst because they were supposed to taste like dirt, not deliciousness. The best part was she'd be super healthy for this little munchkin.

"Besides, Linx's girlfriend is a big deal." Because he normally had lots of girlfriends, but this time it was just the one. That in itself made the situation special.

Courtney turned to the hallway that led to Linx's kitchen. She loved this room in his house because it reminded her of her condo. He hadn't decorated it, but whoever had updated it last used every shade of white—just like Courtney's pad. The rest of his house in Denver was a monstrosity of marble and gold with cherubs painted on the ceiling. It looked like 1990s wealth had vomited all over the place. Linx thought so too and tried to start a remodel, but all that netted him was a huge hole in the wall. At least that added a little character to the place.

"Are you sure you don't want to come back to LA? I got to thinking, if I were pregnant, I'd send my parents a postcard announcement and then I'd turn off my cell phone for a month," Irina announced. She paused, then continued, "Though, at this stage, it wouldn't be a gender reveal, we'd have a father reveal. That would be interesting, wouldn't it? We could do it Maury Povich–style. At least you know who the dad is, that's a huge win."

"Hey, heads up, there's no way I'm having a gender reveal. Don't even think about planning one," she said. Because Irina loved a good party, and any excuse for a party was Irina's idea of a good time.

"Right, you don't want one, but Bax might want one. I can throw it for him instead."

Irina had never even met Bax. Never had a reason to. Even when she'd come to some of the concerts, she'd avoided Bax on the principle that Courtney hated him.

"Irina, no. No gender reveal."

Irina sighed, but Courtney was pretty sure she didn't mean it. "Go forth and tell your family. I'm on standby if you need me to come crack some skulls."

By crack some skulls, Irina meant fly to Denver, crack open a case of wine, and keep pouring until none of Courtney's family cared about anything other than Linx's wall hole, his new girlfriend, and his cat, Gibson.

"Maybe I should go take one more test." Courtney turned to head back toward the guest room that Linx kept for her.

She should probably buy stock in pregnancy test manufacturing because she took approximately two pregnancy tests every day to be sure she actually was pregnant. She'd become attached to this idea of a little grain of rice growing into a chickpea in her belly. She might know nothing about being a mom, but she was ready to crush motherhood like a boss.

The voices from Linx's kitchen carried down the hallway toward Courtney. There was laughter. Some chatter. Mom's and Dad's voices mingling with Linx's and girlfriend Becca's.

How should she say this? Ease them in with assurances and charts? Or just pull the bandage off and let it rip?

"No more peeing on sticks. Let's take the bandage route. Rip that sucker off." Irina added some Velcro-like noises for effect. This was easier for her to suggest because Irina wasn't the one having to do the ripping.

But she wasn't wrong. Courtney said her goodbyes because first things first—this conversation about the baby didn't have to be weird. Truly, it didn't.

Had Courtney known that Linx had a girlfriend guest staying with him in his new Denver pad, she never would've dragged her parents here for the big revelation news.

Actually, scratch that, she totally would've brought them anyway. But she would've given Linx a touch more of a heads-up and probably told him the news first.

"Where's Courtney?" Linx asked as she moseyed around the corner to the kitchen, where he was pouring himself a cup of coffee that smelled really amazing.

While the doctor had said that she could have a cup a day, the stuff now gave her horrible heartburn. Wheatgrass juice with cucumber, however, sounded heavenly, which totally sucked shrimp tails.

"Courtney's right here," she said, hoping no one had swiped her cherry-flavored seltzer because it was one of the few things that actually settled her stomach these days.

Linx glanced at her, paused, and raised his brows. Uh-huh, she probably looked like she got hit by a semitruck and then smeared over the concrete by a rock star. She'd tried her best with some concealer and a hairbrush, but decided it wasn't worth it after about thirty seconds.

Now, she was questioning coming down to the kitchen, because the stench of bacon had her stomach roiling.

Motherhood apparently gave ample opportunity for her to reevaluate the things that had once given her joy. Things like coffee, clubbing, bacon, and sleep.

"Courtney is speaking in the third person." Linx handed over his coffee.

That was sweet, but she shook her head and headed for the fridge. The seltzer she'd put there last night was still there. Hot damn, maybe today would be her day.

"Are you okay, sis?" Linx asked.

"Okay" could mean oh so many things. She poured her seltzer into a glass and firmed every ounce of resolve inside of her. "Hey." Courtney sipped at the liquid fizz. Best to just get this out there so she could escape from the scent of pork and find a cucumber to juice. "I have something I need to say."

"What's up, sweets?" Dad paused where he stood at the stove cooking bacon.

"Here's the thing." Courtney cleared her throat and fidgeted with the napkin holder in the center of the island. She glanced at Linx, then Becca, then Mom and Dad. "I need you not to freak out. Because I'm not freaking out."

"Now we're all freaking out, Courtney," Linx said, full freak-out mode engaged.

"Honey." Mom reached for Courtney's hand. "What's going on?"

Bandage time… One. Two. Three.

"I'm pregnant," she said, extra cheery even though the words sort of stuck in her tonsils. She cleared her throat and sallied forth. "Before anyone says anything, I already decided to keep the baby."

There. Boom. Done.

They had to say something now.

She waited as the bacon crisped and crackled. However, no one said anything. The only other sounds were the dripping coffee she couldn't drink, an electronic pressure cooker letting off steam, and her stomach gurgling at the bacon.

Her gag reflex engaged, and oh crap. She was going to throw up. For real.

Excellent, if she did that, she'd just get it over with early today, then, and be able to move on without worry of puking.

Oh, who was she kidding? She dropped to a chair next to

her mom and did the deep breathing thing that Dr. Carol had her do when she'd found out herself.

"Who is the father?" Mom asked gently.

Courtney's cheeks heated. She quickly shook her head. She couldn't tell them. Not yet. Because—

"He won't be involved."

Why did she have to go and say what she was thinking? She was pretty sure he wouldn't be involved. But this wasn't one of those 100 percent certainty times.

She'd tell him to give him the option, but she knew Brennan Baxter too well. He wouldn't be part of this, and that was A-okay.

"Doesn't seem like he has much of a choice," Linx said, breaking through the moment. Linx seemed pissed, which was a little sweet.

"It'd be better if he's not involved." Courtney wished the coffee didn't give her heartburn. "He's not the fatherly type."

Which was good for her, since she preferred to do things by herself.

"Does he know?" Dad asked. He'd ripped off his T-shirt sleeves like Linx had the night before when they arrived. Linx could pull off the style because Linx was Linx. Dad? Not so much.

"I'll tell him once I'm further along, once we know it's going to stick. They say the first trimester is the riskiest. I figure I'll tell him after I'm through it. I'd like to keep it just with the family for now—and Becca, obviously." Courtney traced a thin stream of condensation down the edge of her glass with a thumbnail.

Given the way that Linx looked longingly at Becca, Courtney had a suspicion that she'd officially be part of the family soon.

"This is going to be wonderful." Dad clapped his hands in a one-two, one-two-three pattern. "I'm going to be a grandpa. This calls for celebration."

That was the spirit she wanted, but maybe they could wait until things got more settled?

"Dad…" Courtney stared at the bubbles in her not-coffee seltzer. "Let's not do that."

"How can we support you?" Mom asked, always knowing just the right thing to say.

"Just… you know, don't make a big thing about it." Courtney needed to find the new normal. She couldn't do that with hovering or awkward family moments. "And don't fry bacon around me in the morning." That would be the biggest help of all.

Linx strode to the pan of bacon, grabbed it with a pot holder, strode to the back door, and tossed the whole shebang outside. "Done."

Uh. That wasn't exactly what she meant. Just because the kid didn't like the scent of bacon didn't mean they should waste it. At the end of the day, it was still bacon.

"I was going to eat that." Dad crossed his arms. Pre-pregnant Courtney could relate—what just happened was sacrilege.

"Not if it's making Courtney sick." Linx frowned and fiddled with the pressure cooker. Then he met her gaze straight on, the worry clear. "Oatmeal okay, sis?"

Oatmeal was fabulous. She loved her brother. Gah, he was fantastic. Her kid was going to have the best uncle in the world, and that choked her up.

"Oatmeal is great." Courtney tried not to let the tears fall, but her body sort of did what it wanted right now, so she had to work to blink back the wet. "Can we change the subject?"

To something that wouldn't make her feel like she'd just watched a Folgers' commercial.

"Becca." Dad turned his attention to Linx's girlfriend, since she'd just been inaugurated into the family chaos. "What do you do for work?"

Becca nibbled at her bottom lip. "I'm a therapist."

Oh, well, wasn't that a great turn of events? Talk about luck.

"I think that skill set might just come in handy today," Mom muttered, filling up a cup of coffee for herself.

Wasn't that just the truth?

Becca took in a deep breath. Then she let it out.

"Uh-huh," she said with a rueful smile.

That was the first morning that her family knew about her addition. The first morning that she got to spend time with Linx's new girlfriend. All wrapped up in a blanket of opportunity.

THE OPPORTUNITIES for growth didn't end there. No, no, they didn't. Because that would make things rather comfy. Courtney's life was not about comfy, but rather growth and enrichment and staving off murdering the band manager.

"Seriously, how did you already know this?" Courtney asked, staring at Hans. Hard.

Well, she more interrogated him versus asked. But he and his otherworldly knowledge of everything Dimefront deserved this interrogation.

That was why they were having a mocktail at Brek's Bar. Brek was the former manager of Dimefront, who actually left the business when he got married to the love of his life and started a family in Denver. He retired and bought a bar. Apparently, this had been a dream of his, though Courtney never would've guessed. When Brek retired, he left Dimefront in Hans's very capable hands.

So, yeah, uh-huh, Hans was in Denver. Linx had found some new bandmates—guys that Courtney had met and seriously dug—and Hans was triaging the situation. Meaning, he was there to ensure that Linx and Dimefront did not fall apart because Linx had found new guys to make music with.

That was the first reason that Hans was in Denver.

The second?

Hans knew about the baby.

"It's my job to know things," Hans said, like this was not new knowledge.

While this was not brand-spanking-new knowledge, HIPAA covered this type of thing. While she often thought Hans must have an in with the medical professionals of the world—because he always knew everything—she didn't really believe it. This time though…

"You're one of the people I take care of." Then he paused, waiting for her to say something more.

That would not happen because—

"I'm not having this conversation until you tell me how you found out." Courtney leaned back in the booth they'd snagged for their chat. She crossed her arms. They both knew she could outlast him.

She raised her eyebrows at him.

He raised his eyebrows at her.

Eyebrows raised all around.

Mercifully, the server brought Courtney her cranberry juice with soda and Hans his beer. First thing after this baby was born, she'd have a beer. A delicious hoppy brew with only a little foam and a lot of yum.

Hans caved first, like she knew he would. She withheld the evil laugh that seemed appropriate for this conversation.

"I talked to your dad today, and he spilled your baby beans," Hans said.

That was a flipping relief because she could still trust her doctor. And yet—

She tossed her hands up, choking a little on her cranberry juice. "Is nothing sacred with my family?"

A wry smile sketched across Hans's lips.

"You need to tell Bax," he said gently, like her mother had spoken to her that morning.

"How the hell did you—"

"I did the math." Hans lifted his shoulder. "The timeline of Bax's liaison lines up." He studied her for a long beat. Thankfully, she didn't have to ask more questions. "Bax told me the gist of what happened."

She lifted an eyebrow.

"He didn't tell me the details." Hans shook his head and murmured, "Thank fuck for that."

"Well, thank goodness Bax didn't give *all* the dirty details," she said with a huff. Hans didn't need to know that she had developed a thing for long, hot showers.

"I'm worried about you," Hans said.

She was seriously getting tired of people talking to her like she might break. She was pregnant, yes, but she was still her badass self. A more *badass* version of herself that was actually building a tiny human while drinking cranberry juice. She'd finally become the epitome of a multitasker.

"I'm going to tell him," she said, instead of responding to his statement. "Right now, he's in Bermuda, so it's a bit of a trip."

"What do you have planned for the future?" Hans asked, again with the frustrating gentleness.

Make no mistake, the two of them didn't do gentle. They did professional and often a lot of sarcasm.

"Since I'll be toting a mini-me around, I haven't decided what's in store for me," she said in total honesty.

"The little one could be a mini-Bax," Hans pointed out. "Not a mini-you."

That was possible. Even likely. Knowing Bax, his sperm was probably just as pushy and would shove her DNA out of the way to make room for his own.

"I guess we'll have to see, won't we?" Courtney said, hoping that a few pieces of her made the cut. "I'm taking things step-by-step. Day by day. Taking things as they come and processing them like the queen I am."

That sounded really healthy. She bet even Linx's new therapist girlfriend would be all over supporting that kind of self-talk.

Hans didn't answer.

"You really think you can salvage Dimefront?" she asked. Because after meeting Mach and Tanner—the guys Linx was making music with in Denver—she was thinking Dimefront might really be done this time.

That would, of course, not be the worst thing for her. That would mean Bax wouldn't be part of her everyday life and her work.

"I know I can salvage Dimefront." Hans got a twinkle in his eye, like his plan was already in motion.

"The cogs of the wheel are turning, and the ringmaster is happy with the tigers," she said, not making a bit of sense by mixing her metaphors. Though, in a way, it totally made sense.

"I'm thrilled with the cogs of my tigers." Hans tilted his beer to his lips.

"Then I think I have to leave the band," Courtney said, though she didn't want to. Hell, she'd been there from the beginning. Leaving was not her favorite choice, but…

"You're not leaving the family," Hans said, and oh boy, did he mean it—what with the way he got rumbly when he spoke.

"It's just a band." She said the words but understood that they were not the truth.

"Tell yourself whatever you need to. The truth of the matter remains the truth."

Did it though? She wasn't entirely convinced.

Chapter Seven
BAX

WELL, fuck him on a Friday.

Bax hadn't expected to get pissed when he heard Linx and the guys onstage at Brek's Bar. But they sounded good. Better than good.

He also hadn't expected to know the woman that Linx called his girlfriend. Becca.

Becca and Bax had a brief history. Once on the Penny Pincher tour years ago, they'd nearly hooked up. Instead, they talked all night.

Since he knew the woman, and he knew Linx, he could say for certain that they were a good fit together. He hoped like hell his friend didn't fuck it up.

Which had led them here, with Bax and Linx and Knox hashing shit out about the band in the back room of Brek's Bar.

"The guys I'm playing with want to meet you." Linx shoved his hands on his waist. "When we're done here."

Bax didn't sit, because he was edgy as hell. He wanted to throttle his friend and bass player. Wanted to grill him about where Courtney was and what she was doing.

He did none of that. Instead, he leaned against the wall.

Trying to go for ease, but anyone who knew him could probably read that he was on edge. Pissed that he'd let his life come to this.

"You seemed cozy up there onstage with them," he said to Linx. Damn, but his tone was not kind. He didn't mean for it to come out as an accusation.

"Take it down, Bax," Hans said.

"I was." Linx crossed his arms. "They're good guys. Excellent musicians. They'll sign with a label soon."

After hearing them? Bax didn't doubt it.

Knox grabbed a chair, flipped it around, and straddled it. "I'd like to meet 'em."

Of course he would. Knox wanted to meet them so he could complain to them about something.

"Don't like the look of what was happening up there." Bax stared straight ahead. "Felt like it was more than just a set with noobs."

"They get the music," Linx said with a shoulder shrug. "They perform for the sound, not because of what it can do for them."

Well, that stung.

"You're saying that's what I do?" Bax asked, his level of pissed ratcheting up to ticked without any actual intent on his part.

No one said anything.

Bax didn't know about the rest of them, but he worried that if he said something, it'd really ruin shit.

Finally, Hans piped up. "Talked with the guys." He jerked his thumb toward Bax and Knox. "We're ready to get back to work."

"Oh, well, then, by all means, let's get back to work." Linx stretched his arms wide with fake excitement that turned Bax's stomach.

Bax didn't want this to be the end. He was ready to move forward like Hans said they could. "Figured we'd come tell you in person." He paused. "Didn't expect to find you having extracurricular fun with another group."

Except he had. He knew that Linx was moving forward. That was the part that rubbed. Bax made plans to move forward, and yet he was stuck.

"If we're going to keep taking a hiatus from Dimefront, I'm going to have to find a new gig." Linx said this like he'd been rehearsing the words for years.

"You should know that Em left him." Hans folded his hands together on the table, keeping his focus on Linx. "You all have been doing your own shit, and Bax's world collapsed."

Wasn't that the fucking truth?

Linx looked at Bax with pity.

Bax did not love the pity. The question in Linx's eyes was clear.

Bax nodded.

Linx ran his hand over his hair. "Fuck, man. I'm sorry…"

"Just cut him some slack, yeah?" Hans asked.

Knox kicked back in his chair until it was on two legs instead of four. "There's shit he needs to catch you up on."

Bax glared at Knox. There was no shit he needed to bring to the table. Not now. Never. Some things were best left in the shower.

"I'm sorry she took off." Linx moved forward and clapped Bax on the shoulder, leaving his hand there in apparent solidarity with his bandmate. "That fuckin' sucks."

"We've all got crap to deal with." It sucked. He'd moved past it. Was ready for a different future. "A lot can change in a couple of months."

"You think we can call a truce on whatever this is with you guys?" Hans asked. "Because I don't like it."

Bax nodded. He liked the idea of a do-over. "I'm game for a truce."

"When we go back to work, we need a new agreement."

Linx dropped into a chair across from Knox. "Something that spells out vacations, time off, everything. So I'm not stuck twirling my thumbs while you assholes do your own thing."

"Fair." Knox nodded.

Bax's shoulders lost a whole lotta tension at that. They weren't a lost cause.

"Fair," he said.

"I see that you met a girl." Knox gave Linx a knowing, sage grin. "I wanna hear about her."

"Becca." Linx nodded. "You'll dig her. She's the best."

Bax knew it. Becca was a good person.

"Glad you found that." Bax finally sat on the chair between both of them, cementing the truce. "Seriously. You deserve a dose of happy."

"Mom and Dad are in town." Linx picked at the edge of the vinyl table. "You should stop by the house. There's food."

Bax's throat seemed to swell. If Linx's parents were in town, then Courtney couldn't be far behind.

"Food's good." Knox lifted his fist for a bump.

Linx met it with his own.

"Heads up, Courtney's here too." Linx slid a glance to Bax.

Courtney. He gulped.

Yeah, he needed to see her. To set things right with her. They needed that to move forward with Dimefront. And he was willing to do it.

"Go easy on her. She's having a rough time," Linx said.

"What's up with Courtney?" Hans asked, a little too innocently.

Bax sat up straighter. What the hell was wrong with Courtney, and why was he just finding out?

"Keep it on the down low. She's not telling anyone yet." He leaned in, talking low even though it was just them in the room. "She's pregnant. Keeping the baby. Living with me in Denver for now."

Time stood still for Bax. There was no rotation of the Earth. No breath in his lungs. No blood to pump through his body.

"Fuck," Hans said, kicking off from the wall.

"She's *what?*" Bax asked, the words not sounding like they came from his lips.

Could she be? Well, yeah. They'd not exactly been proactive with prevention. Or active at all. But she hadn't reached out. That was the code, right? If a guy knocked a girl up, she let him know.

Bax couldn't sit. Couldn't stay still. He stood. His chair clattered to the ground. He moved to set it upright. He needed to see her. Needed her to tell him this herself. But deep down? Deep down, he knew.

And he knew why she didn't tell him.

"Where is she?" he asked.

"You wanna tell me what's going on?" Linx asked, eyes darting between the rest of them in the room.

But Bax only had one thought. *Courtney.*

"Is this the part where you tell Linx that you banged his sister?" Knox asked with more than a little resignation. "Or should I?"

Fuck. Fuck. He needed to see her. "This cannot be happening."

"Tell me you didn't sleep with Courtney," Linx said, stalking forward like he was going to kick Bax's ass.

Bax deserved it, but he wanted to live long enough to tell Courtney that he was sorry. To make things as right as he could. He held up his hands. "It's not what you think."

"Linx, take a breather," Hans said in the periphery, but Bax's world was still upside down and backward.

"Is that why Em left?" Linx asked, the question punching a hole through Bax's chest.

No. He shook his head. No. He'd never done that to her. Never would've done that to her.

"Courtney and I hooked up after Em left," he said, running his hands through his hair. "I didn't fuck around on her."

"Em did." Knox stood, moving between Bax and Linx like he could actually stop Linx from killing Bax.

"It's true." Hans moved next to Knox. "She was the one with a side gig while she planned her wedding to Bax."

Now that, that fuckin' stung.

"That's not what this is about now," Bax said. Clarity cutting through the chaos of the room. "This is about Courtney. She's pregnant? I need to see her."

"No." Linx shoved his hands on his hips, spread his stance, and met Bax's eyes. "She comes to you. When and if she's ready, she makes the move. You leave her the hell alone."

No. That wouldn't work. "Can't do that."

"Can we *please* take a breather?" Hans asked.

"You knocked up my sister!" Linx yelled the truth, flinging it at Bax like a weapon. A weapon Bax had readily supplied him with. "*You* jacked with the band!"

"Linx, breathe," Knox said, though it didn't really seem to do any good.

"Dimefront is done." Linx slashed his hand through the air like a dagger.

Bax flinched.

Knox shook his head. "Not accepting that."

"Serious. Over. *Done.*" Linx had never sounded so sure of anything since Bax met him as a kid. "Bax wanted to talk about contracts. I read the goddamned contract. Any of us want to call it? It's done. I'm calling."

"Whoa." Brek strode through the door and held up his hands.

Bax should've taken that opportunity to bolt. To go find her. Find out what was really going on here.

"I thought we agreed no decisions until I came to referee?" Brek asked, his hands on his hips.

"That was before Bax knocked up my sister." Linx closed his eyes, apparently unable to even look at Bax.

"Tell me this isn't real," Brek said to Bax.

"We don't know for sure." Knox stood. "We'll have to talk to Courtney."

"No one talks to Courtney until Courtney makes that move!" Linx shouted.

"The kid is mine." Bax studied the laces of his boots. He swallowed against a whole throat filled with guilt. "I need to talk to her."

"That's not happening until she says it happens." Linx shoved his finger toward Bax. "Stay the fuck away from my family."

Bax shook his head. He couldn't do that. Wouldn't do that.

Linx marched out the door.

At that moment, a lot of things weren't clear. But the one thing that held an abundance of clarity? He'd single-handedly destroyed his band.

Chapter Eight
COURTNEY

THERE SHE WAS, minding her own business while watching *Manifest* on Netflix, when her phone rang. She glanced at the screen and picked it up immediately. "Hey, Linx."

"Bax knows you're pregnant," Linx said, quick as hell.

Say what now?

Courtney pulled her eyes from the current episode and refocused her attention on her brother's voice.

"What?" she said. Okay, really, she sort of yelled it.

"Everything okay, Courtney?" Mom hollered down the stairs.

Uh. No. "I'm fine. Just got a surprise, that's all," she said, already planning how she could turn this around and convince Bax that she'd been the first to tell him.

"Apparently, there's a little something you left out of that announcement, little sister," Linx continued, and he sounded pissed.

Oh, no, he didn't get to be pissy about this. Her mouth like sandpaper, she said, "I thought we agreed this was something only family needed to know?"

"I thought he was family. He's not. Family doesn't do this to my sister."

Well, technically…

"Uh…" What was up with her family and their inability to keep a fucking secret locked up for longer than half a day? "To be clear, the next time I say family, I don't mean everyone that anyone knows." Not that there would be a next time that she trusted any of them with anything. Except maybe babysitting? Because she didn't really have any other options there. And while she couldn't trust them with a secret, she could probably trust them with the kid.

"I'm gonna kill Bax. I just haven't decided how," Linx continued, like he'd been wronged in this scenario.

"Uh… No. You're not." Killing Bax was a bad idea for many reasons. One, even rock stars got pinned with felonies. Two, Bax couldn't really pay child support if he was dead. Three, the band couldn't tour without their lead singer. Could they? Hmm. Maybe one of the new Denver guys could take that place? That one might not be a point after all. She'd have to wait and see.

And four—this was the big one—she held out a sliver of hope that maybe Bax would want to know his baby too. He couldn't do that if he was skipping over the rainbow bridge.

"Don't kill Bax," she said, and she meant it. "I'd very much like my little chickpea to meet the most awesome uncle in the history of uncles." Also, maybe the daddy.

"He touched you," Linx said, soft and ominous.

"Well, if you're going to take out every man who's ever touched me, I should start a list." Not that it'd be a long list. But it would, in fact, be a list. Over two people on it, and all that. "It could be worse. It could be Alan's baby."

Alan and Courtney had dated for a while, and Linx hated that guy. Courtney thought he was nice enough, just not the kind of guy with sticking power.

"This isn't funny," Linx said, but his anger had diffused a touch.

"Of course it's not funny. And we touched *each other*. It

wasn't the *whatever, man, don't touch my sister, she's a little lady* bull-shit you think it was." Stupid, yes. Consensual? Also, yes. There had been a lot of touching going on, but it wasn't only Bax.

Linx probably didn't want to hear too many details, so she shut her mouth.

"You were off-limits," Linx continued, but the fight was out of his words.

Because she was right.

"Cedric Lincoln, you don't get to choose who I am off-limits to." Wasn't she the one who got to be angry in this situation? Also, "Any idea where Bax is now?"

Because now would be the time that she should connect with him. Lucky for her, because her family liked to jibber jabber, the initial baby-daddy shock would likely have worn off.

"He knows you're at the house. My guess is he'll be there soon," Linx said. "Do you want me there for this? Want me to call the police to haul his ass away for trespassing?"

"Absolutely not." The last thing this conversation needed was her big brother going banana pants on the guy who just found out that he got a girl pregnant, or a police officer showing up at the door that was definitely not a stripper. The only police officer she ever liked at her front door was the Strip-O-Gram that Irina sent her two birthdays ago.

No strippers tonight though. Tonight, she had to deal with a reality that didn't come with a playlist and a thong.

Gah. She needed a minute. Thus, she hung up on her brother. Laid down on his sofa, alone in his living room, giving herself a few moments of peace before—

The pounding on the front door started.

"Who on earth is that?" Mom asked, trotting down the stairs of Linx's house like it was her house.

Mom checked the peephole as the pounding on the door came harder. "Courtney!"

Bax.

Not that she didn't know it was him. She'd put two and two together on that front. Still, the blood seemed to drain from her head, making it excessively hard to think and plan and come up with a communication strategy.

Dad, thank goodness, had lived with rock stars and their shenanigans most of his adult life, so Bax and his pounding didn't faze him.

He moseyed over to the door, past Mom.

Unfortunately for Courtney, Mom's attention was settled on her. And in that moment, Courtney knew that Mom knew who knocked her up. Linx, with his inability to hold anything close to the chest, had probably told her too.

Ugh.

"Oh my God, I have to call Cherie," Mom squealed, and ran up the stairs.

Right, so Bax's parents were going to know too. This was good information to know—anytime Courtney wanted everyone in the world to know her secrets, she only had to tell her family. They'd handle the rest.

The knocking was still happening at the door, but had ratcheted up.

"Hold your horses," Dad said, pulling at the waistband of his pants before yanking the door open.

Clearly, Bax was not expecting to see her dad.

That stopped him short, but only for a second. He scanned the room, his gaze settling on Courtney and clearly —given the expression sketched across his face—seeing straight through any excuses she was subconsciously drumming up in her mind.

"Hey, Bax." She gave him a little wave and started to run her hand over her abdomen. She stopped before she made the gesture that had become something of second nature lately. Her T-shirts were getting tight, so she blamed it on that. "Good news, yeah?"

He dropped his gaze to her stomach. But she wasn't really showing yet. Still way too early for that. Sure, she was a little poofy around the middle, had a massive craving for carrots—

"You're pregnant." He said this not as a question but as a statement.

"I know, it's such a surprise…" Courtney took some deep breaths as she spoke, trying to figure out how to spin this even a little. "I know this is so not what we planned…"

"Brennan?" Dad looked Bax up and down. "You're the mystery man?"

No, this wasn't Brennan. The fire in his gaze, the unfeeling expression… yeesh… this was Bax.

"Bax is the mystery man." Courtney made some jazz hands.

"Cherie wants to know your due date?" Mom called from the top of the stairs. "And, Brennan, dear, your mom says hi."

"My mom knows?" Bax asked, as confused as Courtney felt about this turn of events.

"Hi, Brennan," his mom said from the speaker on Courtney's mom's iPad. Oh, look, they were video chatting. "Your father and I are so excited!" Cherie shouted, as though they couldn't hear her over the miles between wherever they were floating in the ocean and Denver. "What a great surprise this is!"

"Yep, surprise! Now, I need to sit down." Courtney headed toward the sofa and sat, dropping her head between her knees so she didn't lose consciousness. This seemed like a bad time for that, and if Linx found out, he'd blame Bax and it'd be a whole thing.

Mostly, by utilizing this maneuver, she also didn't have to look anyone in the eyes.

Abruptly, Dad said, "I want ice cream. Let's get ice cream, honey. Cherie, you come too."

"Ice cream is great," Courtney said, lifting her head from

her knees. In her defense, she also really wanted some ice cream. *Sue me.*

Dad shook his head, grabbing his coat. "Only room for two and the iPad. Let's go on a date, girls. What kind should I bring you back, Court?" he asked, pulling on his coat.

Traitor.

"Raspberry, please," Courtney said. "With chocolate sauce and sprinkles and whipped cream with a cherry."

Now she really wanted that ice cream, with a side of carrot sticks and cucumber.

When her parents left, she bit her bottom lip. Should she just come out and say it? But he already knew. So she didn't really need to say it. More like just acknowledge that the baby was his. He'd probably want to know. That'd probably be the question. Because, of course, he wasn't sure if she'd been with anyone else.

While, no, she hadn't been with anyone else, because everyone else seemed like an unflavored popsicle next to the sprinkled raspberry deliciousness of Brennan, he didn't know that. He also didn't need to know that, since his head was already plenty big.

"It's yours," she said, deciding to just go all in and get it out there. "I'm keeping it." That seemed important to share, so he didn't make a suggestion that might make her angry. "You don't have to be involved if you don't want to be." She said this in a chipper voice, like she was ordering more ice cream.

"It's mine," he said, saying what she'd already confirmed, and moving into the room. She didn't even get to nod her head before he continued, "You're keeping it."

This time, she nodded. Though she said nothing because he looked like he still had more to say. Usually, she didn't mind cutting Bax off, because it was kind of their thing, but this time she didn't particularly want him more agitated than he already was.

"I don't have to be involved if I don't want to be?" There seemed to be some steam coming out of his ears, which made no sense, given that she was letting him off the hook as far as any responsibilities and he'd had the entire car drive to process the news.

This is where he should say, *Thank you for being so awesome.*

"I talked to the label and Hans. If you'd prefer, I can switch my assignment away from Dimefront. That way you don't have to… see me." She probably should stop speaking because Bax looked like he might short-circuit at any second.

Maybe this would be a really good time for her to pretend to lose consciousness? She didn't particularly want to be conscious through this anyway.

"I want to make this easy for you," she said, because she did. Also, she wanted to make it easy for her too. She wasn't totally selfless.

He turned away from her. Dropped to the other end of the sofa, his head going to his knees this time, and started breathing heavy through his nose and out his mouth, sort of like he'd done right before he came in the shower—

"Nothing about this is easy," he said to the wall.

"Except me." Levity seemed like a good idea. A little joke at her expense.

It had the opposite effect, and Bax turned toward her. "Don't say shit like that about the woman who is having my baby."

Oh.

Huh. So he accepted it just like that.

"I thought you'd want to do the paternity test thing. They can test as soon as we're ready, but I was going to wait until after the first trimester, just to be sure nothing goes wrong with the pregnancy."

Bax wasn't moving. Breathing, sure. But his breaths were shallow.

"Something's wrong with the baby?" He stared at her abdomen like it was something super special.

That one gaze made her warm and squishy inside.

"No. Of course not. It's just..." Courtney bit her lip. "This is my first time being pregnant. There's no reason to think things won't go well. But there's no way to know. You have to admit I'm me, which makes me kind of a disaster, so..."

"You're kind of a disaster?" he asked, monotone and like he was trying to process what she'd said. "You're not a disaster. I'm a—"

"Do you want a minute?" Courtney didn't touch him, because if she touched him, she'd probably want to take him up to the shower. But she also didn't want him to fall off the couch either. Then she'd have to be the conscious one, and that wasn't something that sounded nice. She'd end up at the hospital with him, and then she wouldn't get her ice cream sundae and the day really would be shit. "I can give you a minute."

On that note, Bax shook his head and dropped it back against the sofa. He repeated the word "fuck" repeatedly.

Here's the thing. She didn't really expect him to jump up and down at the knowledge that she was going to be a mother, though she'd allowed a few daydreams like that. Then she squashed them because they weren't reasonable. What was happening now was more likely and totally in line with Brennan Baxter and the way he avoided things that were hard.

Perhaps he needed a pillow? The banging of his head thing really didn't look like it felt super great.

She should get him a pillow.

Look at her, being motherly.

She totally had this thing.

She snagged one of the throw pillows off the sofa and

scooted toward Bax. When he lifted his head, she slipped the pillow there.

He stilled. Head against the pillow, he stopped, stared into her eyes straight through to her soul. He lifted his hand to her jaw and touched her there, the pad of his fingertips against her skin.

"Brennan," she whispered into the side of his palm. "I wanted to tell you myself."

Though she hadn't quite made her plan to tell him yet, this method would not have even remotely made the short list of options.

He continued stroking the column of her jaw.

She let him, because it felt really nice, and at this point, not a lot of things felt nice.

"I want to be part of this," he said, that croak back in his throat as he dropped his hand.

The croak thing was sexy in a baby-daddy rock star kind of way.

"We've got time." She situated herself beside him. A little distance so it wasn't weird. Though, actually, the distance made it feel odd. Not better.

"If you want to be part of this, that's great," she continued. "We'll make it happen."

"Tell me everything." He looked up at her, eyes soft like he was a kid again, helping her climb up into the treehouse at the park up the street. Like they had been transported right back to a time when things were so much simpler.

"How long have you known?" he asked.

"Not long." She nodded. That much was true, at least. "I seriously just found out, like, a few days ago." A week, but who was counting?

He looked like he wanted to drop his head to the pillow again. Instead, he lifted her hand in his and held it there, threading their fingers together.

At the sight of his hand holding hers, she gave him a look. One that she hoped broadcasted, *Uh, what the hell?*

Though she didn't say it out loud.

"I want our baby. We're gonna make this work." He squeezed her hand like he was making a promise.

Of note, he had not said that he wanted her. He wanted the kid.

That was fine though. She didn't really want him either.

Not really.

Right?

Chapter Nine
BAX

WELL, hell, this was awkward.

"Hey." Bax stood on the top step of Linx's front walk and held his hand out to Linx for a shake.

Linx crossed his arms, totally blocking the doorway of his house, totally leaving Bax hanging. Bax had really screwed the light socket, so he understood. He still shook his own hand because he couldn't leave himself hanging like that.

"Courtney invited me to the appointment." Bax glanced behind Linx, but Courtney was nowhere to be seen.

Linx grunted.

That was about where they stood, and Bax had to fix it because he'd fucked it.

Bax understood, got why Linx was ticked. He didn't have a sister, but if he did and Linx had gotten her pregnant after years of bickering, he'd be less than accommodating too. "I'm sorry, man."

"My sister's life is totally upside down, and you're sorry?"

"I am. I am so sorry."

Linx said nothing.

"I've spent way too much time in a fog," Bax said, genuine, hoping he didn't fuck this up, because he really didn't want to lose his friend over this or his band or… Courtney. "But I realized something in that fog."

Linx didn't move, but he quirked an eyebrow.

"*This* is exactly what I need in my life. I need Courtney to kick my ass on the regular and our kid to keep me centered."

Linx had a look of a man not buying what Bax was selling.

"Serious, man, I want to do right by Courtney and our kid, and I'm willing to do what I need to do to make that happen." Whatever that was… as long as it didn't include walking away. That was the one thing he couldn't do.

"My mom always said something—you know, you were there a lot. 'You can be sorry, but unless you change the behavior, your remorse is only a show.'" Bax's tongue felt a little heavy as he spoke. "I am sorry, and I am not going to be the same guy around your sister. I'm not arguing with her. Not pissing her off because I can. And I'm going to support her, because that's what she deserves."

"And if Em shows up tomorrow asking for cash?" Linx asked, looping his fingers in the waistband of his jeans.

"Em's not in the picture anymore." Bax had moved on, and now he had a new focus. Two of them, in fact.

This baby was a not-so-small nudge in the right direction. He'd been wandering like a lost fool, and now he wasn't just drifting. There was a big ol' foam finger pointing the way.

"I want a family," he said, meaning it. His parents had wanted more kids, but only had the one. He'd always wanted to fill a whole house with clomping feet and love. "My original plan didn't pan out, but for some reason, I'm getting a second chance. The right chance."

He didn't like to think too hard about Em and his original plan, because then he'd get an ache in the center of his chest.

Linx said nothing, just glared.

So this would take a bit more effort and a helluva lot of time. Bax would wait it out.

"This baby is the answer to a question I didn't even realize I'd asked." He held Linx's stare, not breaking the link between them. "I will not screw up things with your sister."

He'd already decided that he wanted to be in with her for more than the baby-daddy bit. He wanted to give her time to adjust to the idea that maybe the two of them could be the real deal, an actual couple who cared about each other.

"Courtney's confused," Linx said. "I don't like it when she's confused."

Bax shoved his hands in his pockets. "Me neither."

"Which means you can't fuck this up anymore, because that would hurt her, and I can't have that."

"I'm not going to." Bax held up his hands in surrender. "I'm letting her take the lead. I want a shot to show her how good we can be together and how this can work out for everyone. I'm willing to give her the time to come to that conclusion."

"And if she doesn't?" Linx was being a hard-ass about this, but Bax mostly respected him for that.

"Then I guess we'll figure something out. She's Courtney. You know her, she's amazing." Bax kicked at the edge of the step with his sneaker. "I just didn't see it before because she sees…" He looked up, didn't want to say it, but understood deep down that he had to. "She sees me. I don't like it when people see me. I like to be Bax, but she sees Brennan sometimes too."

"I see Brennan." Linx dropped his arms, finally engaging. "Always have."

"But I didn't get you pregnant, did I?" Bax shook his head because that wasn't the correct thing to say. "I'm sorry that I broke code, but I'm not sorry that Courtney's pregnant. I want this like she wants this. We'll take things slow, and find our way."

"And you won't go poking your dick where it doesn't belong?"

"I'm not going to be seeing anyone else."

"No handing out bracelets?"

Who did he think Bax was? "No. That's over."

"How serious are you about my sister?" Linx leveled a big-brother stare that ate clear through what was left of Bax's veneer.

"Serious enough to keep it in my pants until I convince her that I can make her happy."

Linx frowned. "And if you break that promise?"

"Then I'm scum." But he wouldn't let that happen— would do everything in his power so that it wouldn't.

"You're not scum," Linx said through gritted teeth. "But I'm still pissed. I don't know how to forgive you."

"Then let me prove to you that I mean what I said. Let me prove it to Courtney too."

Linx nodded and reached for the door. "She'll be out in a minute. Nice hat."

The door closed, and Bax stood there like a teenager waiting for the girl he was taking to prom. A guy full of pent-up energy and hope. So he paced beside the Range Rover. Three long steps to the tailgate, three long steps to the hood. Repeat. And again.

He had that feeling in his gut like he did before going onstage at a massive venue. Like he was jonesing for what came next and having a hard time keeping that type of energy pent-up.

Because today he would get to see the little dude or dudette on the ultrasound. Maybe there'd be multiple dudes or dudettes. He wasn't saying his sperm was superhuman, but he was confident that he wasn't a slouch in that department.

Courtney needed to get out here because left alone with his own thoughts and Linx's ultimatums was not a great place to be.

"Should I knock again?" he asked the driver he'd hired as part of his security detail in Denver.

Chet, also known as Driver Dude, leaned against the hood and shook his head. Chet didn't say much, but he had to have caught most of what went down with Linx.

"You sure?" Bax asked, again with the pacing. "You think it's weird that Linx didn't ask me in?" Bax paused his pacing. "I mean, what does that say?"

"Says he didn't invite you in," Chet responded.

Right.

Bax would do his part to save Dimefront, fix his relationship with Linx, and show Courtney that they could be more than a team. What that meant at the moment was staying the fuck away from Linx so he could deal with his anger, and not push Courtney so she could realize he wasn't a total selfish asshat.

"Not my call what's weird or not weird," Chet said, all Chet-like. "I'm just here to take the bullet and drive the car."

Well, wasn't that frightening? Chet had the look of a guy who'd been in more than a few street fights. Crooked nose, scars along the temple, lots of muscles. The kind of guy who made a good security detail because everyone was a little scared of him, including Bax.

"I mean, she invited me to this appointment. That means something," Bax rambled as he resumed his pacing. "We used to be friends, you know? Back in the neighborhood where we grew up. Used to talk for over ten minutes without arguing about something that doesn't really matter in the long term."

Now, he was ready to put aside his arguments for the sake of the kiddo and their future.

Then the front door opened, and Courtney stepped out, sucking the air right from his lungs. She was... wow.

"Hey," she said, giving him a once-over that was most definitely a little awkward. Stilted. Like *Ew, who are you?* Or *Ew, so this is what I got myself into.*

Also... where did he miss the memo that this was a dress-up gig? He should've worn something other than jeans, a black tee, and a novelty hat he'd bought that read, "Call Me Daddy." This seemed appropriate for the meet-the-kid appointment.

But here he was dressed like usual while Courtney wore a knee-length yellow dress with floaty sleeves. She'd pulled her hair up into a heap of a bun that must've taken a helluva lot of time to get it to appear so perfectly messy.

She started down the stairs.

Should he offer to hug her? Should he help her down the stairs? That'd be the nice thing to do. But Courtney probably didn't want his help.

What the hell did a guy do in this situation?

Apparently, nothing, because that was what he did.

Chet, meanwhile, opened the back door of the vehicle for them. At least he had something to do with *his* hands.

"Thanks for the ride," Courtney said, slipping into the car.

This she said to Chet.

Chet didn't reply, as was his way.

"Thanks for inviting me," Bax said, because he knew well enough that she didn't have to.

Yet ever since he'd said he wanted to be involved, she'd been nothing but accommodating. Inviting him to her doctor's appointment? Check. Texting him when she felt the baby move for the first time? Check. Texting him to tell him that apparently it was just gas? Also, check.

He felt very… unable to reciprocate. Which also led to this pent-up, pacing-the-floor energy inside him.

This was not a feeling he enjoyed. Which was weird because he usually liked it when others did shit for him and left him in his own head.

"Super excited to meet the little dude or dudette," he said as he climbed into the seat beside her.

Were the circumstances ideal? No, they were not.

"What's with the smile?" Courtney asked, waving her fingertip toward his face.

Up close, she was even prettier than when she'd come outside. Her cheeks were pinker than usual. This pregnancy agreed with her. Not just the plump tits and ass, which he noticed but didn't mention, but the glow of her skin and the way her eyes seemed brighter.

"What smile?" he asked, intentionally moving his lips into a frown.

"That goofy grin you've got going on." She squinted at him, evaluating.

Oh, that smile. Yeah. He actually felt… giddy about the whole prospect of being a dad. Giddy and unsure of what to do. They didn't write books for rock stars who knocked up their friend's sister in a one-night-shower stand after breaking up with their fiancée and imploding their band.

"What's your angle?" she asked. Again with the criticism in her tone.

"I don't have an angle." He didn't. Also, he wouldn't argue with the woman who was going to be his baby mama. That was his new rule.

So he said nothing. Because apparently saying anything led to her wanting to argue. She said nothing. Chet said nothing.

A couple of other security guys met them at the medical plaza where they did these scans. They were discreet enough. As discreet as two beefy guys in black suits could be.

"Security?" Courtney took in the security guards, then turned to Bax and gave him a slow blink. "Are you serious right now?"

He was 100 percent serious. There was no way he was risking anything happening to her or the kid. Or him. Not to leave him out of the equation.

"He's serious." Courtney answered her own question,

apparently not appreciating his efforts to protect her or their baby.

Chet opened the door, and Bax slipped out onto the sidewalk. He held his hand out for Courtney. She did not take it, because apparently he now had cooties.

"You know how things get when we go out," Bax said, shoving his rejected hand into his pocket. "Fans can get weird."

As their publicist, Courtney knew better than most how things could go badly when they went out.

"When you go out," she corrected. "When I go out, things are fine."

"But you're with me," he said. Actually, that might be the first time he'd said those words. She was with him. They were in this together. And that meant certain precautions needed to be taken.

"This entire production is totally unnecessary," she said, fidgeting with the edge of her skirt, smoothing and fiddling some more.

Damn, he wished he didn't have cooties, so he could reach for her hand. Soothe away the nerves. Promise that things would be just fine because today they got to see the inside of her uterus. But that'd be a weird thing to say, and if he reached for her, she'd probably just swat him away.

"Not unnecessary." He said it. He meant it.

Courtney clearly didn't like it.

"You're being unreasonable," she said with a huff.

You're being unreasonable, Bax. Em's words floated through the air. That'd been part of the last argument they'd had. The one after he caught her with the neighbor guy.

You're being unreasonable...

"Think you're thinking of yourself, sweets," he said.

To Em? To Courtney? He couldn't be sure. What he understood for certain was that the buzz he'd been enjoying today had come to a screeching halt.

"Brennan, seriously," Courtney murmured. "Don't be this guy."

"Court." This time, he reached for her hand. Cautiously, because if she didn't want the touch, he'd let it go. Let her go. Let her have her space.

She didn't let him go though. Allowed him to link his fingers with hers.

There it was, that buzz of excitement again. Except this time it was about holding a pretty girl's hand. When the hell was the last time that had happened?

"You've seen what can happen," he whispered, so he wouldn't spook what seemed like a truce between them. "The fans who take a very vested interest in us need a reminder to keep some distance."

She grunted in reply.

The grunt shouldn't have been cute—she probably didn't want it to be cute. Yet there it was, being cute.

Some of those fans and groupies and followers forgot that rock stars were people too. He made it a point to protect his family. Courtney might not think of herself as his family, but he'd always thought of her that way. Ever since she rode her Soft 'n' Sweet bicycle down the sidewalk as a seven-year-old and biffed it in front of his house. He'd been twelve, and he'd wanted nothing more than to make the scrapes on her knees disappear.

His parents still lived on that street.

Linx's parents might have moved away long ago, but his parents didn't see the purpose of leaving what they knew.

Not when they'd already paid off the house. So Bax ensured that security was provided. Since the band's first record hit platinum and the shadow figures started emerging from the alleyway every-fucking-where.

Twice security had had to step in.

Twice he'd been grateful as hell that he'd placed them there.

Because the thought of the alternative?

Not an option he would entertain.

"You're the target," she mumbled. "Not me."

He gave her hand a squeeze. "Because I'm a target, you could be."

She turned to him. This time not arguing, but clearly her hackles were raised. "I've been Linx's sister the whole time, and no one has ever targeted me."

"You've never been pregnant with the lead singer of Dimefront's kid," Bax said. This changed things. Changed her position with the band. Her position with the fans.

Was it him, or did the skin on her chest get a little red?

"Next time I guess I should go for a drummer, huh?" A tickle of a grin twitched her lips.

"No drummers." He gripped her hand harder. "We're in this together. Let me be in this with you."

She squeezed back, and dammit all to hell, that felt amazing. Like they were a dysfunctional football team that didn't know how to play the game but wound up on the field anyway.

"You know what?" Courtney held up her hands in surrender. Unfortunately, this meant she let his hand go.

He didn't like that.

"Fine," she continued as she brushed a small piece of hair from her forehead. "You want to hire a driver for me, and you want to bring along a security detail? Fine."

Well, this was progress, wasn't it? Slow progress. But progress just the same.

"The thing is, you could've mentioned it before. Talked with me about it. Given me a heads-up so it didn't blindside me." This she said under her breath.

"You're blindsided?" he asked, trotting to keep up with her.

"I thought this was just us," she said, under her breath. "I didn't realize there would be an entourage…"

The light bulb over his head seemed to click on.

This was private. This was them. Not the world.

Right. His bad.

"Fuck," he said, rubbing his hand over his face.

"Yeah," she replied, pushing the button for the elevator.

Neither of them said anything for a beat. The only sound was her breath and his heartbeat thudding in his ears.

"I got so excited about today that I wasn't thinking straight. You're right, I was wrong about this. Should've told you my plan." He made a mental note not to do that again. "I'm sorry, Court."

Looked like he'd be saying that a helluva lot.

She tilted her head to the side and studied him. "Don't do that."

"Don't do what?" Wasn't he supposed to apologize when he fucked up?

Fuck up. Then apologize. Then don't do it again.

"Don't say things to appease me because you're worried about my blood pressure." Courtney went back to waiting for the elevator.

So, in this case, he shouldn't apologize?

Fuck it, this whole pregnancy and doing the good-guy thing confused the hell out of him.

"I'm recognizing that you are right about something because you're right," he said cautiously. "I should've consulted you."

Her chest started heaving like she was holding back tears. Which, damn it to hell, was not what he wanted.

"Don't cry, Court," he said, wiping a tear away from the apple of her cheek with his thumb, even though that was not his place. Yet these were tears because he'd messed up. His to make. His to deal with. "I promise I won't do it again," he continued as the tears came faster. "All future security decisions go through both of us."

"I'm not crying," she said, even as another tear trickled down her cheek.

Okay, he wouldn't argue that point with her.

"I've done a lot of shit for you to be mad about," he said. While he was admitting the truth, maybe he should just tell her that it was him who accidentally ran over her new bicycle when he was sixteen and barely knew how the reverse feature worked on his dad's station wagon.

"I want to be mad at you, and you won't even be a dick so I can be mad at you in peace." She hiccuped. "I don't even know why I'm crying right now. It makes no sense. It's like I have no control over any part of my body."

The elevator opened, and he and Courtney stepped inside.

"Okay," he said. "I'm sorry about the body thing. That sucks. But uh… you want me to be a dick so you can still be mad at me?" he asked, because this seemed like one of those times where he didn't fully grasp what the hell was going on.

"It'd make things easier, yes." She swiped at her cheeks. Then she turned to him. "Just be you for a while. Bossy and grumpy and telling me things that piss me off. At least until we know the baby's okay."

Alarm bells started going off in his brain. "Do you think something's wrong?"

"It's not that I think anything's really wrong. But... I'm scared to hope."

Well, he had some thoughts on that. "Reason number one, we're in this together," he said. "We both fuck shit up on the regular. But two negatives make a positive, which means our kid is destined to be the next Hawking or Einstein or Beethoven."

"You think a lot of your little swimmers, don't you?" At least she smiled and the tears stopped.

"I just said I'm an idiot. You're an idiot. That means our kid's gonna be a genius."

"You just called me an idiot." She pursed her lips.

He glanced at her belly. She wasn't so swollen pregnant yet that it popped a ton, but he had noticed the slight bump.

"I called myself an idiot too," he said. "Does that help my case?"

"Thank you, Bax." A little smile tickled the corners of her lips.

"For what?"

"For being a dick when I need you to be."

Oh, well, if that was all that was required of him, perhaps he'd do excellently at this new daddy gig of his.

Chapter Ten
COURTNEY

MORE. Sterile. Paper. Against. Her. Tush.

Courtney seriously hated this part of the doctor's office.

At least this place had comfortable cloth gowns to change into, but, sheesh, so much for dressing up for the confidence boost.

The exam room wasn't large, but not small either. Enough room for the patient table, a couple of screens, cupboards.

Bax in his baby-daddy hat pushed some buttons on the expensive-looking machine beside the exam table.

"You should stop touching things," Courtney whisper-hissed.

Bax paused where he was fiddling with a knob on the machine.

"Why?" he whispered back.

"Because you might break them," she said, hoping that would be enough to get him to cease and desist with the button pushing and knob turning.

"I won't break anything." Of this, he sounded convinced.

Her? Not so much.

"You don't know that." And why were they still whispering? "And we might need that knob for the appointment."

"Okay." He moseyed away from the machine and opened the cupboard above the sink.

"Are you always like this?"

"Like what?"

"You know, with the opening and closing and touching and—" She gestured to where he was currently digging through the cupboard.

"Curious?"

That was not what she would've called it, but she said, "That's one way to put it."

"I always thought I might've been a doctor if I wasn't in Dimefront," he said, standing on tiptoe, apparently to see what was on the top shelf.

"Seriously?" Courtney had never—not once in her life—considered that Bax would've been anything except the lead singer of a band. Definitely not something that involved years and years of medical school, internship, and residency.

"Yeah." He pulled out a small box and opened it up. "Huh. Condoms. A little late for that, yeah?" He shook the box.

"Going through the cupboards isn't any better than pushing buttons," Courtney whisper-hissed again. "Put the condoms down and pull up a chair."

"Negative." He shook his head, but he did put the box of condoms back in the cupboard. "Too much pent-up baby-daddy energy to sit." He did the bounce-hop thing he usually reserved for right before going onstage. "Baby daddy, doo doo doo doo doo doo," he sang to the tune of "Baby Shark."

Oh my God with the baby-daddy bit. She wanted to claw off his hat and run it through a shredder.

"How do you feel about using a different term?" she asked. Something less annoying that held a bigger punch.

"You don't like 'baby daddy'?" He paused his wandering around the room.

"Yeah, Bax." She shivered. "The baby-daddy thing, it's kinda creepy."

"So I can't call you my baby mama?" Aw, he looked a little sad at that.

She didn't want him to be sad. Also, she didn't want to be referred to as his baby mama. Motherhood was so conflicting.

Thankfully, Bax shoved his hands in his pockets as he noodled on her request, which at the very least prevented him from touching anything else.

"Let's just try something else on for size," she said, as cheerful as she could. "See what happens."

"Ten-four." He rolled up on his toes and gestured between them. "Then we need to figure out what we're gonna call each other."

"I was thinking I'd call you Bax, and you'd call me Courtney." She fussed with the edge of the gown. "That seems to have worked so far."

He shook his head. "That's no fun. Can I at least have a pet name for you?"

"Yeah, you can call me Courtney." She flashed him a grin. "And nothing else."

"No fun. No fun at all," he muttered, and went about examining the posters on the wall. There was one illustrating the stages of fetus development, from embryo to delivery.

Unfortunately, he wasn't wrong. Since becoming pregnant, her fun factor had significantly declined. She should let him have a pet name for her, something perky and exciting.

"Hey," he said. "Take my picture." He struck a pose, pointing at the photo of the baby at seven weeks—right about where she'd be.

"I'm not taking your picture." Though he looked kinda sweet there, studying those illustrations with awe.

"Can you believe we're here?" he asked, still looking at the poster.

No, no, she couldn't, but she didn't say that.

Bax finally—thank fuck, finally—sat down in the chair beside her. His foot bounced with pent-up energy. The guy either needed to perform onstage or get laid.

That thought made her tongue feel funny. Sandpaper funny.

Was he still seeing other women?

He could. There was no reason he couldn't.

For what it was worth, she could see other men too. But that would be weird and lead to a conversation she definitely did not want to have with anyone.

Also, the thought of being with someone else made her chest ache and had the same effect as smelling bacon—great and wonderful pre-pregnancy, but not so much now.

Bax lifted what looked like a long microphone from the side of the machine.

"What do you think this is for?" He held it near his mouth and started singing one of the Dimefront classics that was really about giving a blow job, but most people assumed that it was about taking a walk. Those who were really Dimefront followers knew that it wasn't gum in the song girl's mouth.

A quick tap-tap on the door and the new doctor breezed in.

New doctor paused, made a sound like she'd eaten a squeaky toy, and then turned, walked out, and closed the door.

"Shit." Courtney turned to Bax, who hadn't removed whatever the wand thing was from near his lips. "She's a Ten." Ten was the pet name for the Dimefront groupies. "That woman is not delivering our baby."

The door opened again, and the doctor lady seemed to have gotten herself together a little bit more because this time she held her hand out to Bax and said, "Brennan Baxter. You're Brennan Baxter."

"I am." He nodded, totally used to the fangirl schtick.

Courtney totally checked the doctor's wrists for an I-bagged-a-Bax bracelet. Thankfully, she didn't wear one.

"I'm Courtney Lincoln," Courtney said when the doctor just stared at Bax in that groupie trance. "Your patient," she added, rubbing her tummy for good measure.

"Right, right, right. I'm Dr. Pepper." The woman held her hand out to Courtney, but still stared at Bax.

Yeah, she wasn't going to be delivering the kid.

Bax fumbled, putting the wand back in the hanger slot thingy.

"I really shouldn't do this," Dr. Pepper said, staring straight at Bax. "But I just have to say… Oh my gosh, I shouldn't do this…"

Then don't…

"I just want to tell you how much I love your music," she gushed.

Okay, well, of everything she could've said, that wasn't the worst.

"I lost my virginity to a guy who looked just like you, but he's actually a podiatrist now." *Yup, there was the worst.*

Bax did his standard thank-you, making the fan feel important, but somehow—and Courtney wasn't entirely sure how he did this—he didn't make Courtney feel left out. He glanced at her often, even as he spoke to Dr. Pepper. Those little moments of eye contact reassured her that she was important. That they were here as a team.

She hadn't realized how much she craved that, wanted that… needed that.

"So," Dr. Pepper said, staring at the clipboard in her hand but obviously not actually reading it. "Ultrasound day?"

Courtney nodded, and they made it through the preliminary questions as Dr. Pepper side-glanced at Bax every few seconds and flicked her hair over her shoulder.

"And who is this with you?" Dr. Pepper kept her eyes stuck

to the paper as though she was asking a question on the list, but Courtney had her number.

"This is Brennan Baxter," Courtney said, sliding her gaze to Bax, who only shrugged his shoulder. "We established that, I think."

"His relationship to the mother and baby?" Dr. Pepper asked, still staring at the paper, pen held ready to scribble.

"We had sex, I impregnated her. She's my…" He looked at Courtney. "What did you decide to be called?"

"Uh…" They hadn't quite sorted that out yet, and he should never call it *impregnated* again.

"Mother Goose?" he asked, apparently on the fly.

Okay, what?

"Seriously? You went from baby mama to Mother Goose?" she asked. "Find whatever would be between those two things and call me that."

"She's *my Courtney*," Bax said, pulling her to him so their temples touched.

That was nice, seriously nice. Whooshy belly nice.

Dr. Pepper did look up then, and whatever crush she'd had on Bax seemed to dissolve. Meanwhile, Courtney's heart was a puddle of mush.

Something about the way he said "my Courtney" made her not really care what else he called her, because it was sweet, super sweet.

Finally, questions answered, Dr. Pepper strode to the cupboard and pulled out the box of condoms. She grabbed one.

Okay, well, Courtney wasn't one to judge anything, but that was a little forward if she was going for a bracelet at Bax's first baby-daddy appointment.

Gah, no, she would not start calling him that.

"Let's take a look, shall we?" Dr. Pepper asked, opening the condom package for a reason that Courtney seriously did not understand.

Bax also had a *what the fuck* look drawn across his face too, so at least it wasn't only her.

Dr. Pepper lifted the wand thing, and everything got clearer when she rolled the condom down the shaft of the wand.

"Uh," Bax said aloud.

Yeah. That.

"Have you ever had an internal ultrasound before?" Dr. Pepper asked, turning knobs and flicking switches.

Courtney glanced at Bax whose eyes seemed to be as wide as her own. "No. Never."

"Should I step out?" Bax asked, already inching toward the door. "I should step out."

"Don't you dare." Courtney pierced him with what she hoped was a *sit your ass down* stare.

He moved closer to her, leaning in and whispering in her ear, "This seems like a private moment."

She tilted her lips to his ear, so only he could hear. "Do not leave me alone with your Ten and that wand."

It must've worked, because he sat his ass down.

Dr. Pepper gave the instructions for positioning, and Courtney did as she was told, scooting her bottom down to the end of the table.

Once the probe—it was no longer considered a wand as far as Courtney was concerned—was in place, the black-and-white image flickered on the screen.

"Oh," Courtney said as the *swish, swish, swish, swish, swish* sound came through the little speakers.

"That's the heartbeat." Dr. Pepper stopped, did some stuff with the machine, and clicked a bunch of buttons. "You can't see much now. Still pretty little, but this is a healthy rock star of an embryo."

Courtney's gaze fixed on the screen. She couldn't seem to say or do anything other than watch the monitor.

"Wow," Bax said, and his hand somehow found hers,

holding her palm against his. She squeezed, and holy, holy, holy shit. This was an actual human growing inside of her. Not that she'd expected a litter of puppies, just that—

"Wow," she repeated.

Dr. Pepper started humming one of the early Dimefront songs about breaking up with a too clingy girlfriend. *Nice choice.*

"I made that." Bax remained oblivious to Dr. Pepper as he pointed at the screen and grinned like a lunatic.

Uh… say wha?

"Excuse me?" Courtney asked, with what she was certain was the appropriate amount of *What the hell?* "Which one of us is puking all the time?"

"Right." He pinched his lips together like he used to do as a kid when he messed up and got caught. The move was adorable and reminiscent and… she hoped their baby did that same thing when they got older.

"You made this." He tapped the monitor. "I had nothing to do with it."

Well, he had been present for the main event. His unwillingness to spar with her was really starting to become a nuisance.

"So you had *nothing* to do with this? That's what you're saying?" Was she picking a fight? Yes. Was it working? To be determined.

"I don't know what the right answer is here." He squeezed her hand as he said this.

That little squeeze sent butterflies to her tummy.

"So I'm just going to say the answer is whatever is the right one." He did the smile thing again, and she totally melted.

Dr. Pepper sighed a melted-butter sigh.

"I mean, I was there for the exciting part at the beginning," he said like an eager Labrador retriever. "But you're doing the heavy lifting now. I only did it the one time."

She tilted her head to the side.

"I mean, not heavy lifting, just a little lifting." He turned to Dr. Pepper. "The shower, you know how it goes?"

Oh hell, Dr. Pepper did not need to have that vision of Bax. Courtney rolled her eyes and went back to watching the *swish, swish, swish* on the screen.

"Everything looks great," Dr. Pepper finally said. A few more button pushes and she removed the probe so it could go back to being just a wand for Bax to sing into. "Questions so far?"

Oh, all the questions. None that could likely be answered at the moment.

Dr. Pepper handed over a few prints of the little bean growing in Courtney's stomach. She said something else before leaving, but Courtney didn't really hear, because she was staring at the image. This little blip was everything all wrapped up in a mistake.

"We made a cute kid," Bax said, pressing a kiss to her temple.

No, that wasn't Bax. This was Brennan. Brennan with the softness and the tenderness, and maybe there would be more Brennan in this baby than Bax. Maybe that was what she'd end up with. She couldn't complain about that.

Bax's phone buzzed in his pocket.

"Do you need to get that?" she asked, still not pulling her gaze from the image.

He checked the phone. Then clicked it on.

"Hey, Hans," he said. "What's up?"

He paused. She glanced from the pictures to him. His eyebrows furrowed, and he'd gone from Labrador retriever to scared puppy in the blink of an eye.

"Yeah. I'll be there." He paused. "Yeah. She's good. Really good."

Courtney sat up from the exam table. This time the paper hadn't ripped.

She moved to grab her clothes and head to the little bathroom off to the right. Once she finished dressing, she came back out to Bax staring at the images.

"Can I keep one?" he asked, tracing his finger along the edge.

"Of course." Courtney shook off any residual feelings from the temple kiss. "What's going on with Hans?" She picked up her purse and slung it over her shoulder.

Bax paled a little. "He asked me to stop at a studio to meet with the guys."

Oh, well, that could be good. Or it could be bad.

"It might not be over," she assured. "I've been talking to Knox and Hans. They're thinking about moving to Denver. Knox has been over at the house. He's cool with Linx. And Hans works magic, you know that."

And yet did any of them really know? Linx hadn't ever wanted to walk away before, but now…

"Hans won't let me down." Bax nodded. "Do you mind if Chet takes you back?"

"I don't mind." She reached for his arm and gave it a squeeze. It didn't feel weird this time. "Are you okay?"

"Uh-huh," he said.

Call it her newly minted mother's intuition, but she wasn't buying it. Bax was terrified.

Chapter Eleven
COURTNEY

HANS CALLED her immediately after their meeting to confirm the logistics of a "Dimefront is officially moving operations to Denver" announcement. The two new guys—Tanner and Mach—were initiated as bandmates. Linx wasn't sulking, Knox wasn't complaining, and Bax didn't look like he'd eaten a ghost.

The chat was not of the breakup variety. As Courtney had hoped, Hans worked his magic.

All in all, things looked promising for the band.

Linx even invited Bax back to the house after their studio chat. Bonus—this time he wasn't looking at him like he was going to murder the guy in his sleep with a swizzle stick. They gathered around the kitchen island—Tanner, Mach, Bax, Knox, Linx, Becca, Courtney, and the parents (even Cherie on video call)—the marble counters and travertine tile floor a far cry from that first meeting they'd had in the garage at her parents' old house.

"Everything okay?" Linx asked, just for her to hear.

"Uh-huh." She pulled the photos from her purse. "Baby's totally healthy, and we got pictures." No one else seemed to have a *holy crap, this is happening* reaction. Ah well, they weren't the one growing this tomato plant.

"I don't get it." Knox picked up the photo and turned it upside down. "Where's the kid?"

Bax pointed to the bean-shaped fleck in the center of the image. "There."

"You sure? That looks like Courtney ate a funky-shaped gummy worm." Knox handed the photo back. "Congrats all the same."

The kid did kind of look like a funky-shaped gummy worm. Courtney turned the photo right side up. Yup, still gummy.

Gah, now that she'd seen it, she could not unsee it. She frowned because, damn, she didn't really want to see it. The photo was better when the kid was just a kid.

"Have you ever seen a transvaginal internal ultrasound? Because I did today, and I did not know that was a thing." Bax tipped back his cherry seltzer water like he was gulping beer.

Make no mistake, the other guys drank beer, her mom was drinking beer, even Bax's mom on the iPad video call was drinking a beer. But he'd asked to have what Courtney was having.

She wasn't sure how to feel about Bax and his seltzer. The gesture was sort of sweet, since she really couldn't have a beer. But also kind of off because it wasn't like they were a couple, and he'd been dishing out a whole lot of sweet lately. The kind of sweet that made sense for a girlfriend or a significant other, but not for Courtney.

So, instead of choosing one of those options, she elected to feel nothing about it and let Bax drink whatever he wanted. If that was cherry-flavored seltzer, then she'd just buy more.

"I have not seen one of those ultrasounds." Mom held up the iPad. "Cherie, have you seen one?"

"It's sick," Bax said, getting animated again with that

explosive energy taking over. "They just put it on up there, and then boom"—he smacked his hands together—"kid."

"Isn't that sort of what happened when you made the kid?" Knox asked under his breath.

Thankfully, everyone ignored him. His mom, however, looked seriously confused.

"Sick?" she asked, leaning into the camera.

"By 'sick,' he means 'awesome,'" Courtney replied. "No one has an infection or anything like that."

"I checked out car seat options today." Bax pulled up a browser on his phone and held it up for Courtney. "Wanted to get your opinion before I make a purchase."

She hadn't even gotten to picking out maternity pants, and he was already at the car seat level?

"Bax." She took the phone and thumbed through the options. "This is a little premature, don't you think?"

"We already ordered one," Mom said, holding up Cherie on the iPad. "Cherie and I bought it when we bought the crib."

So they had a car seat and a crib and absolutely no maternity pants?

"Mom." Bax leaned in so his face filled the iPad. "Wait until Courtney chooses. She has to say what she wants because, well, she's... the mom." He stilled. "Can I say that? You good with that?"

Courtney was having squishy inside feelings again, and warmth seemed to settle her nerves. "I am the baby's mom, so yeah."

She was totally having a moment here over Bax and car seats and cribs and moms overstepping and—

"Okay, good. I wasn't sure after the entire conversation today." He took another pull of his seltzer. "Don't want to fuck it up again."

"What conversation?" Linx asked.

"Court here doesn't like to be called baby mama and takes issue with me being called baby daddy."

"Bet the hat isn't helping with that." Knox eyed said hat.

No, it wasn't. Also, of everything Courtney wanted to do, having this conversation was not one of them. Didn't even make the top one hundred.

"Bax." Courtney waited until he met her gaze. Then she shook her head. "I'm the mom. You're the dad. No other labels needed." *Or wanted.* She didn't actually say that last part, only thought it.

"Was thinking we should come up with something to call the little tyke until he or she is born," Bax said. "I made a list."

Color Courtney surprised, because Bax had actually made a list of pre-baby names. He'd written them down and everything. Also, he'd categorized them into boxes called "Favorites," "Courtney Will Like," and "In Case She Hates Them All."

"Just 'the baby' doesn't work for you?" Because she was totally fine with calling the baby that until the munchkin had an actual name.

"It's just a little *normal* for my kid." He stopped. Swallowed, and glanced around. "Your kid. Our kid. The kid in your uterus." And he'd officially read too many posters at the obstetrics office.

"Okay... Just..." Courtney didn't read off the list. She'd just go with asking, "What do you think we should call him or her?"

"Something like Atlas or Tiny Badass?" Bax suggested. "That's my favorite."

Hah, what the—

"No." Courtney shook her head.

He shrugged, going back to his seltzer. "Okay, your call."

"Oh my God, stop doing that." She enunciated every word.

He stopped mid-gulp, sputtering, "Doing what?"

"Being so agreeable." She shoved her hands on her hips. "We've already had this discussion. You don't just go along with what I say because I said it. If you want Tiny Badass and I say no, then you lay out the reasons you're going to call Tiny Badass, Tiny Badass. Then we argue about it."

"I like McFluffin," Mom said. "It's on the list under 'Alternatives.'"

"Team Baby Shrimp over here." Knox raised his hand.

"Somebody hold up the list," Cherie said.

"No to McFluffin," Courtney said to her mom. Then she looked at Bax. "Also, no to Atlas."

"Squirt," Linx read from the list, nodding. "That's cute."

"Especially since, you know, that's how this whole thing started," Knox oh so unhelpfully added.

Courtney pointed at him. "You're not allowed to talk anymore."

"What'd I say?" he asked.

"I've decided," she said, taking control of the situation like a badass. A badass growing a little badass seed. "We are going to call this child Tiny Badass, but not because you came up with it." She pointed to Bax for clarity. "But because it's a really cool name and I like it."

Bax glanced around the room at the other stunned faces, even his dial-in mom.

She may have taken that a *scooch* too far.

"What I mean is that you and I came to a mutually agreeable decision because I am also on board with the name Tiny Badass." That framed the situation much better.

"Does anyone know what just happened here?" he asked.

"I am also confused." Knox held up his hand.

Linx grinned and tapped the bottle of his beer to Bax's can of seltzer. "Looks like we have ourselves a Tiny Badass."

"I'm using McFluffin. It's cuter," Mom said, flouncing

away from their group over to where Dad and Hans were yapping. "I don't care what anyone else thinks."

"Team McFluffin over here, too," Cherie yelled—even though they could hear her just fine.

Well, grandmas had their prerogatives too.

Courtney glanced away from the fizzy seltzer, suddenly having an intense craving for a cucumber and carrots with hummus.

Bax was looking at her funny. Like he couldn't quite figure out what to do with her.

Funny. She couldn't figure out what to do with him either.

Chapter Twelve
COURTNEY

Two Months Later

"I SHOULD GET MY OWN PLACE," Courtney said to Linx's cat. A cat that lounged on the pillow of her bed, his foot over his left ear so he could lick his junk.

Today Gibson wore a Mister Rogers–style sweater vest, so Becca must've dressed him. When Linx dressed the cat— yeah, they did that—he usually went for something leather. This was the stage of her brother's relationship: they both dressed up his cat.

Gibson paused the licking to glance at her and meet her gaze with narrowed cat eyes.

"Am I interrupting? By all means, continue." She yawned and sat on the side of the bed. "I'm so confused. What should I do?"

Gibson dropped his leg because he knew this dance and apparently understood that she wouldn't stop talking anytime soon. She should call Irina and talk to her instead. Or run downstairs and chat with Becca. Maybe even Linx or her mom. But people talked back and didn't always say what

Courtney wanted to hear. So instead she chose Gibson, who just licked at his penis while she blathered and brainstormed.

"I don't know what Tiny Badass is going to want. The grandmas already bought the crib, but we've got no place to put it yet." Did the kid prefer to live in Cherry Creek or Arvada? Condo with a pool or lots of land to run around on? Who would take care of that property? Would she need a handyman or would handy Bax take care of it?

So many questions.

"Maybe we start with what we know?" The one thing she knew for certain—they'd land in Denver. Irina had gone into serious pout mode when Courtney informed her that she'd be moving out of LA, but Dimefront getting serious about making music and therefore moving to Denver meant this was where Bax would plant roots.

As much as the nerves twirled whenever she thought of what co-parenting with him would look like, they needed to be in the same town to give it a solid shot.

He wanted to know the baby.

Really, his desire was convincing.

All that to say, Linx had this massive mansion with a room he kept for her—because he was an exceptional big brother—so she sat tight, talked to the cat, checked out real estate listings, and tried to figure out what a kid needed for a life of happy and healthy.

Gibson hopped from the bed and meandered toward the door, tail held high. With his back to Courtney, he plopped down and went back to town on his tongue bath.

She got the message—the cat didn't want to talk. Irina would be willing to dissect the issue, but... yeah, no, that would include pouting. A little nap sounded perfect. Napping was her new favorite pastime because she wasn't that flexible, and she didn't have anyone to lick *her* junk.

She lay down on the blue bedspread, let the mattress mold to her body, and allowed the lead weights that seemed to be attached to her eyelashes pull her eyelids close. She even did the deep breathing thing that usually helped relax the muscles of her back.

This was her second favorite kind of nap—a midday, full-bed snooze. This was only second to a sofa nap, which she preferred. But Linx and Becca were downstairs, so it made little sense to fall asleep where it'd interfere with whatever they'd planned for the day.

Mom and Dad would be in and out too. They were also looking at Denver properties. Probably with Cherie in tow via iPad. Of course, the boat that Bax's parents were on returned, and they'd come for a short visit before heading back to Tennessee.

Rolling onto her side, a pillow tucked under her leg, Courtney drifted. Let her thoughts do a tango until they could settle.

They did not settle. Nopers, they bounced right into the shower and the vision of Bax with his hand on his erection, that smirk on his face and the invitation to join.

Just like that, the pulse between her legs thrummed.

Grr. This was not nap-appropriate thinking.

No Bax allowed.

She opened her eyes, blinked any memory of him away, and closed them again.

Cherries. She loved cherries. Cherries were her favorite. Especially those cherry-flavored Puffle Yum toaster tarts. Those were divine, and they didn't make her feel sick like most of the other sugary sweets she used to enjoy.

The flaky crust and warm center.

A vision of Bax feeding her toaster pastry flitted around in her subconscious, and, dammit, now she wanted sex *and* a toaster tart. Maybe with a dash of argument. Bax straight-up refused to bicker with her, something that drove her bananas.

What she'd do for a small bit of arguing with him. Just a little bickering over whether cherry or strawberry was the better variety. Nothing too intense. Just semi back to the way things were between them before, back when things were normal.

Sex and Bax and toaster tarts and bantering about who was right… now she was seriously turned on.

"Courtney?" Bax's voice came from the stairs outside her door, because apparently God had a sense of humor.

A light knock on the door followed.

She rolled onto her back, her arms spread wide across the comforter. "Come in."

Bax slipped through the door, looking way too yummy in his jeans and well-worn Fleetwood Mac T-shirt. His long hair fell well past his ears, but he didn't tie it up like her brother.

Gibson bolted for the hallway, paused, turned, and licked himself between the legs some more. The cat was halfway to being a full exhibitionist.

Bax's gaze trailed to Courtney spread out on the bed.

"Shit." Bax backtracked. Literally moving backward out the door. "I didn't mean to wake you."

She shifted toward his direction. "I wasn't asleep yet. Come on in."

Cautiously, Bax moved to the bed, but he didn't sit.

Mom had implemented a no-shoes rule in the house—even though it wasn't her house—so Bax was barefoot in her bedroom. The bare feet thing felt oddly domestic. Also, he sort of had sexy toes. Were sexy toes a thing?

Nuh-uh, sexy toes were not a thing. She was just so turned on from trying to go to sleep that he could've come in wearing a cupcake Halloween costume and she would've wanted to jump his bones.

Bax feeding her frosting from a cupcake wouldn't be a bad thing. If it were a carrot cake cupcake, that would actually be a pretty good thing. Creamy icing she could lick from his fingertips—

"Are you okay?" Bax asked, still standing beside the bed,

glancing over at her and apparently not having the same problem with cupcake porn that she was.

"No," she answered honestly as she moved her arm to fling it over her forehead.

He moved to her side of the bed, moving her arm to place his hand over her forehead. His touch felt amazing. Even his temperature-checking skills were sexy as hell.

Unfortunately, the touch made her want to play dirty doctor with him. He could be the doctor, and she could be the patient. He could take her temperature and then slide his hand along her cheek and then do… other dirty doctor things to her.

Her breath came a lot shallower, and she was pretty sure her pupils dilated. That was how turned on she was by the thought of Doctor Bax.

She swatted his hand away because she didn't need a repeat of the shower.

"Court." He sat on the edge of the bed. "What's going on?" His eyebrows furrowed, and he was genuinely concerned.

That was nice. Sort of sweet. Probably because he worried about the kid though.

"Nothing's going on," she dodged.

"You're acting all kinds of off."

"You're acting all kinds of off," she huffed. But added, "Baby is fine. I'm fine. Just…" You know what? She should just throw it out there. This was half his fault too. "Just super aroused right now and no good way to release that pressure."

"Uh…" Bax glanced at the door like he was contemplating how much time it would take to flee.

She understood that. It wasn't like she was really on her A game these days. When she wasn't working, showers were intermittent, napping was the priority, and she'd finally shopped for maternity pants, since she couldn't button her jeans anymore.

"That wasn't me asking you to do anything about it," she murmured, refusing to be embarrassed. Not her fault that there was a whole ton of blood flow below her waist. Well, not *only* her fault.

"You need sex?" He scratched his neck like he wasn't sure what to do with this information.

"No." She shook her head. "I need a pressure release. No sex necessary."

"Oh." Bax frowned. Then he gave her two thumbs-up. "If that's what you need, I'm here for you."

"Bax?" She pushed herself up to sit.

He stared at her chest. Another side effect of pregnancy? Her breasts had grown two whole cup sizes.

Bax seemed lost in a trance, staring at her cleavage. Probably because the overnight transformation had shocked him too.

"Bax?" She said his name again.

He seemed to pull himself from his cleavage trance. "What? Yeah?"

"Why are you here?" She studied his face for any clues as to what had brought him here. Not that he hadn't been by frequently. Usually, he texted her first or had a handful of baby-gear brochures to show her.

"What do you mean?" He scrunched his eyebrows together. The movement was adorkably cute.

"I mean, why are you physically in this room with me?" She gestured to the room. "Did you need something?"

He nodded. Said nothing, but frowned.

She sort of wished this were a baby-gear-brochure talk because whatever was going on with him was definitely not the normal they'd gotten used to. "Bax?"

"Yeah. Uh. Actually." He stood. Paced to the window and ran his hand over the back of his neck.

Her pulse started to glitch. "You're freaking me out. What's going on?"

He took a huge lungful of air. Let it out. Then did it again. Finally, he turned back to her. "We're going on tour."

"Say what?" Courtney sat all the way up at that. A band did not just decide to go on tour without consulting their publicist first. Or at least giving her a heads-up the discussions were even happening.

He held his hands up in a gesture of surrender. "Rocky Mountain region only. Something small. Enough to get Tanner and Mach into the groove, give them the full Dime-front experience."

Why was she not looped in on this discussion? "When?"

Because there was a lot of coordination she needed to do on the marketing side of things. Updating the website, for starters. Scheduling interviews, coordinating with local promotion teams. A band like Dimefront did not simply decide one day to go on tour. This kind of thing took planning and careful consideration.

"Thinking we'll do an impromptu thing. Hans said he could have venues ready in three weeks, so we're gonna roll with that." Bax didn't seem to know what to do with his hands, so he shoved them in his back pockets.

Okay, well, with that timetable, they'd need quite a lot of marketing materials—promotional photos to take and a crap load that she needed to get moving.

Looked like it'd be a while before she could actually catch another nap.

"I'll call Hans." She kicked her legs over the bed.

"I…" Bax ran his hand along his neck. "We only decided just now—literally thirty minutes ago. I volunteered to talk to you. Figured it's better you're pissed at me, since you can't come along this time."

The thing he'd said that caught her attention—

"Why can't I come along this time?" she asked.

He glanced at her abdomen, and she totally noted how his eyes snagged on her breasts again. "Tiny Badass?"

"I'm pregnant." She pointed to her belly. "Oh… I'm pregnant. Right."

He seemed sheepish at that and nodded.

"Why can't I come along?" she asked, because she was pregnant, not dead.

"Hans said you shouldn't have the stress of a tour bus." Bax said this with the same caution a person would use to defuse a bomb.

Which was good because this conversation definitely had the potential to go sideways. This kind of conversation was not conducive to napping.

Not at all.

Chapter Thirteen
COURTNEY

COURTNEY SCOWLED. "HOW MANY STOPS?"

"Six," he said with another whole heap of caution.

"I can handle that." She could. Six stops was totally doable. A world tour? No. But she could do a mini-tour, easy peasy.

Instead of arguing, sorting through their shit, Bax said nothing.

"I can handle it," she assured. "It's not a world tour in the third trimester. It's a brief run during the second. I'll be fine."

Bax seemed unable to meet her gaze. "Linx was thinking…"

Oh, no, no, no. Her brother didn't get to think about this. "Linx can think all he wants. But if the band's going on tour, I'm coming too."

"That's, uh…" Bax scratched the back of his neck.

"That's, uh, what?"

"Linx, Hans… they told me to smooth this over so it wouldn't be an issue." Well, that call was really not for them to make. "I feel like we're heading into issue territory."

"It's not an issue. Really, it's not. I'll look forward to

talking to Hans about the details." She'd also have a little chat with her brother.

She stood. Smoothed the comfy T-shirt and wished they were having this conversation in an office someplace where she wore business attire to work and there was a whole wide desk between herself and Bax.

"Court." He said her name like it meant something. Like she meant something.

That caught her attention. "Bax?"

He licked his bottom lip, which was something he used to do right before saying something to piss her off totally and completely.

That shouldn't have turned her on again... except... she needed a good Bax argument.

"I'm going." She strode three steps forward and pointed straight at his chest. Which meant she touched him. Which also meant her little horndog nerve endings perked to attention.

"I don't want you to overdo it," he said. Unfortunately, he said this with concern she couldn't quite shake. "Can't you sit this one out?"

"That's what you think?" she asked.

He nodded.

"Noted. Now, if you boys think you can cut me out of the Dimefront reunion, then you've got another conversation coming." She turned, pulled at the band in her hair, and paced away from him so she didn't jump him. "Do you want to have another conversation coming?"

"No." He shook his head. "I really don't want that kind of conversation."

"I mean, we've got to figure out how to work Tiny Badass into our lives long-term," she went on. "Might as well start now." Then she turned back, marching toward him. "I'm coming. Got it?"

He didn't move. Didn't argue.

Dammit, she wanted him to argue. The air buzzed *waiting* for him to argue.

"Promise you'll ask for help if you need it?" he asked instead of planting his feet and taking a stand. "Me. Just me. Promise me that if you're physically not okay, you'll tell me? I know we've had our problems, but you've always mattered to me." The way he said that? Sounded like she mattered, not just their baby… but her.

"I matter to you?"

He nodded as his throat worked against some kind of emotion she'd never seen on him before.

Well, that totally diffused the angry mood she'd been stoking and made her chest feel tight in a good way, the hopeful kind of good.

She reached for him, took his hands in hers. "Bax, I'm fine. The pregnancy is fine. Our baby is totally fine."

He didn't move other than his Adam's apple bobbing.

She stroked his hands with her thumbs. "I solemnly swear I will tell you if anything is off with Tiny Badass."

Bax nodded. "And you."

"And me." Now her throat was thick.

Again, he had that uncomfortable aura shift around him. "I wanted to talk to you about us."

"What about us?" This was dangerous territory because technically there was no "us" and now she didn't want to fight with him. Definitely not about that.

"I wanted to see if you might want to…" He was remarkably off-kilter.

She stepped into his space, closer, still holding his hands that now gripped hers too. "Want to whhat?"

"If you might want to try it." He pulled his hands away and gestured to himself. "With me."

"Like try me and you?"

"Not just like we've been. Not just a team." He looked at the carpet. "More than that."

Did she want that?

She didn't not want that.

"Like date?" she asked.

"Like try the couple thing. See if it takes." He shrugged like it wasn't a big deal either way, but the words wobbled a bit, and she could tell this mattered to him.

"See if it takes…" That wasn't the best come-on line she'd ever heard, but coming from Bax—

"Just think about it?" he asked.

She didn't answer. Simply blinked excessively hard because how was this her reality? Okay, she was in, and she'd try the couple thing. They could totally do that.

"About the other issue. I can… I can help with that too." Bax looked at the bed. Back to her.

She mattered to him, the baby they made mattered to him, but how could this be real when he wouldn't even argue with her? Wouldn't engage past some imaginary line he'd drawn for himself.

"Your dirty talk needs some work," she said, aiming for light and teasing. She should probably take some time to think about the tour and think about what "see if it takes" really meant.

Bax scowled. "You've got a need. I want to take care of it."

That was not sexy at all.

This was Bax. She'd heard him talk dirty to women all the time on tour. Never to her, but she knew he had it in him. He might not have gone to medical school, but the guy practically majored in getting underwear off the women around him.

"You want to provide for my sexual needs?" she asked, trying very hard not to giggle.

"Uh-huh." He nodded. Bax had never been self-conscious. Never. "I'm around," he finished.

She shoved at his shoulder with a light thud. "Seriously,

stop before I laugh and make us both uncomfortable. Don't be a goober."

He nodded. "Well..." That was all he said before he strode to the door with purpose. Then he stopped, hand on the knob. "I wouldn't mind if we..." He gestured to the bed. "You know."

She shoved her hands on her hips, willing him to walk back to her, tell her something super dirty, and then *do* that super-dirty thing.

Or... tell her that she mattered again. Reassure her he meant it. They'd both have the same effect, truly.

"You can't even say it. How do you expect to do it?" she asked gently with genuine curiosity.

He thought way too hard about that. "I guess I figured I'd take off my pants. Then your shirt—"

She held up her hand and chuckled. "Stop. If you want to do the dirty talk, I know you can do better than that."

His cheeks pinked adorably. He cleared his throat. Lifted a shoulder. "I'm just putting it out there. You need me. You call."

"Bax, I'm so confused right now." She shook her head. "I shouldn't have said anything. I'm sorry I made things weird between us. I..."

Something in the air shifted. He seemed to struggle with the doorknob, then he clicked the lock button.

She didn't move, because she wasn't entirely sure what was happening here.

He turned on his heel, stalked toward her, and suddenly she was seriously concerned. In a good way. In a not pathetic get-in-her-pants attempt.

Maybe she misread before. Perhaps he wasn't looking at the door like he wanted to leave. Maybe he was looking at the door to see if it locked?

That made more sense.

"I'm so confused," she admitted. Confused about everything.

His expression turned cotton-candy soft. "How do you think I feel?"

"You're just being so nice all the time." She didn't know how to handle this Bax. Brennan was gone, this was still Bax, but she didn't understand this guy.

The jerk version? She was a professional. This guy? Gah. He was like a Bax and Brennan fusion that she couldn't comprehend.

"So you want me to be a dick to you and then get you off?" he asked, but he wasn't mean about it. The words were low and for her only and—

Was that too much to ask? Seriously? That was the foundation this relationship—or whatever it was—was built on.

"You want to know what I want to do?" he asked, moving to stand wickedly close but not actually touching her.

"Yes," she said on a breath. Well, it sounded a little more like a croak. But, hey, it worked.

"I'm going to kiss you everywhere," he said. "Starting here." He pressed a kiss to her temple.

The brush of his mouth there ignited every nerve ending in her body.

"Then moving here." He dragged his lips along her cheekbone to the column of her throat.

She made a gurgling noise because words weren't really happening then.

"How far down do you want me to go?" he asked, nipping at her earlobe as he spoke.

"All the way." Of this, she was certain. "All the way down."

He ran an arm around her waist as he kissed his way down her body. Down the column of her throat, to the top of her chest where her T-shirt met skin. Stopping briefly at her breasts and pressing open-mouthed kisses over her shirt to her nipples.

This was so much better than arguing.

He spent a lot more attention there than she'd expected, sucking her through the cotton fabric. Hoo boy, did that feel nice. Maybe he needed to work on his dirty-talk game, but he definitely had the oral-fixation game down.

The pressure between her legs continued to grow and build with each suck and nip.

She held him by the hair, tossing her own head back as he continued to tongue her through the wet cotton.

As his mouth worked her, his hand slid between her legs, and she was his. There was no doubt about that.

"Do you want me to fuck you?" he asked her chest.

"Mm-hmm." She made affirmative noises, since she couldn't exactly form coherent syllables at the moment.

"I won't do that," he said, still working her with his hand, his mouth against hers now.

"Why?" she asked on another croak.

"Because you're not a quick fuck, Court."

"I could be." What? Well, she could, and why did she love it so much when he used that word like this?

"No." He continued working her with his fingers. "But I'll go down on you until you beg me to stop."

"I won't ask you to stop." She ground herself against his palm between her thighs, the pressure nearly peaking.

His hand still working her over her shorts, he took her mouth. Pressed her body against his—wet nipples against cotton, his palm against her sex, and a trip up orgasm mountain.

He slid his fingers inside her shorts, finally touching her with no fabric between them. His fingers worked their magic, brushing against the pulsing bundle of nerves.

She moaned.

He groaned. Slipped two fingers inside as his palm continued to work against her sweet spot.

"Come for me," he said as a command. "Come on my hand."

She didn't really have a choice then, because he did a gentle pinch and flick that took her right there.

She pressed her face against his neck, letting him absorb the noises as she finished with only his hand. Did she snort? Maybe. She was a little out of it, and it'd been a very long time since she had this type of attention.

Bax held her against him, his erection pressing against her thigh through his jeans. She continued breathing hard, letting the scent of him—sandalwood and rain and musk—invade her space. She gripped his shoulders for support, even though he didn't seem to have any intention of letting her go.

"That was…" she said against the column of his neck. "Thank you."

He grunted something that sounded like "You're welcome" and "My pleasure" wrapped up in one word.

His erection twitched. She totally owed him. Seeing that he'd given her what she needed, and given that his erection was ready to rip through his jeans, she ran her hand down to cup him.

He lifted it away to press a kiss to her knuckles. "Not yet."

Uh. What?

"This isn't about me," he said, his voice husky and rough. "This is about *you*."

"I should take care of you too." She leaned in to kiss him on the mouth, something he allowed for the briefest of moments before lifting her and laying her back on the bed, her head against the pillow.

Then he pulled the blankets up to her chin and tucked her in tight.

Uh.

What the hell?

"Bax?" she asked.

"Get some sleep, Court." He brushed his lips gently across her forehead. "I'll tell Hans you're coming along and that you're napping."

She reached her hand up to cup his face. "But…"

She glanced at the erection still bulging.

"When you're ready for my dick, it's got to be when neither of us wants to even think about walking away." He leaned in, his breath brushing against her cheek. "Honestly, you ready for that?"

Yes. Oh, yes. But also, "No."

He nodded. "Didn't think so. But when you are, I will be too. When that happens? I'll do more to you than we ever thought of in that shower."

That was interesting, because she'd pretty much done everything she'd ever thought of doing to him in that shower.

Her breath stalled in her lungs.

"You know where to find me when you're ready." The way he said that? There was no mistaking that if she wanted to find him, he'd be oh so very ready for her.

"What if I'm ready now?" she said, breathy and sated from the orgasm to end all orgasms.

"Are you?" he asked.

She wasn't sure. Yes, because she didn't like being indebted to him. Also, no, because she was trying very hard to uncomplicate her already complicated life.

"You need my hand again? Any other part of me but the main event?" He pressed a kiss to the top of her head. "Just ask."

"Bax, you're being ridiculous—"

He pressed his fingertip to her lips. "Let's just get this out there. Things changed for us, and I want more. I want you and the life we didn't mean to start. I'm not compromising that for a quick roll in the sheets. You mean a helluva lot more to me than that." Whew. The seriousness of his gaze. "So if you're feeling like you need me to get you off, I'm down for that. But the rest of it? We'll get to that when you're ready to take that leap with me."

Well, huh. That was not what she expected.

Truly, it was hard to focus after she just came like she hadn't done in forever.

Then he turned and left. Left her sated and tired and frustrated. Mostly, however, he left her content. And… dammit. Now she had a *new* favorite kind of nap.

A Bax nap.

Chapter Fourteen
BAX

"YOU CAN'T JUST BUY a house, Bax." Courtney's eyes sparkled with humor. "That's not how it works. You have to go through escrow and sign contracts."

"Yep. Did that." He nodded because he'd totally bought a house. Bax decided he was tired of living life slow. Things happening fast was working for him, so he'd just embrace it. The opportunity arose, he jumped on it, and he really hoped Courtney might decide to move in.

"Like, today? You up and bought a house *today*?" Courtney asked, realization that this could actually happen apparently sinking in. "*Nobody* just goes and buys a house."

"I did." Linx raised his hand. "Bought it for Gibson." Gibson lounged on his bed in Linx's living room. He paused licking his paws long enough to look up at the mention of his name. At least he wasn't lapping at his penis—he saved that for Courtney's pillow.

"Hello, everyone." Linx's mom, Linda, strolled through the front door with Becca and his mom... on the video call.

"Mom, why don't you just come stay for a while?" He snagged the iPad and held it up to his face.

"Your dad and I decided we want to give you space while you and Courtney sort things out," Mom said.

Linda leaned into view, then looked at Bax. "Hank and I decided the opposite. We're not going to give you space to muck anything up."

"Hey, everyone. What'd we miss?" Becca asked, stopping to give Linx a peck on the lips then going in for a little extra.

Bax glanced away because while he was happy for his buddy, he felt a twinge of jealousy that Linx had what Bax wanted. Not Becca, but the woman, the house, and the potential for more.

Granted, now Bax had the woman and the house, but they were separate and not yet tied to a future together.

"Did you know that Bax bought a house?" Courtney turned, her growing belly making the motion adorably disjointed.

"Which one did you decide on?" Becca pulled her sunglasses up to the crown of her head and sat on the edge of the sofa next to Linx.

"I hope it was the one with the guest house," Mom yelled, even though they could hear her just fine.

"Did everybody know about this?" Courtney asked, clearly confused.

He didn't mean to confuse her—he also didn't want to give her the opportunity to talk him out of it.

"The one across the street." Bax pointed in the direction of the house he'd closed on that morning. "Figured it was the best option, since it'd be close to Courtney and Tiny Badass."

"I'm not staying here forever." Courtney frowned. He really hated when she did that. "I figure I'll get an apartment soon."

Linx shook his head. "Why? We've got loads of room here. Bax is across the street. Knox is going to be up on the cul-de-sac."

Courtney did the owl-blink thing he'd become pretty fucking fond of. "Knox bought a house here too?"

"Not yet," Knox said. "Working on it."

A grin teased Bax's lips. Knox was going to stay with him until his pink house was ready. Which, given the amount of work to be done, would be a bit. Unless Knox hung onto the pink bathroom carpet.

"Tanner and Mach don't have the funds yet, but after the tour, we were thinking we'd buy 'em the house next to Knox's as a 'welcome to Dimefront' present. They can share," Linx said.

"No one has ever bought us a house before," Mach said. "I'm not sure how I feel about it."

"You'll feel awesome about it because eventually you'll buy each of us a house, and we'll be even steven." Linx grabbed his guitar and started playing some new song while watching Becca.

"Have you boys lost your marbles?" Courtney asked, finally closing her jaw. "Because you can't just go around buying mansions whenever you want for whoever you want."

"Why not?" Bax asked. "The owners were good to sell."

"Was it even on the market?" Courtney asked, because she had not seen a "For Sale" sign out front.

"Nah." Bax shook his head. "I had my lawyer pitch them a number. They liked the number, so we moved forward."

"Wait till you see Knox's future house," Linx said with a snort. "Needs a whole renovation. Everything's pink and pastel purple."

"It's not that bad." Becca rolled her eyes. "Nothing paint can't fix."

"Paint and carpet and a lot of demolition." Linx shook his head. "That place is a money pit."

Bax grinned. Knox got that house because Bax had already offered on the sleek modern villa across the road. The other neighbors on the street weren't ready to sell this week, and Knox had no patience to wait.

"I want to see these houses." Courtney pulled herself up to stand.

Bax stood too, moving behind her just in case she needed a hand or anything. "I'm thinking we hit up Knox's house first because then my place will look even better."

"Let's go." Knox stood and jingle-jangled a set of keys in his hand.

"If you haven't bought the house, how do you have keys?" Courtney asked, adjusting her shirt over the belly he'd really grown to dig.

"I asked." Knox lifted a shoulder.

"It's not like he can make the carpet smell more like piss," Bax said under his breath.

Knox's house came from the estate of an older couple who decorated it in the 1960s and never looked back. Pink tile, pink appliances, pink carpet in the bathroom that smelled like it'd been pissed on for the last sixty years, and pastel purple curtains everywhere else.

Epic shit that could be on one of those HGTV lifestyle demolition shows.

Not to say that Bax hadn't sent photos of the place to TMZ. Bax had totally sent photos of Knox's new digs to TMZ. He should probably mention that to Courtney, since she'd probably want to play defense on that one.

"You are all buying houses before we go on tour?" Courtney used her not-a-good-idea tone. "Now you have to get house sitters."

"Just one because they're so close to each other," Linx said.

Courtney shifted, rubbing her stomach like it hurt. Which made Bax stand at attention like a guard dog.

"Where have I been while you went house shopping?" she asked, still rubbing the little bump.

"Working." Bax pursed his lips. He didn't love the hours Courtney was putting in for tour prep. Between that and catnaps, she hadn't asked for a repeat of their bedroom groping session. He'd seriously reconsidered his abstinence declaration until she was ready to try for more than just a bedroom fling. Not because he needed to get off—he had a working hand. But because he wanted to be with her. Have the ability to hang out while she slept and not feel like a total creeper.

But the argument that had started all the fights between them nagged at his conscience. He needed to address it, apologize for it.

He'd not been the best guy when she caught him with a groupie behind the stage. Cleo—he still remembered her name because he wasn't a total asshole—had been all in for bagging a rocker, so it wasn't like he'd taken advantage. They'd both taken advantage of each other for different reasons.

The way Courtney dressed him down though? The clear disappointment in who she thought he was had pissed him right the hell off. Made him rethink his decision. He didn't want to rethink that decision and resented that she'd called him out. Brennan may have gotten called out, but no one called out Bax for being Bax.

The part of him that was Brennan didn't resent Courtney because she was wrong, but because he was terrified she was right. They'd never had that kind of a fight before, and he'd never been so wrong. Therefore, being doesn't-give-two-fucks Bax was easier. He went that route.

Growing up, they'd always gotten along about most everything. They argued about little things, but the friendship wasn't like that. They'd coexisted just fine.

He tired of that groupie gig and realized Courtney was right about things. Their friendship was over—and he wasn't willing to admit she'd been right to anyone but himself. So he found Em. He thought he was ready for a life of not being that guy anymore. And then shit went down, and things got fucked.

Courtney yawned and stretched.

"Do you need to lie down? Maybe you should get some rest." He wanted to touch her hair. Kiss her temple. Pick her up and tuck her into bed.

Courtney clearly had other ideas, what with the way she rolled her eyes. "I'm fine. Thanks though. I've got houses to see."

He wanted to argue his point, but he didn't. He only lifted his chin in response.

"We're looking for a permanent place," Linda, Courtney's mom, said. "Anyone want to buy us a mansion?"

"Sure." Linx nodded. "Pick it out, and it's on me."

"We wouldn't say no either!" Cherie yelled through the screen.

"You don't have to yell, we have the volume turned up," Linda yelled back.

"I have a guesthouse," Bax said, because he did. Tucked on the back acreage of the property, the guesthouse had its own pool.

"Oh…" Linda perked up at that. "It's so close to Linx and Courtney too."

"I'm sort of hoping Courtney and Tiny Badass will be closer because I'm hoping they'll move in." He paused. "With me," he clarified.

The room went silent.

Right. He should probably have talked to her about that before announcing it in front of their friends and family.

"When she's ready. If she wants to. Eventually." He should've offered her the guesthouse first because that would've made sense. Then she'd have her own space, and he'd have his own space.

But he didn't want his own space.

"We should talk about it and think about it," he added when no one said anything.

"Excellent idea," Cherie said. "Somebody take me over to see the guesthouse."

Everyone but Gibson took that opportunity to evacuate to check out the other houses, but he and Courtney didn't move. She sort of stared at him like she didn't know what to do with him. This wasn't disappointed, and it wasn't excited... she was confused.

Which made his chest tight, since he'd sort of hoped for excited.

"When do you move into the new digs?" Courtney asked, crossing her arms.

Nope. Crossing arms was a bad idea.

"Bought most of the furniture with the joint, so I'm staying there tonight." He'd hired a service to get it spic-and-span before he moseyed across the street to try out his brand-new movie theater room. "There's a room there for you if you decide you'd like to come visit. Use the pool. Jump on the trampoline. Play in my pirate ship." Uh-huh. The place came with an in-ground trampoline and a pirate-ship-themed tree house. He figured Tiny Badass would get a kick out of it when the kid got older. "Best part about it? It comes with me."

Courtney didn't smile, but she did shake her head and frown. He seriously hated the frowning.

"You actually bought a house with a pirate ship?" she asked.

He nodded. "Is it really a house if it doesn't have its own pirate ship?"

"Bax?" She said his name like she was operating with extreme caution.

Nope, he didn't like that.

"You don't have to make a decision right now, but I've got space for you there if you decide to…" He didn't quite know how to finish, so he shoved his hands in his pockets and stared at the floor.

"Let's say I come stay with you." She gestured across the street.

"I'm on board with this." He was. He really was.

"You'd strangle me within three months." Courtney held up three fingers to illustrate her point. Three totally unnecessary fingers.

"Would not." He wouldn't, but he would convince her to stay long-term in those three months.

"Here's the thing though. If I were to win this bet, I'd end up strangled. I don't like to be strangled." The words were light, but her tone was serious.

"Don't let this be something it's not," he said. "I only want a place for you and Tiny Badass. The guys and I? We'll live on the same block, like when we were kids, but with bigger houses and better parties."

She bit her bottom lip.

"Think about it." He'd put every single one of his Cadbury Eggs in this basket of *let her decide, give her space, don't push too hard*. He hoped to hell it worked.

Knox didn't knock. He let himself into Linx's house with a, "Are you two coming or are you arguing?"

"Not arguing and we are coming," Courtney said, but she didn't make a move toward the door.

Knox got the message and left, closing the door behind him.

"I need to think about this," Courtney said, crossing her arms under her breasts. "I don't want to make the wrong decision here."

He nodded. "Yeah. When you're ready to make your decision, I'll be hanging out on my pirate ship." He stood, already making plans for a night alone. He'd order kale chips and dinner from Just BE Kitchen and enjoy his own company.

Maybe he'd even take it on himself to go get a haircut. It'd been, what, like three years since he'd last cut his hair?

Yeah. That sounded good.

Look at him. He had plans.

Chapter Fifteen
BAX

BAX WAS A SINGER. He didn't enjoy playing instruments, but was okay on the piano thanks to ten years of lessons, and he'd written a few songs here and there.

The byline helped with his rocker credibility, but drafting didn't come naturally to him, which was why he rarely had to scratch the itch of song creation.

Today was different. After taking Courtney on a tour of the houses, and then spending a night in his new digs, he'd found himself sketching out some lines. In the light of day, he tried his hand at that new song gnawing at him.

Strike that. This was not a song.

Only lyrics.

Once he got them sorted, he'd hand it off to Knox or Linx, and they would turn it into actual music.

The lyrics weren't gritty like their last album, didn't push any envelopes.

Also, not sunshine and rainbows. That was what he should be writing. He was going to be a dad. Things were good. He should focus on the good. The part of his life he looked forward to.

A tour.

The baby.

But that wasn't what his brain spewed onto the paper. No, this song was a breakup song. Something he should not have been working on. Something that wasn't part of his current life.

He was not in a relationship. Was not heartbroken. So what the hell was up with the breakup lyrics?

Yeah, he didn't know either.

"Bax?" Courtney's voice carried through his brand-new backyard into the pirate ship where he'd set up his makeshift office. No desk or anything, but he'd brought his pencil and notebook, so he figured it counted.

"In here," he called back, ducking his head out the window of the ship next to a cannon.

Was it really a pirate ship if there weren't a pirate flag and cannons? The answer was no, it was not.

Courtney strode toward him in cutoff denim shorts and a red tank that accentuated her newfound curves. Her brown hair flowed free today, held back from her face with barrettes he didn't realize he found supremely sexy until right that moment.

As she came closer, she squinted at him.

The haircut took a little getting used to. But he'd kept the stubble, so it wasn't too much of a change.

"What the hell did you do?" Courtney's expression changed from searching to fury.

"Uh." He glanced around to ensure she was talking to him. Last time he checked, he'd done nothing to light the spark of her fury. "No idea."

"Your hair." Her eyes big, she marched toward him like she was going to glue every strand of hair back on his head.

Interesting, because Courtney'd never cared about his hair before. Last he checked, the cut was even. A little short, but good for the tour. Less maintenance.

"What are you thinking?"

"Uh." He pointed to his scalp. "You're talking about the hair?"

"Yes!"

"I got a haircut."

"I see that. Have you lost your mind?"

"You don't like it?"

"Of course I like it! I never liked your long hair as much as I prefer it short." That admission seemed to pull her up short. She stopped. Deflated a little. "It messes with the marketing for the tour." She closed her eyes. Opened them again. "You guys already did photos. Ads were designed— sent out to the world. Ads with your hair as it was yesterday."

Oh.

Shit.

He probably should've thought about that before he found a lady wielding scissors and shears.

"I fucked up," he said. "Shit."

"It's okay." She nodded, as though nodding would make that statement true.

"You want me to wear a wig?" He shouldn't offer things he didn't really mean.

"You wouldn't actually wear a wig."

"You're right. I wouldn't." But he'd say he would, and then she could say, "No, don't worry," and then everyone would be happy.

"I'm becoming wise to your mind powers, Bax."

"That is a real bummer." He gestured to the door. "You wanna come inside my pirate ship?"

"You don't have to keep using those words," she said as she did, in fact, come inside.

"But it's so fun to say." He moved so she could sit on one of the little kid chairs that came with the boat. "About the hair—"

"I'll figure something out. Graphic artists always have ideas, and I have a guy."

"You have a guy?" Nope. Didn't like that she had a guy.

"A graphics guy. He's good. He can probably give photo-Bax a haircut."

"This guy makes your life easier?"

"Uh-huh." She'd lost her mad. Made sense because turned out being pissy in a pirate ship was difficult.

"Matey, wha' brings ye t' me pirate ship today?" The other awesome thing about having guests visit his ship? He got to practice his pirate speak.

Courtney smiled. Soft. Gorgeous. "You've been waiting to say that."

"I 'ave."

That got him a full grin. "You'll have to teach me how to do that."

"At yer service, lass."

Her top teeth bit into her bottom lip. "You're going to be a great dad."

That hit him right in the feelings.

"Ye're goin' t' be a great mom." He chucked her under the chin.

That got him a slight chuckle. Not enough of a laugh. He'd need to work on that.

She glanced at her hands in her lap. "Can we be serious for a second?"

"I'm always serious," he said seriously.

Then she gave him a full smile. Full sunshine. All Courtney. "You were just speaking like a pirate."

"Good point." He sat in the kiddie chair across from her, his knees going up to his chest. "Whatcha got for me?"

"Well…" Again, she glanced at her hands.

She'd painted her nails since yesterday. Good. She needed to take a little time for the things that mattered to her.

"I was trying to sleep. But I kept thinking about your offer of a place to stay," she said as cautiously as if she were creeping through a construction zone in a stretch Escalade.

But that didn't sound like a no. "Annnd?"

"I think we could try it." She stopped wringing her hands, placing them on the acrylic table between them with a treasure map etching. "But if things aren't working for either of us, we've gotta be honest about it. I don't want Tiny Badass to have parents who fight every second of the day."

Good news, he didn't want that either.

Don't get him wrong, this wasn't the reason he'd gone on an arguing-with-Courtney fast, but it wasn't a bad by-product of that decision.

"Agreed." He nodded. "Not saying we'll never argue in front of the little badass, but we can make it a point that it's not habit."

"But that doesn't mean we can't disagree," she added quickly.

"Right. It's about how we handle those disagreements." He ran a hand over his newly cut hair. "Check it out. I'm being an adult."

"Oh my God, Bax." A sly smile hit her lips as she continued, "That's the thing."

"What's the thing?"

Then the smile disintegrated, and she got way too serious for pirate ship discussions. "You don't argue anymore. Even when I can see you have a strong opinion about something, you drop it. I don't like it."

"Don't like which part? The strong opinion or the dropping it?"

"It just doesn't feel right to me." She shifted in her chair. "Like, we used to have our thing—it wasn't a healthy thing, but it was ours. Now I don't know where I belong in us."

"Give me some examples." Real-world experience dictated how he should move forward. Helped with the communication.

Again with the fucking adulting. He was going to be the best dad ever.

"Tiny Badass?"

"It's a great name."

"Me moving in?"

"A fabulous idea."

"You didn't argue your point on either of those things."

"By the look of it, I didn't need to."

"Bax."

"Court. I'm not going to go for conflict only because you like to disagree for the sake of disagreement."

"I don't like to disagree for the sake of disagreement."

"Okay."

"See!" She threw her hands up. "That's what I'm talking about."

She'd pushed him about as far as he could go without saying something that might hurt her feelings.

"Okay." He leaned in, popping her personal space bubble. "You've got a lot of pent-up energy again. Energy you used to release by fighting with me. But now that I'm not fighting, you don't know what to do."

Her breath came shallow. The skin above her collarbone turned red.

"Would you like me to help you with this?"

"You cannot just get me off instead of communicating with me."

"Getting you off is communicating."

"What if I want to get you off?"

"You know the cost. You ready for that?"

She closed her eyes. She seemed to not breathe. Then she opened them. "You're not in this for me. I'm really struggling with that."

The vulnerability in her expression tugged the pirate shenanigans right out of him. "What are you talking about?"

"The only reason you're not arguing with me is because we're going to be parents."

He wasn't really sure where this was going, but it didn't seem to be a good place. "That's not true."

"I get it, Bax." She moved her palms to his chest, gripping the cotton of his shirt in her hands, pulling him closer.

That movement? It felt fucking good.

The entire front of her pressed against the entire front of him. Her belly just an added curve to the gorgeousness that was Courtney.

"I just don't want to always come in second." She released his T-shirt. Smoothed the fabric.

He caught her hands. Held her gaze with his own.

"Who says there's a line?" Because last he heard, there was only her.

She flinched. "You want our baby. I'm only part of the package. Like a bonus you didn't really want."

"Yes." Dammit. That was not what he meant. He shook his head. "I mean, no."

She pulled her hands away.

No. No. No. Red alert, Bax. Red alert.

"I mean, you're not a bonus," he blurted.

The hurt in her eyes. Fuck a fucking French fry.

If there was a medal for screwing up, somebody could hand it right on over to him.

"What I mean is…" He picked up her hands. Held them to his chest. "You're enough on your own."

She pulled away, but he gave her the slightest squeeze.

"If I wasn't part of the package, then you'd still want the baby," she said. "But if there wasn't the baby, then you wouldn't want me."

Well. Fuck.

"Court."

"No. I mean it when I say I understand. We're forced into this box together and need to figure out how to maneuver together. That won't change. I accept that. Own it. I was there in the shower with you. I didn't stop you."

"Court." He shouldn't have done it. Dammit, playing dirty wasn't his style. Nevertheless, he leaned in and started singing some old-school boy band—New Kids on the Block.

"You are the worst."

"I think you mean the best."

That got him a crack of a smile. "We have to navigate this together. You want in. I want in. That's why I agree I should come stay with you to try for some stability." She squeezed his hands. Frowned.

Nope. He didn't love the frown.

He should offer her the guesthouse, but—

"I figure we can use the guesthouse for all the grandparents. Either set can come to Denver to hang with Tiny Badass…" He paused. "And us."

She glanced up from under her lashes. Were they wet? They were totally wet.

"I have an idea." He wrapped his arms around her, pulling her into him. "Let's make a deal. We only have our disagreements in the pirate ship."

"Are you serious?" She leaned back, but he followed.

"Yeah. It'll be our space. Whenever we need to have a private mommy and daddy discussion, we'll come here."

The hair on her shoulders bobbed as she shook her head. "*That's* a ridiculous idea."

"I don't think so." He smirked. "See? It's already working. I'm happy to disagree with you in here."

"I will not agree to only argue with you in *your* pirate ship."

"*Our* pirate ship." He lifted his eyebrows. "I mean, if you're moving in here, it'll be your ship too." He gave her a squeeze before letting go. "Great. Now that we've decided that, is there anything else you want to discuss?"

"I don't know that we finished that conversation."

"Did you have more to add?"

"Not really."

"There you go."

"I don't really enjoy arguing with you in the pirate ship."

"'Cause I'm right. I get it. I wouldn't wants t' argue wit' me either in this here ship."

Courtney looked at the ceiling. Unfortunately, all it held in this cramped space was a wooden roof. "It is impossible to argue with you when you talk like a pirate."

He grinned. Looked like the pirate ship would work just fine.

Her eyes went wide. "Tell me that is not your plan."

Well, it hadn't been until right then. Truthfully, he had given little thought to the use of pirate speak to end an argument. Good to know that it would work. He'd use it more often.

"Wha' are ye pissed at me about? I'm openin' the discussion so we can work it out in Ye Arguin' Sails."

"That's what you're naming this place? Ye Arguin' Sails?"

Hell, she laughed at it, so that was officially going to be the name. Maybe he'd even have a boat-christening thing where they smashed a bottle of good champagne against the bow.

Although, given that this was a children's ship, perhaps they should just go with sparkling cider? He'd ask his mom. She'd know.

"Aye. That's ye ol' name."

"Oh my God. You cannot talk pirate when we are having a serious discussion." She smacked his chest, light and with no real feeling.

Almost… playful.

He liked playful Courtney. She didn't come out to chill with him often enough.

"Fair enough. What's the problem?" he asked, way too seriously and without a dash of any pirate. Not even a smidge.

"Your baby is demanding that I eat salad. *And* vegetables.

And I wanted tofu today." She tossed her hands up like this was the greatest affront of all the affronts that ever affronted. "Tofu! Who wants tofu?"

"I like tofu." What? He did.

"Exactly. You and your baby. That's who."

"My kid enjoys tofu, huh?" Good to know. He sort of dug that about the Tiny Badass. They ate veggie sushi with tofu. That should be fine for a toddler. Also, delicious.

"My mind wanted a burger, but my body demanded tofu." Her hands drifted to her hips, and she glared at him like he should have an answer to this problem.

"I'm so sorry, Court." He wasn't, but it seemed like the right thing to say.

"What do I do about this?" She seemed to want an answer.

"Uh… I can show you how to marinate tofu? You put it on a salad with some soba noodles and a little ginger dressing." So fucking good. His salivary glands were working overtime.

"I hate that this sounds amazing." She crossed her arms. "At the same time, it sounds awful."

"Is that a yes on the tofu salad?" Because he was getting mixed signals on this one.

She let out a low growl he really liked. "Sure. I'll eat it. I'll like it. But I won't like that I enjoy it."

He nodded because he actually understood her logic there. "I can live with that."

This was sort of like Knox and his garlic bread sexcapades.

"I'll also bake up some kale chips." This he actually sang to her. Hell, it seemed like the thing to do.

"Ew." She pulled a disgustedly cute face.

"Tiny Badass is gonna love 'em."

"Probably." She pursed her lips.

He moved to her. Slung his arm around her shoulder. "You might not hate them."

"Don't count on it." She looked up at him, and in that moment, everything felt like it clicked into place.

No breakup songs necessary. No arguments. Just her and him and some understanding.

"Sometimes I eat them with bacon," he said, because everybody loved bacon. He couldn't wait to introduce Tiny Badass to bacon.

She gagged. Actually gagged. Full-on, not-a-joke gagged.

How could a guy go wrong when he talked about bacon?

"Now I can never move in here." More than a little greenish pale, she started for the door.

"What did I say?" He followed her out into the mountain air of the Denver suburbs, catching up to her quickly—because, really, she wasn't moving quickly.

"Don't say the "bacon" word around me. The whole sizzling. Fat. Pork. And…" She turned a lot more green at that. "Bax? Your baby does not like bacon talk."

"Noted." He rubbed her back while she heaved big lungfuls of air, and also made some gagging noises that weren't adorable but seemed necessary given her shade of golf-course green. "Tofu talk only."

Her body seemed to lean into his touch. Hell, he'd take it. Savored it, even.

"Do you want to come inside?" he asked.

She nodded.

"I'll show you what could be your very own room." He'd picked it out, right across the hall from him.

"Does it have a mini-fridge for cherry seltzer?" She leaned into him as they moved toward the back door.

"It will after today." He inhaled the scent of her—coconut and the scent of sexy showers.

"Can I steal my mattress from Linx's house? It's a really great mattress." She glanced up at him then.

"I will personally carry it."

"I could get used to this." She didn't look so pale and green anymore.

"Used to what?"

"You being nice to me."

"I could get used to it too," he said. Because it was a helluva lot better than writing breakup songs in the arguing pirate ship.

With Courtney at his side, he showed her into the house. Into the future that he hoped could be theirs.

Chapter Sixteen
COURTNEY

DEEP BREATHS, *Courtney. Deep breaths.*

"Please. Hear me out." Bax stopped and turned toward her, his eyebrows furrowing deeper.

The problem with his words was that they were overprotective, ridiculous words. "I'm listening to every word you're saying."

She could see the war happening inside him—they could not slip into argument territory. It violated their cardinal rule. But the pendulum was swinging, and he wanted to take a stand. She could feel it.

While she usually appreciated a good row with him, she was kinda tired and didn't really have the stamina for it.

Also, their arguing ship was clear across the house and yard.

She really would've preferred to lie on the sofa and eat some of the chickpea chip things she'd found in the junk food section of the health food store. They had one. It was epic.

"I don't think Bax is gonna love this." Linx's voice drifted from Bax's kitchen.

They had company, but they always had company.

Bax growled. He actually growled. That was pretty cute, really.

She was certain that Linx and Becca and her parents continued showing up as observers for when things imploded. There was probably even a bet going as to when it would happen. She hadn't asked. But she sort of figured it sounded reasonable. It was what she would've done if she were them.

Knox was always there because he had moved into the spare bedroom. The spare bedroom on the other side of the six-thousand-square-foot house.

"What am I not gonna love?" Bax asked as they turned the corner to the ginormous kitchen, still in epic grump mode.

Here's the thing. Bax's kitchen was the bomb. If she were the type of woman who loved to cook, she'd be in heaven.

She wasn't a woman who loved to cook; she was a woman who enjoyed heating things up. All the same, she could appreciate the attention to culinary detail that had gone into this room. Slate-gray cabinets with white quartz countertops, dark hardwood floor, and backlighting in the glass-front cabinets. Everything was clean lines and seamless edges.

"Have you seen the new ads?" Linx asked, slipping his gaze to Courtney with a *what the fuck* look she'd become accustomed to as a kid.

Right. The new ads. Courtney's graphic artist had played a little with Bax's hair, and honestly, she thought the concept was awesome. Hans thought so too. So they ran with it.

Made an entire campaign around Bax and his haircut.

"New ads?" Bax moved to look at Linx's phone—where he was apparently flipping through the new advertisements.

Bax's expression went slack.

Yep. The ads were *that* exceptional.

"What happened to my hair?" he asked, mirroring Linx's *what the fuck* look.

"Your hair is fine." It was. Still looked great.

"Courtney." He heaved a breath. "I appreciate you are doing such a great job with the publicity." He paused, as though seriously considering his next words. "What did you do to me?"

She had done nothing. But graphics guy had experimented with various hairstyles and that had sparked a concept of "Where's the real Bax? Rock out. Find out. Buy your tickets now!"

Each ad had a different version of Bax: Cowboy Bax. Construction worker Bax. One where he wore a firefighter's hat. One with his old long-hair style. One with the new. Another with Bax's face replaced by a T-Rex head—that one was Hans's idea. The one with him in pirate garb—that'd been hers.

The other guys, of course, stayed the same in each ad.

If the campaign took off, Hans had a T-Rex head for Bax to wear when they wrapped up their tour in Telluride.

Courtney hadn't said a peep about it, because it *was* Hans's idea. She had minimal involvement—other than instructing her graphics guy and ordering the costume head. That was it. The extent of her involvement.

Also, she figured Hans would've told Bax by now.

"Can I just say that it's nice to hear you two bickering again?" Knox kicked back on one of the kitchen chairs— balancing himself by leveraging his feet on the table.

"We're not bickering," Courtney assured. "Just talking."

They couldn't be bickering, because they were not in a pirate ship.

"Well, it's good to hear you two *talking* again." Knox rolled his eyes.

"I'm not convinced that sounded like talking." Linx shook his head. "I could grab Becca though. She's sort of the expert on talking and communication. She'll know for sure."

"Courtney"—Bax said her name like he was trying to

strangle it with his tongue—"appears to have issues with my trying to ensure the safety of her and Tiny Badass."

Courtney shook her head. "That is not true."

"Maybe you should pick up where you left off?" Knox suggested, leaning in like he was ready to give advice. "Right before Real Bax met T-Rex Bax."

"That would be when Bax mentioned he didn't feel like I was hearing him out." Courtney tried to make his name sound like she was strangling it. But it didn't work. "Of note, I was actively listening to him when he said I wasn't hearing him out."

She'd listened the entire time he told her that he wanted to hire a medical provider to come along on the tour. A medical provider who would be there specifically to *babysit* her and ensure she drank enough water. Courtney did not need someone to take her blood pressure or remind her to do anything. She was a grown-ass adult who could take care of herself.

Bax wasn't keen on just any medical provider—he wanted to spend an obscene amount of cash on a traveling obstetrician.

A doctor who would be incredibly bored the entire time because Courtney was absolutely fine. The doctor had cleared her and then cleared her again—just to appease the label.

"I appreciate Bax's concern, but an obstetrician does not need to come along on this tour." Also, Courtney was more than a little annoyed that Bax had waited until days before they left to have an anxiety storm about this. They weren't in the pirate ship, and she was tired, so she hadn't gone there with him.

It didn't matter, though, because his plan wouldn't work for oh so many reasons.

The first? There was no more room on the crew bus.

The second? The cost would eat up funds that didn't need to be spent.

And the third? She did not freaking want it.

Bax's hands went to his hips, and he was breathing a little heavy. Like he wanted to get angry, but also didn't want to get angry.

"I'm medically cleared." Calm understanding. That was what Courtney channeled. "It would be wonderful if we didn't change the plans right before we leave. Trust me to drink enough water."

The blood vessel at Bax's temple throbbed. "I would very much like to go hit the argument deck."

Fine. If they were really going to argue about this, they couldn't do it in the kitchen. Well, they could. But it was technically against the one rule they'd put in place.

"That works." Courtney pushed out of the kitchen, heading for the ship.

"I appreciate your understanding that I want to be sure you and Tiny Badass are safe," he said, walking alongside her.

"And I appreciate your wanting to take care of me." She did her best to keep her tone level. Reasonable. Even.

"And I appreciate your willingness to allow me to care for you," Bax agreed.

Now for the nitty-gritty. "That said, I also appreciate that we are traveling through large cities with hospitals and medical providers, and we don't need to spend the money on a traveling doctor."

"*That said*, I have the money, and that's not an issue. I also appreciate that when I'm onstage, I'd feel more comfortable knowing you have help if you need it."

Crawling through the miniature door was getting harder each day because her stomach was not getting smaller—that was for sure—but she managed it.

Bax followed her in. They both stood, but Bax had to hunch over, given that he was about two inches taller than the roof.

"Becca will be there." Courtney pursed her lips. Realized

she was doing it and tried to stop. "She can get help if I need it. This is ridiculous."

He took some deep breaths in through his nose. "I need to know that I can do my job and everything else is taken care of."

Dammit. She needed his focus to be on the tour and not on her. He needed to do the things he did when he toured—except the groupies.

There had to be a middle ground here, but looking at Bax, he wasn't in the headspace to let this one go.

Fine.

"I get to pick the provider," she said.

Bax blinked hard.

"It's ridiculous. But whatever. This is important to you, so I get to pick the provider. Fair enough?"

"Uh."

"You're getting your way. I'm getting a little of mine. I'll select the person to come with us." See, everyone won.

"Okay, then." Bax nodded carefully. Cautiously.

Which was probably not misplaced caution, given that there was no way she would have someone staring at her while she peed or drank fluids or any of the other stuff she figured a medical babysitter would observe.

Besides, she preferred to follow actual medical advice versus Bax's pre-tour panic.

"Okay," she replied, ready to call Irina and see if she was between gigs… and what she knew about *not* having to deliver babies on tour or give Courtney shit about how much water she drank or didn't drink. Courtney squatted so she could crawl out the door.

"Do you want to have dinner tonight?" Bax asked, like they hadn't been having dinner together every night since she'd moved in.

She turned, glad she hadn't quite made it out, because then she'd have to come back in. "Huh?"

"A real dinner." He seemed adorably uncomfortable asking her this.

She squinted at him, trying to figure out his angle. "Like a date?"

He nodded. "Like a date."

"A *date* date, where we go out to determine compatibility with one another?" To be clear, because otherwise it could be uncomfortable.

He nodded again, and he was a little pale this time.

"Are you allowed to ask me out on a date in the pirate ship?" she asked, sort of savoring the request because it turned out being asked on a date by Brennan Baxter was pretty exceptional.

"Figured you'd probably want to argue about it a little, so we're in the right place for that."

His logic was sound.

"What are we going to be eating?" Because that was really the only determiner whether they'd argue.

Was that hope in his expression? It totally was.

Her whole heart seemed to warm up.

"There's a new vegan place downtown I've been wanting to try," he said. "Or if Tiny Badass is letting up on your dietary restrictions, me and *my Courtney* can hit up a burger joint."

Her tummy fluttered at his use of "my Courtney," but there wouldn't be a burger joint. Tiny Badass was not letting up. Courtney's cravings for whole foods, naturally sourced options, were getting a little out of hand. "A vegan place sounds perfect."

"So that's a yes?" Apparently, he needed to confirm this.

She was happy to give him that confirmation. "That's a yes."

Chapter Seventeen
BAX

BAX DIDN'T GET NERVOUS. Not anymore. He played stadiums full of people and had the confidence to pull that shit right off, so he shouldn't have been nervous.

There was nothing to be nervous about.

He and Courtney spent a helluva lot of time together. Had now lived in the same house for weeks.

But tonight was different.

Tonight, they went public with their relationship. Tonight, he dressed up—seriously, in a suit jacket and everything. Tonight, he wanted to show her and the world that he was ready for more. Hoped to convince everyone that *they* were ready for that.

"Yeah. No. That won't work." Courtney was speaking into her phone as she came around the corner into the kitchen, where he waited in his best dress-up clothes. His shoes were even polished, and that never happened.

She glanced up from the call and full-court stopped. Her jaw dropped a few millimeters, and her eyes gentled.

That made a guy feel good about his decision to strangle himself with a button-down shirt all night.

"I'm going to have to call you back," she said into the

phone. She didn't seem to wait for an answer before turning it off and shoving it in her purse.

She'd gone with a short blue sundress that accentuated the bump and the brown of her eyes at the same time.

"I should probably not wear flip-flops to this dinner, then." Her eyes never left his, even as she spoke. They seemed pinned there, which he really dug.

"Wear what you want to wear," he said.

Colorado was more of a come-as-you-are kind of state, and they were making the rules for themselves. At the same restaurant that you'd find a guy in a full suit, you'd also find a guy in Wranglers and cowboy boots. So, if Courtney wanted to wear flip-flops, that was fine. Setting their own tone for who they were together made all the sense in the world.

"One sec." She turned and hustled back toward the direction of the bedrooms.

His gaze trailed to the window so he didn't watch her ass as she left. That had become something of a problem for him. Really, watching every part of her—the quirk of her mouth, the way she fidgeted with her jewelry—had become part of his regular viewing habits.

"Do you mind helping me buckle these?" She held two strappy sandal wedges in her hand.

He nodded. "Yeah. Of course."

She sat on a chair beside the table and slipped her right foot into the shoe. He knelt down to get the buckle, only fumbling a little when his hand grazed the skin along the back of her ankle.

"My belly is making it impossible to tie my shoes or buckle them." She sounded like this really bothered her. Also, it made sense why she only wore slip-on shoes lately. "And heels hurt now, which sucks for my Louboutins. They're feeling neglected."

Still kneeling before her, he gently pushed her foot into the other shoe, letting his hand linger against her ankle as he pulled the strap through the buckle. He traced the curve of her ankle up to her calf. A light touch, nothing invasive. Still, goose bumps trailed up the inside of her calves to the back of her knees.

Honestly, he had goose bumps too.

Once the shoe was buckled, he lifted her foot and kissed the top of her left shin. Subtle, and only a brush of his lips, but seriously, he'd never helped a woman put on her shoes before. Never knew it would make his throat get thick and his pulse beat harder.

"Brennan," she whispered his given name, and he liked it. Liked that when he turned her on she called him the name he reserved for only those who mattered most in his life.

Like a clock hand finding its way to midnight, everything about this moment whispered perfection. The kind that isn't screaming or overbearing... it's just there. You don't even realize it's there until it shows up.

"We're going to be late," she said, but she didn't seem invested in her statement. "I've sent in the tips, and there should be cameras ready for you."

"For us," he corrected, standing and offering her his hand. "Then we should go, shouldn't we?"

She took it, her chest heaving, and nodded. "We should."

Funny thing, she didn't release his hand the entire ride to the restaurant.

THE MOMENT they hit the sidewalk, he knew *they* were screwed. *He* was screwed.

Because two of the women who met them on the sidewalk had Bax bracelets.

Son of a bitch. His method had seemed like a good one at the time, but that was before... back when he was an idiot.

He pulled Courtney to his side, hoping she didn't notice,

but she absolutely noticed. She said nothing, but the little hitch in her step said everything.

"You're the one I'm with," he whispered, only for her. "Don't let them get in your head."

She nodded. "It's easier to direct other people than do this myself."

"Good thing I'm a professional." He winked at her, then he pulled her into his arms, and just like they'd planned, he kissed her like he meant it. Like he couldn't get enough of her.

This image of them would be splashed all over the tabloids, and Courtney would control the narrative. It was what she did best.

"Good job," she said against his mouth. "It's like you've been practicing."

What could he say? They'd totally been practicing.

"Bax?" a familiar voice said from near the front door.

He turned, and the narrative turned on its head because Em stood right there, as though she just happened to be at the same place at the same time.

Fuck.

She even wore her Bax bracelet.

He caught the moment of dawning for Courtney the second it happened. Noted the way her eyes scanned Em, and Em scanned Courtney.

The photographers missed nothing.

Courtney was not a little pregnant anymore—there was no doubt looking at the woman that she was going to have a baby.

Em looked as amazing as she always had—perfectly put together and as fake as could be.

In Los Angeles, this would be the time for maneuvering on the hostess's part. Send them to a table away from the lookie-loos.

He knew in the depths of his gut that was not what would happen.

"Oh my God, it's Dimefront Bax!" Someone behind Em shrieked.

Not the words. She didn't scream the words. She said the words, then she screamed—high-pitched and entirely too over-the-top.

Every pair of eyes in the restaurant and every camera lens swung to them.

Fuck on the first date and not in the fun way.

He seemed to lose feeling in his limbs because whatever came next would not be helpful. Of this, he would bet his star on the Hollywood Walk of Fame.

"This is awkward," Em said, totally committed to her role as jilted fiancée.

"Is your girlfriend *pregnant?*" hostess lady said entirely too loudly. Brittney, her name was Brittney. That was what her name tag said.

Bax moved to get in front of Courtney, block her from view. But Chet was already there, scooting them both back to the SUV with practiced ease and the authority Bax had hired him for.

"What's it like carrying the baby of a rock god?" Brittney shouted as the door closed behind them.

"Fuck," Bax whispered under his breath.

Courtney turned and gave a wave.

"It's spectacular," she said. "Bax has always deserved happiness without strings attached."

Damn, did she just burn Em in the middle of this with Em's own fire?

And could he be any prouder?

Courtney followed Chet's instructions and direction, with Bax right behind. Chet's extraction technique worked, and he had them back in the vehicle before either could process the enormity of what had just happened.

Courtney was a little quicker on the uptake than him,

because he was still stuck on the "carrying the baby of a rock god" part of what Brittney had shouted.

"Call Hans," Courtney said with the same authority as Chet. Meanwhile, she was whipping through social media apps and searching for hashtags.

Bax called Hans. Relayed the information. Listened as Hans did the deep mouth-breathing thing he did when he was not happy. The guys thought it was hysterical how Hans deep breathed into the microphone of the cell like he was in a freaky-ass horror movie.

Tonight, Bax didn't find it particularly amusing.

"The news is going to come out anyway. Might as well tell everyone yourself," Hans finally said through the speakerphone.

"But how did she know? Who told her where we'd be?" Bax was taking the temperature of the back seat, and Courtney did not look like she was happy with the turn of events.

"We're on Instagram." Courtney held up the app, and sure enough, there was a photo of gorgeous her and suited-up him at the hostess stand with screeching Brittney and Em.

Chet let out a string of cuss words.

"Don't worry, they cropped you out," Courtney assured half-heartedly. Then she let her phone fall to her lap, slumped against the back seat of the car, and pressed her palms to her eyes. "Shit. They're twisting things. I'm the villain."

No, Bax didn't accept that.

"You're too close to this, Courtney," Hans said, gentler than Bax had ever heard. "We both know the narrative is yours to control. You've got the upper hand. We'll pick a different photo and make it grow legs."

Bax didn't entirely know what making a photo grow legs meant, but he figured it was more of a Courtney and Hans thing.

Courtney nodded, even though Hans couldn't see her. "I know you're right. That's what we have to do."

"Make it happen how you see fit," Hans said. "I'll let the other guys know. Ask them to play a minor offense. Linx might even start a bar brawl and get arrested to take some of the spotlight."

Honestly, it wouldn't be the first time.

Bax finished up the call while Courtney stared out the window at the lights of Denver and the spring rain pelting the car.

Finally, she said, "We spin it in favor of the tour. Take the attention—even the not great attention—while it's given and make it about the tour." She seemed to be speaking to herself, not to him. "Use this to sell tickets for your show."

Hold up. He wasn't sure he liked that idea. She might have been the publicist, but he didn't enjoy using her for publicity like *this*.

"We do that? You're paparazzi bait." He said it, and he hated it. The whole idea made his stomach sour.

She nodded. "Yep."

"Not lovin' that idea." He pressed his knuckle against his lips and willed his brain to think of a better alternative.

"Me either." Her chest rose and fell, hiccuping a few times. But she didn't make a sound.

He reached for her hand, lifted it to his lips, and breathed a kiss there like he'd done to her shin not too long ago. "You don't want fame."

"Nope." Her brown hair caught against her necklace as she shook her head. "But it's what I've got."

She loved the band. Loved the guys—that much was clear. Now that he thought hard on it, whenever photo ops came around, Courtney was absent.

"Are you hungry still?" He asked what appeared to be the only safe question.

His attempt got him a smile. "Always."

"Is Tiny Badass down for a little frozen pasta bake?" Because he'd stocked a few of the frozen meal things he'd seen in Courtney's freezer back in LA.

"Does it come with a side of carrots?" Courtney asked, lines around her eyes that he hadn't noticed before showing themselves. The indentation under her eyes darker than usual —even with makeup to cover them.

She looked tired. Like she could sleep for a month and still need more. But at least she had a small smile twitching at the edges of her lips.

"Doesn't everything?" he asked. "Carrots are the shit."

"Then, yeah." She nudged his arm with hers. "Pasta sounds great."

"Then we'll have pasta." He squeezed her hand and pressed a kiss to the side of her neck.

He couldn't make everything better, but he could throw a bag of pasta into the microwave.

They made it home. She ditched her shoes at the front door with an assist, and he changed into sweatpants because when the world was fucking him, he preferred not to be in the discomfort of a suit.

Changing clothes took little time, but when he returned to the kitchen, Courtney had already fired up the microwave.

"I was gonna do that." He strode to the fridge and snatched one of the multiple bags of carrots he'd purchased.

"It's just pushing buttons." She stared at the buttons like they might say something important.

"I'm good at pushing buttons." He pressed a kiss to the side of her neck because he didn't want to lose the connection they'd started to build. Didn't want it to disintegrate like cotton candy in a vodka martini that he'd seen Courtney order once at one of the clubs she loved so much in LA.

She hadn't known he was there. He'd made sure of it.

As soon as he saw her there with her flaming cotton candy martini, he'd hightailed it out and hit up another joint.

Today he regretted that maneuver. Today he realized there was something seriously special about Courtney Lincoln and the way she made a guy feel the things that mattered. Something he wished he'd seen long before he knocked her up.

Digging through the cupboards, he found a cutting board and placed it on the counter.

"This is true." She climbed up the step stool and sat on the countertop while he chopped carrots.

"What's true?" He'd totally lost track of what they were talking about.

"You're good at pushing buttons." She crossed her ankles, her legs dangling.

He didn't argue the point, because they weren't in the pirate ship, and also it was true.

"You know," he said, "this whole thing with the paparazzi and fans and social media… it can just be about you and me having a baby. We don't have to spin it for ticket sales."

She reached for a sliver of carrot and popped it into her mouth, nodding. "I know. It's what makes sense though. What's best for you and the band."

"When has anything we've ever done made sense?" Because as far as he could remember, there wasn't much that did. Pausing from the carrots, he took two side steps to her.

"Open," he said, a small slice of carrot between his fingers.

She opened her mouth, and he slid the carrot onto her tongue. But he didn't remove his fingers right away. Instead, he pulled them from between her lips and traced there with the pad of his index finger, wishing it were his mouth and not his fingertip.

Their gazes held as she opened her legs, and he stepped between them. He'd never found vegetables particularly erotic. They were something that just had to be eaten. It had to be done.

But watching her throat as she swallowed that bite of carrot gave him a hard-on like he hadn't had since…

Well, since he touched her last time and brought her to completion.

"Can I?" he asked, holding his hands just above her belly.

She nodded, her eyes not moving from him as he splayed his hands over her abdomen and moved closer to her, right between her thighs.

"How are you feeling?" he asked, moving his hands from her abdomen to the edge of her dress and lifting the hem a few inches. Testing the waters. Seeing where she was with things.

"Right now, I'm feeling really turned on." Her voice was husky with desire.

He could relate. Every inch of his skin seemed to be extra sensitive when they were in the same room.

The microwave beeped, announcing the completion of the cycle.

"Hungry?" he asked.

"More turned on than hungry." The words came from low in her throat and rumbled through the air, straight to his groin.

"Can't have that." He lifted the hem of her dress higher to the crease of her thighs, and reached up so his hands were at the waistband of her panties.

Then he kissed her. Or she kissed him. They were both actively involved in every aspect of that kiss, so it was hard to say who did which part. Somehow her panties came off—the logistics were a little fuzzy given that she kissed him silly while he maneuvered the soft cotton over her thighs.

"Funny." He kissed a trail along her inner thigh, up to the curve of her hip, then back to the V between her legs. "I'm feeling hungry now."

"Then you should eat," she said, breathy. He settled her

deeper on the counter, hooked her legs over his shoulders, and tasted. Savored. Built her up with his mouth.

Her hands gripped his hair, giving their own version of instruction, pulling him tighter when he hit a good spot, redirecting when she was ready to go to the next level.

He loved this. Loved being in control, but also loved giving it over to her. Giving it when he knew intuitively that she would show him what she needed.

"Holy shit, you two." Knox's voice cut through everything.

Bax stopped sucking and licking.

Fuck.

Fuck. Fuck.

Courtney's whole body seemed to freeze in place, her legs holding his head in a vise.

"Could you at least put a tie on the goddamned door or something?" Knox hollered, but his footsteps were carrying him farther away. "My eyes. I'm blind. Fucking blind. I can't ever unsee *that*. And I have to eat in that kitchen. What the fuck? Why do you both hate me so much?"

"I think we should probably use a room with a door and a lock in the future," Courtney said, horror infusing each syllable.

"That's it," Knox continued. "I'm going to the pink house. I don't even care if the pink carpet smells like piss. No one will be giving head on those countertops unless it's *me*!" The front door slammed.

Courtney's grip on Bax's head lessened enough for him to remove his face from between her legs and resettle her skirt.

"Did he see anything?" she asked.

"Uh." Bax wet his lips… for what he'd been doing, suddenly they seemed pretty dry. "My face was covering." He made a circular motion around her groin area. "I think he just saw the back of my head and the… positioning."

"I have to move to Antarctica," Courtney said, a little dazed.

"I think we should probably eat some pasta and call it a night," Bax suggested, because with the way this night was progressing, they needed to nip it in the bud.

"I've had some fucked-up dates," Courtney said. "Done some really weird stuff."

Okay, what now?

"But this is the strangest night I've ever had."

Him too. As far as first dates went, this one was a doozy.

Chapter Eighteen
BAX

SOMEBODY–PROBABLY Knox—left the lights in the hallway on.

Bax rolled out of bed to see what the hell Knox was up to now. His earlier exodus only lasted about twenty minutes because the pink house had a fairly invasive urine-carpet scent in the bathrooms. Also, he figured that amount of time gave Bax and Courtney long enough to get themselves together.

Read: remove his face from between her legs.

With Knox's return, sudden fatigue hit Courtney, and she crashed as soon as she'd eaten half a bag of carrots and two bites of pasta.

Huh. No Knox in the hallway, but Courtney's door was open.

Bax probably should've put pants on before going in, but he wasn't in the mood to get dressed just to go back to bed and get undressed again.

He knocked on the doorframe. "Court?"

The nice thing about the house was that the rooms were big enough for a bed, some space for furniture, and massive closets. He dug it.

Also, didn't smell like piss.

Winner, winner, chicken dinner.

This room came with a white carpet he oddly did not hate, light-gray walls, and lots of art with big white and silver flowers.

"Hey." Courtney sat curled up on the lounger by the window with a cup of what appeared to be hot tea.

Her long brown hair was pulled into a low ponytail, and her pajamas were the comfy kind. Nothing particularly sexy about the sweatpants and sweatshirt, but the fabric hugged her new curves, and she might as well have been wearing a negligee with the way his heart sped up at the sight.

"Sorry I woke you," she said, eyebrows furrowing. "I didn't mean to be so loud."

Well, she wasn't making a peep, so she had the quiet thing down.

"No." He shook his head. "I woke up, saw the light on, came to see what tomfuckery Knox was up to this time."

"It's just me." She smiled, but it didn't reach her eyes. "I can turn off the hall lights. You go back to bed."

"Are you going back to bed?"

"No." She shook her head, sipped at the tea, said nothing else.

"Courtney, what's going on with you?" Something was off with her. Something he didn't care for one bit. "Can I come in?"

She nodded, gestured for him to enter. "Sure. Do you want some tea?"

"Not so much into tea. More of a coffee with whiskey kinda guy." He pulled the door closed behind him, just in case he ended up going down on her again.

Not that it was in the plan for the rest of his night, but he figured if the two of them were alone in a room, they should probably close the door in case things got sexy. Otherwise, Knox would probably wander in by accident.

"What's up?" he asked, heading toward her.

"Nothing's up," she straight-up lied to him.

"It's one a.m., and you're awake." He sat on the edge of her bed. Not too close, but not too far either. "There's no club to dance at. No drinks to drink. And you seem really into sleep these days. So spill it."

"I always get edgy before a tour." She lifted a shoulder, and the collar of her sweatshirt fell low. He was like a Pavlovian dog ready to go down on her just because she showed him some biceps. "It's my normal," she continued. "The edginess before tour."

"What about it makes you edgy?" He had a solid grasp of what made him edgy, but he couldn't speak for everyone.

"Honestly?"

"We're being honest, aren't we?"

"It's too late to go to the pirate ship." She sighed. He didn't care for that brand of sighing. "I don't have it in me to crawl through that door this late."

"That's good because the sprinklers are going off out there, and I don't have any intention of arguing." He leaned in, steepled his fingertips below his chin. "What makes you edgy before the tour?"

"You." Her throat moved, and she seemed to stare at the steam of her drink.

"Me?" What had he ever done to her before a tour? They hadn't even spoken before touring until this one.

Sure, they argued plenty when they were on the buses, but pre- and post-tour, they hardly saw each other. Usually, communication came through her assistant or Hans or Linx. Sometimes Knox, but with him, it was iffy as to whether the message would come through correctly.

"It's routine, I guess." She took a small sip, as though she were testing the temperature. Seeing if it was to her liking.

"That *I* put you on edge?"

"Pre-tour." She nodded. "You usually get a little annoyed

with me as soon as we head out, and I am always worried it's because…"

That wasn't the best place for her to stop speaking. Not when she was about to get to the meat of the matter.

"Because of what?" he asked.

She didn't seem to be able to meet his gaze. "Because I'm me."

Oh.

Well, fuck.

"When we argued before, it wasn't because you were you." Though she could've left some of the sass out of her comments toward him. But that wasn't the point tonight. "It was because *I'm* me. And I was a dick about a lot of shit. I don't want to be that guy anymore. I want to be the guy the band deserves." He looked up from the carpet and said sincerely, "That you deserve."

"No, I get it." She nodded. "We were both itching to fight. Sometimes I'd sit up and think about what our first round would be about. Prepare myself so it didn't shock me when it happened. I'd buy myself a little treat if I was right about who would toss the first volley."

"I'm that predictable, huh?" The truth was, if he really thought about it, he'd done similarly. Not to the extreme of making it a whole routine with a cup of tea… but yeah…

"There's nothing predictable about either of us." She blew at the steam, lifted the mug to her lips, and sipped.

That motion of her lips wrapping around the lip of the cup made him suddenly wish they were in the kitchen or the shower or she was in bed with him—

"I've been thinking about what you said." She glanced up. Met his gaze head-on.

"Which time?" Because he'd said a lot of stuff over the years.

"When you mentioned that if I'm ready to be in, then

you're ready to give me your…" She glanced pointedly at his crotch.

"Yeah. I probably wasn't thinking that through."

"No." She nodded, even though the word didn't match the movement. "You were right. We should wait until we're both ready to make a commitment to each other beyond just going at it."

He nodded, hating that of everything to be right about, this was the one that had stuck.

"I think I want to do that." She nodded. Sipped again at her tea.

"You want my dick?"

"No. I mean, *yes*. But no. I want us to, you know, try. See where we go. Have dinner, not because I live here or for the counter after-party, but because we want to spend time together. Figure out how to do this life we're linked in together."

"I always want to spend time with you." At least now that they weren't at each other's throats every second of the day.

She let out a breath through her nose. "So, what's next?"

"I'm pretty sure we're gonna go at it." Well, that was the truth. At least, if he had any say in the matter.

"C'mon. Be serious." She ran her hands through her hair, pulling it to the side and draping it there.

"Well, I think we do our best talking when we're naked. Don't you?" He said this with a huge scoop of misplaced humor. Adorably misplaced humor.

"Serious for a second?" she asked.

"Sure," he agreed.

"We go public. We're in this. It's not a secret. We do the whole 'please respect our privacy' even though we know they won't."

He nodded. "I'm going to let you make this call. Let me know how I can support the effort."

She glanced at her abdomen, running her hand over the sweatshirt there.

"Why don't we both go to our respective beds?" he suggested. She needed to rest. Needed to think. He understood that. "Get some shut-eye," he continued. "Don't overthink too much. We'll keep this simple."

There was a first time for everything.

He turned to leave. To give her the space she needed to decompress.

"Brennan," she whispered.

He loved it when she called him Brennan. Reminded him he was that kid no one knew existed other than family and his friends. A kid who wanted to be a rock star, but would walk dogs for summer cash while he waited for his big break.

"Love it when you call me that," he said, turning back to her.

"Maybe we should just try the cuddling part," she suggested, setting her tea on the coaster and striding toward him.

He didn't object, because he was either going to get lucky or get some sleep—both things he was good with.

"I could be down with cuddling." He intentionally let his tone hit that low note from "Get Them Blue." That had been one of his few original songs.

He opened his arms so she could move in.

Move in she did. Still standing, she settled between his legs so his face was at her chest.

Honest as fuck, he didn't mind this position, but he wasn't digging the sweatshirt anymore. This felt more like a skin-on-skin kind of moment.

"What do you think the odds are that we can be less than three feet from each other and not want to get naked?" he asked.

She combed her fingers through his hair, and damn, that felt good. If he had any feline in him, he'd be purring.

"Pretty low," she said, her hair falling forward into the space between them. There it was, the husky tone of her words.

Coconut and Courtney and—

"I need you." Courtney adjusted herself so his bare thigh settled between her legs.

"Do you?"

"Don't be a jerk about this." She nibbled at his jawline.

"I'm not being anything about anything." He wasn't quite able to think with the way she ground herself against his leg.

"Maybe be a bit of a jerk. That'd be okay."

She pushed him back on the bed and mounted him, one leg on either side of his hips, the core of her pressing against his crotch.

Her eyelids went heavy as she ground against the hard length in his shorts. Dammit, if she kept this up, he'd probably embarrass himself and come in his underwear.

Hands to her hips, he helped center her, held her steady while she used him for what she needed. Wished there weren't two layers of fabric between their bodies, but willing to give her what she needed.

Right now, she didn't seem to be in any hurry to pull off her clothes.

The problem was, if they kept this up, they'd both be suffering—

"Rug burn, sweetie," he said. "If we're gonna cuddle like this, let's get rid of some clothes, yeah?"

A momentary second of horror hit her face. "Did I hurt you?"

She started to climb off, but he held her hips still. This time grinding up gently against her.

Damn, she felt amazing.

"Brennan." Her pupils dilated further. "Did I hurt you?"

"Not yet." He pinned her gaze with his. "But we keep this up, we'll both be sore."

"Right." She pressed two hands against his pecs and shook her head. "You're right. Of course you're right."

Again, he held her hips still so she wouldn't dismount and run.

"I didn't say we should stop." He pressed the pad of his thumb against her bottom lip, reveling in the tender softness of her pink skin.

She reached for the hem of her sweatshirt and pulled it over her head.

He didn't want to stare, but her breasts had been fantastic before. Now? They were even better. As if he'd thought that possible.

"I'm gonna take care of you," he said in a promise he abso-fucking-lutely meant. He pressed up and ruffled his hands through her hair, pulling it around her shoulders before pulling her to him to drink her deep. Kiss her like she deserved. Like he needed, and he hoped to hell she needed too.

By the time he finished with her mouth and moved along the curve of her neck with his mouth, neither of them were super concerned about rug burn. Bax and Courtney of tomorrow could deal with that.

Bax and Courtney of today were about to have an excellent time.

"I need you," she said when he moved to pull her pants off. "Need this."

Thank hell she did a pants and underwear combo removal. He appreciated the enthusiasm.

"I know," he said, crawling toward her and drawing one nipple into his mouth.

She moaned and mewled and rubbed her core against his.

Here's the thing—Bax had had a lot of sex in his time on this planet. Had it in many, many places. But Courtney deserved better than a quick fuck.

They'd already done that.

This time, he'd wanted to give her more.

So he extracted himself from her arms and pressed light kisses to her mouth as he pulled off his shorts.

Careful not to jostle her as he laid her back against the comforter, he settled her into the bedding before dismounting to head to the bathroom. He hoped to hell there were condoms somewhere in this house.

He should add that to any future real estate contracts.

"Where are you going?" Courtney pulled him back, laced her fingers behind his head, and did not let go.

"Condom, sweetheart," he said against her lips.

She shook her head, lips brushing against his. "That pirate ship sailed months ago."

"I'm clean," he said. He'd taken a lot of tests to be sure after he found out his swimmers had made it to home base.

She was clean because she'd told him.

Hell, he could be down with this.

"Only if you're sure?" he asked. Transparency was important at times like… well… now when they'd just made something of a commitment to each other and were ready to seal that deal.

Instead of answering with words, she answered with her mouth and her hands, legs, her whole body.

He responded the same, and as her moans melded with his groans, he realized this wasn't about releasing tension. This wasn't about sex.

Not to him.

This was about them. About what she'd become to him.

He wanted her to open herself and give him those deep-down pieces of herself just like he'd unwittingly given to her sometime in the recent past. Because, damn, she'd become his world.

He kissed her body… everywhere. Took inventory. Licked and touched and lavished.

She seemed to do the same thing, and there were no words necessary between them.

The gentle caresses turned heated. Her wet center pressed against him. He met her fire with a passion of his own. Met her frenzied kisses with smooth strokes to her breasts, down along the swell of her abdomen, to the bundle of nerves between her legs.

She gasped as his fingers met precisely the right point, rubbing her there as she writhed beneath him.

The first orgasm came quick, but they hadn't been able to finish before, and he wouldn't disappoint. He owed her two.

She cracked the door to her heart for him, and he was going to make his point. Show her how good they could be together.

So, as she rode the orgasm down, he centered himself over her, stared down, and pressed inside.

There, he took his time, holding her gaze with his as his hand worked her sweet spot and he thrust gently.

The thin string of invisible connection pulled tight, and he wouldn't release it. They had this. This chemistry. This depth. This… everything.

She came again, wrapping her legs around his waist. This time, he followed.

Then, as she drifted to sleep in his arms, he decided that this was their new pre-tour ritual.

A helluva lot more fun than a cup of tea, he could promise her that.

Chapter Nineteen
COURTNEY

COURTNEY WASN'T HIDING ANYTHING. She just didn't want Bax to hear this particular conversation. So she hid in the pirate ship to make the call.

"Is this for real?" Irina asked through the phone line.

"Very real." As real as it came.

The silence that followed wasn't assuring.

"You're sure we wouldn't be breaking any laws?" Irina asked. "Not that I'm opposed to breaking certain laws, but I like to know what I'm looking at going in."

"We'll just be careful with how we describe you. Like, you could describe a paper towel as a napkin. That's not illegal, it's just a different description."

"I don't think this is the same thing."

Blah. Courtney needed her for this, because she didn't care for any of the alternative options. "You're only impersonating for my sanity's sake. No one actually thinks you're a professional. It's the same thing you'd get to do on television. But this time in real life. It's like immersive acting."

"I literally went to school for performing, and I don't think that's a thing."

"New genre. You're a groundbreaker. Are you in?"

Courtney asked, hoping like hell that Irina had a free moment to come play doctor with her. Otherwise, she'd have to hire an actual professional. But she didn't need a professional. Didn't want to take a professional away from other patients who actually could use their services.

Irina could use the acting credit for her resume, and Courtney could use a buddy on tour.

Win. Win. Win.

"Fine. I'm so far in I might as well already be in Colorado," Irina confirmed. "I've needed a break anyway. Things here are slow."

Irina went through the Tisch School of the Arts. A brilliant actress who, like many others, had struggled to find her way in Hollywood. Find that breakout role. That breakout anything.

Her résumé was chock-full of community theater, commercials, roles as an extra in blockbuster films. Yet she had never quite made it past that initial level. Which was ridiculous, because Irina was the shit.

She could cry on command. She could do any accent she wanted—probably even give Bax a run for his pirate money. And she was a dab hand with theatrical makeup. She could make herself look twenty years older or ten years younger with just a little purse of makeup.

The problem Irina ran into was that she really loved carbs as much as pre-baby Courtney. That was part of the reason they bonded. All that was to say, Irina didn't fit into the size structure that Hollywood preferred.

Courtney figured if the whole acting gig didn't work out, Irina could probably work for the CIA or something. Though Courtney wasn't entirely certain what the government thought of agents who liked to go clubbing with the same commitment as Irina.

"Well, get your ass out here because we are ready to take off," Courtney said.

"Any special requests?" Irina asked.

"Would you stop by Compartés and grab me a box of chocolates before you head out? It's the only chocolate I've been craving. One of their bars with the fruit and nuts and…" Yum.

"Caramels too?" Irina asked, because this was Courtney, and if there was sugar involved, she was usually in.

However.

Tiny Badass wasn't keen on caramel.

"Stick to dark chocolate and fruit. This kid enjoys anything that looks like it came from nature." What Courtney wouldn't give to crave a French fry.

"I'm never getting pregnant," Irina announced. "I like the bad stuff way too much."

Well, never say never. That was what Courtney discovered.

"Also, I actually meant acting requests?" Irina said seriously. "Any particular accents? Wardrobe? What should we call me?"

"Surprise me," Courtney said. Then she stopped. Rethought that statement. Actually… "Surprise me, but make it believable."

"Consider it done," Irina said with an impressive French accent.

"Oh, and no pink hair. Go with a natural color, please." Courtney hated to make the ask, but given Irina's love of changing up her locks, she could decide to go neon before boarding the plane.

Actually, Courtney wouldn't put it past her to dye her hair while actually on the plane.

"Natural hair. Make it believable. Bring chocolate. Check. Check. And checkity-check." Irina paused, then said, "I'm not actually going to have to deliver your baby, right?"

"No." Absolutely not. "If there is an issue, we'll be in bigger cities. The most you'd have to do is drive me to a clinic or something. I think we could call you my birth guide. What do you say? It's not a lie, and it's not illegal."

"I can totally handle that."

"Bax will also want you to harass me about vitamins and water consumption, but you're not allowed to give me shit. That part is acting. Agreed?" Because the last thing Courtney needed was her birth guide telling her what to do or where to go or how to get there.

"Aw, that's no fun. I'd rather give you crap."

"You give me crap, I'll give you crap." The laughter was clear in Courtney's tone. "No one wants that."

"Agreed." Irina chewed at her bottom lip. "Linx isn't going to tell our secret?"

Courtney shook her head. "Linx took my side on this one."

Irina skedaddled to prepare for her latest gig, and Courtney made the arrangements so Irina could fly in before the big Red Rocks concert that night. Then they'd load up and head to Cheyenne. One wouldn't think that a town built on everything Chris LeDoux would embrace Dimefront. But given that tickets had sold out in a matter of moments, they would be wrong.

RED ROCKS WAS one of Courtney's favorite venues. The band loved it here because it was in Denver. Brek, their previous manager, like to book the old tours through here, so it'd become one of their usual haunts. He'd stop in and see family whenever they came through.

The amphitheater was cut into the side of the mountain, and the place was gorgeous. A backdrop of literal red rocks everywhere. At night, when the bands played, the lights lit up the theater, the giant screen behind them projecting the live video. Thousands of fans streamed into the bench seats.

The whole event was something special. More than the usual Dimefront concerts, which were special in their own ways.

Red Rocks was magical on its own, but when you added the band?

Boom.

"He's so dreamy with the haircut," Irina said, totally committed to the French accent. If Courtney didn't know she was from the Midwest, she'd totally buy it.

Bax *was* dreamy with the haircut.

Courtney turned from watching the band onstage to her best friend.

Her best friend who had gone off the deep end.

"You're here." Courtney flung her arms around Irina. "And what the hell are you wearing?" Courtney was seriously regretting not taking the time to create an entire call sheet for Irina.

"You said I got to choose." Irina struck a Material Girl pose. "I went funky-clunky."

Funny thing, that description was entirely accurate. She wore clunky jewelry, and her dress was a multicolored, bold giraffe print A-line. With fake gemstone–encrusted flip-flops.

Courtney wasn't judging the flip-flops—they were her preferred footwear too. Especially inside. But Red Rocks was outside, and it was spring, and Irina's tootsies were gonna catch a chill.

"I figured I'd go with something I could wear after the gig." Irina smoothed the dress.

Courtney had to give it to her—it was different, but it suited.

"Something French," Irina added.

Irina's style changed as often as her hair color.

"You don't like it?" she asked, deflating a little. "I figured it looked very baby with the animal print."

"It's just not what I expected." It worked though. A traveling birth guide could wear whatever a birth guide wished to wear. There was no uniform. If there was to be a uniform, they'd get to decide what it was. Since they made up the profession.

"You're committed to your role, and I applaud that commitment," Courtney added.

"I even made a name tag." Irina produced the pin and attached it to her collar. She did a shimmy shake to show it off.

"Look at you. Nice." That wasn't even a homemade name tag. She probably had to go to Office Depot to get it.

"I'm going to be the best traveling birth guide who ever traveled." Irina winked.

"You're probably the only one." Courtney loved that she was there. "So you get to set the standard."

"Ha-cha-cha."

As the boys played into the third song, Irina pulled out her cell and opened the notebook. "Tell me the details I'll need to know so I can nag you without actually nagging," Irina said.

"Bax is worked up about hydration." Courtney crossed her arms. The timing of this nag wasn't great, because Tiny Badass had hit a growth spurt and it was seriously causing bladder issues. The only thing that made them worse?

Drinking more water.

"I can understand why. You're literally drinking for two." Irina eyed Courtney's stomach. Then she dropped the accent. "Seriously, that kid must be massive. How are you even standing up right now?"

"Write this down." Courtney pointed to the open notepad app. "'My job is to take Courtney's side on everything, while not calling her massive.'"

Irina smirked. "'Get her to drink water without actually telling her I'm doing it.' Done. 'Tell her she's gorgeous.' What else? Can I plan a gender reveal?"

"No."

"If I promise there won't be pyrotechnics?" Irina tried again.

"No, we're not finding out." They'd already decided.

Irina made an *urgh* sound. "Then what am I supposed to do?"

"Every once in a while, do birth-guide stuff." Courtney waved her hand.

"I don't know what that would be, but I am happy to do some research and find out. I'll probably need a stethoscope and some tongue depressors if we're going to pull this off." Irina seamlessly slipped back into the role of French birth guide.

"What do you need tongue depressors for? Why didn't you bring them with you? What are you pulling off? Why did your accent change?" Knox asked, sticking his head between Courtney and Irina.

Courtney's heart seemed to lodge in her larynx.

"Hell! You're supposed to be onstage." Courtney smacked him on the shoulder. "Why aren't you onstage?" He was just onstage.

He jerked his thumb toward the bathroom. "Had to piss."

"You can't just leave to pee," Courtney whispered, and glanced around to see if anyone had noticed they were missing a bandmate.

"You don't want me to do it onstage, that'd be gross. PR nightmare. I went pee for you, Courtney." He said this with huge puppy dog eyes that did nothing to sway her.

"Liar," she said.

"Touché." He studied Irina for a beat. "The guys barely miss me. I'll get back to it. But first"—he pointed to Irina and then to Courtney—"I wanna know."

Fine, he wanted to know, he could know. "This is Irina, she's my traveling birth guide."

"You're fucking with me right now?" he asked, shoving his

hands on his hips. "Because she didn't even bring a stethoscope."

Dammit, if she couldn't even convince Knox, how would she convince the rest of them?

"Get. On. The. Stage," Courtney said through gritted teeth.

"I'm getting there. You need to spill about this first." He made a motion with his finger like was stirring the pot, then spilling the pot.

Courtney didn't know what to do in this situation. She glanced at Irina, who shrugged and lifted her palms in an *I've got no idea either* kind of gesture.

"Nice to meet you, Mr. Knox." Accentless Irina held her hand out for him to kiss her knuckles.

He stared at her knuckles like he had no idea what to do with them.

"Ladies, I've got to get back onstage," he said, as though Courtney wasn't saying the same thing two seconds earlier. "I don't have time to be fucked with." He popped a breath mint and glanced at the band. They'd jumped into the next song.

"Actually," he said, "I've got about thirty seconds to be fucked with." He glanced at his Apple Watch. "And… go."

"Get your ass back onstage," Hans said menacingly from behind Knox.

"I am getting my ass back. But first I'm talking to these ladies who are trying to hide something." Knox crunched the breath mint and smacked his lips.

"Go." Hans pointed, and his tone said there was no arguing to be had this time.

Courtney made some mental notes because she'd probably need to use a tone like that for this whole motherhood gig.

"Fine. But when this show is over, you're telling me everything." Knox turned and managed a stuntman-esque flip jump onto the stage. He didn't miss a beat, jumping right in to rock out.

Courtney didn't want to turn around. She *really* didn't want to.

But she had to, so she turned to Hans.

"Hey, Hans. This is Irina." She gestured to her bestie. "My traveling birth guide."

Hans kept his arms crossed and raised his eyebrows. "I'm not saying I agree with you. But I'm also not saying I agree with Bax. You two have to sort this one out yourselves."

With that, he turned on his dress shoes and meandered back to wherever it was Hans went during the shows.

"He knows, doesn't he?" Irina whispered, but kept the accent. "He's got that look like he knows."

Oh yes… "He knows."

Because this was Hans.

Hans knew everything.

"I have a question," Irina asked, raising her hand..

"Yup. Shoot."

"You are going to have Bax's baby."

Courtney nodded. "Yup."

"And I'm your best friend."

Courtney nodded again. "Yup."

"So that makes me sort of an aunt to this child."

Courtney was not loving the direction of this conversation because it was starting to dawn on her that—

"Which means eventually Bax will see me outside the role of traveling birth guide."

Courtney pulled her lips to the side. Perhaps she hadn't thought this all the way through.

"Here's what you'll do. You are still my best friend." Courtney crafted the plan on the fly.

"Good to hear." Irina nodded.

"You speak with your normal accent."

"Okay." She still said this with her French accent.

"And you moonlight as a traveling birth guide. This will be your last gig before you hit the big-time."

"So far, I do not hate any of this plan," Irina said with a huge smile.

"Perfect." Courtney shifted on her feet.

"Are you sure I can't use the accent? I've been practicing since you called."

Courtney shook her head. "Unpractice it."

"Method acting is more complicated than that," Irina said with a huff.

One of the spotlights flashed, apparently attempting to blind everyone with theatrics.

Irina flinched. "But I'm a professional, and I will make it work."

Good.

Then they just had to deal with Knox.

Chapter Twenty
COURTNEY

"SPILL YOUR TEA." Knox stood against the door of one of the buses with his arms crossed.

Courtney and Irina had nearly made it to the buses without getting ambushed by Knox. She rolled her eyes. She was tired, they'd had a long day, and she was ready for some Bax time.

"Can you just leave it alone?" she asked.

Knox seemed to think about that for a beat before he shook his head. "No."

"If we tell you, can you promise to keep a secret?" Irina asked, more innocent than Courtney felt.

"Secrets are my favorite." Knox bounced on his toes. "I like knowing things nobody else does. Like how Linx went ring shopping for Becca? No one else knows that little gem."

Courtney glanced at Irina, shaking her head. "He can't know."

"I guess I'll have to do my own investigation." Knox lifted his shoulder. "I'm like the Sherlock Holmes of rockers."

The last thing she needed was Knox poking around, so Courtney clenched her teeth, scanned the area, and came clean.

"Was that so hard?" Knox asked.

"Only if you can't keep a secret," Courtney countered.

"I will keep your secret, but I don't like it." Knox pinched his lips together. "What happens if you actually need medical help?"

"Then I'll call a doctor," Irina said. "That's what my job description says."

Knox harrumphed. "You better be good at your job."

"I don't take time off in the middle of it to go pee, so there's that." Irina totally hit him straight in the nuts.

"Good talk, then." Courtney patted his shoulder and headed to the bus she shared with Bax.

Linx and Becca had their own bus because they were new, and no one wanted a repeat of the Bax-Courtney kitchen counter fiasco.

Bax and Courtney? Also got their own bus for the same reason.

Tanner, Mach, Knox, and Irina shared another.

And the crew shared the fourth.

They loaded up and headed for Wyoming.

There was something soothing about the highway under the wheels as they moved from one venue to the next. A lull that made things focused and fuzzy, all at the same time. How that was possible? Well, that was the secret of life on the road.

"You look exhausted." Courtney stood at the doorway of the bedroom she shared at the back of the bus with Bax. Bax who lay spread-eagle on the bed.

"I wish I were twenty-two again," he murmured as he rolled onto his back.

"Stage life kicking your ass?" She sauntered into the room, already pulling off her shirt to give him a little show.

He grinned. "Maybe I'm not that tired."

"Hmm." She pulled her leggings down and kicked them off so she was just in her skivvies.

"Maybe my twenties were overrated," Bax said, propping himself up on his arm, his erection filling up his fly.

Courtney's pulse thrummed a little harder, and she moved over him on the bed, unbuckling his belt and working his jeans down his thighs.

Then she took him into her mouth—deep and long and oh so very Bax.

He moaned, holding her hair in his hands as she gave him a reward for a job well done.

"You," he groaned, as she worked him with her hand and her mouth. "I want you, Courtney."

He held her eyes with his as the wheels turned behind them, and she removed her panties, mounted him, and took him for a ride.

This wasn't a quick fuck or a frantic bull ride... this was long and slow where she took the reins and rode her rock star.

When they both came, she was on top of him, her knees on both sides of his hips, and he had a wicked grin that made her heart swell.

He pulled her down to him, settling her on her side and nuzzling her neck. Somewhere between Denver and Fort Collins, they'd lost the rest of their clothes. Now, it was him and her and... peace.

She grinned. He smiled.

And this life they had together did not suck.

THANKFULLY, Bax didn't question Irina. He said his hellos, remembered her from the photo on Courtney's apartment wall, but was too overwhelmed with the fans and the signings for more digging.

The Cheyenne concert went as well as Red Rocks. Even better, some might say, since Courtney ensured that Knox used the facilities before hitting the stage.

The concert finished, the guys tromped offstage. Bax kissed the hell out of her on his way by.

She dug that. Dug that he didn't mind the public display of affection or the photos that would turn up online afterward. Dug that he stopped long enough to think of her. Do something about it. And make a promise for later.

"I won't be tired tonight. It's my turn to take lead." He kissed the tip of her nose. "Wait up for me?"

Well, duh.

She nodded.

He got shuffled away with the crew and had to break the connection with Courtney to pay attention to where he headed. Backstage was a mix of cords and equipment storage boxes in various stages of unpacking and packing. A person had to watch their feet so they didn't biff it.

"Hey, Courtney." Knox settled in beside her, draped his arm around her shoulder, and pulled her against him.

She moved along with him toward the exit that led to the VIP tent, but she had no intention of going in.

The band would prepare for their VIP meet and greet. She was preparing for them to get mobbed, so she could grab Chet, and Irina, and maybe Becca and head for her favorite Wyoming milkshake stand.

She'd called ahead, and they would have a vegan milkshake and a smoothie waiting for her.

"Hey, Knox." She glanced up at him. Grinned. "What do you want? Do you need to go potty again?"

He scrunched his nose and shook his head. "No. Thanks for asking though."

"What do you want?"

"I have a request."

"Okay. Shoot." Hopefully it was a publicist-type request. That was all she was going to handle before heading out.

"You know how I'm keeping your little secret?" he asked. "I need a favor in return." He slowed.

She didn't like that. "What kind of favor?"

"I want to check your cervix." He stopped because she stopped, because straight up? What. The. Fuck.

"Hear him out." Irina hurried to their huddle. "He's actually got a plan."

Again with the what the—

"I don't care what his plans are, as long as they don't involve my cervix." A sentence she never thought she'd need to utter. Ever. To anyone other than maybe her gynecologist. "No one is touching my anything." Only a physician, and that was solely when necessary.

"Mach and Tanner, Knox and I, we stayed up late last night on the bus researching how to deliver a baby." Irina slid her gaze around. "Just in case, you know?" Her gaze landed on Courtney's stomach.

Uh-huh. She knew.

There was so much to digest here.

First...

"You told Mach and Tanner?" Courtney mouthed, "Everything?"

"Oh, no." Irina shook her head. "I just did a training seminar. YouTube for the win. Totally standard procedure for a traveling birth guide. We prepare those around us for any birthing emergencies." She pulled up the notes app on her phone. "Check it out. I made a list of everything we do. How sick is that?"

Courtney blinked. Blinked again. Again.

Maybe she should've just hired an actual professional.

Back to digesting this... The second point...

Tiny Badass kicked her in the ribs, and she couldn't really remember the second point suddenly.

Third...

"You want to check my cervix?" Courtney asked, staring hard at Knox to get an idea of what the hell was wrong with him. "Why?"

Knox nodded, looking way too excited for his own good. "So I have a baseline."

"Why would you need a baseline?" And why was she still asking these questions?

"So I'll know when you dilate." He looped his thumbs through the loops of his jeans.

Where the hell was Bax? And why was he right that she needed a professional on the tour? She hated he was right.

When Bax was right, it tasted metallic. Yuck.

"Please," Knox added, like that would actually get him somewhere with his request.

"No." Courtney strode away. Then turned back. "Ask Irina if you can check hers instead."

"It's not the same," Knox called. But Courtney decided not to listen to him anymore.

About anything.

Ever.

That milkshake was looking better and better. Or maybe the smoothie. Of course, Tiny Badass would prefer a smoothie. Probably with lots of vegetables inside.

"Hey." Bax kicked off from where he waited by the exit door.

"Hey," she replied, grouchy because her cervix was the topic of anyone's conversation.

"Why do you look like you want to strangle someone?" He pushed a piece of hair behind her ear, and her nerve endings perked right the hell up.

"Because I want to strangle someone." Her breaths were huffing and puffing because she was hurrying in case Knox had any other stupid requests, and she had a baby pressing against her rib cage. And now she was aroused on top of everything else.

"Tell daddy about it." Bax reached up to trace her jawline.

"Ew. Don't call yourself daddy like that." She shivered. "Ever."

"What's up, Court?" he asked, still trailing his fingertip along the column of her neck.

"Irina had a lesson last night with Knox, Mach, and Tanner. Reviewed what to do if I need someone to deliver Tiny Badass," Courtney said, trying to keep her opinion out of it but unable to remove it completely. "While we're on the road."

Bax tilted his head to the side. "That sounds really smart."

Yes, well, Irina was probably trying to get an idea of exactly how a person gave birth. Where the baby came from. Came out.

Courtney ground her molars together again. She really needed to stop doing that, or she'd need a dentist and a medical professional to travel with them. "Knox wants to check my cervix."

"Your cervix?" Bax seemed confused.

"You know." She leaned in closer. "Where the baby's going to come out."

"He what?" Bax yelled, clearly as appalled as she was.

Uh-huh. She could relate.

Bax made two fists and scanned the backstage area. "I'm going to kill him."

She reached for his shoulder. "You can't kill him. If you did that, you'd go to jail, and our baby would never know you."

"Fuck." Bax apparently did not love that he couldn't commit murder.

Knox, unfortunately, took that moment to saunter by.

Bax tapped him on the shoulder.

Knox raised his eyebrows. "Good show, man. Nice work out there."

Bax stepped forward, right up in Knox's face. "The only guy checking Courtney's cervix is me."

Well, not exactly, because she wasn't even going to let him—

"We clear on that?" He patted Knox on the shoulder and mimed wiping dust from the cotton fabric.

Knox glowered at Courtney.

She glared right back.

Neither of them really meant it.

"Fine. You do things your way. But if things go south, don't say I wasn't trying to be prepared." He pointed his middle and index fingers toward his eyes, then at Courtney, as though saying, *Comprende?* But with finger motions instead of words.

"I can live with that," Courtney called as he hit the exit.

"Walk with me?" Bax asked, holding his hand out for her.

She threaded her fingers with his as they moved outside, past a couple of golf carts to the entrance of the VIP tent.

She'd need to make her move soon, or she'd get caught up in the VIP wave. There weren't many aspects of touring she disliked. The VIP tent and the meet and greets were two of her least favorite activities, however.

The guys loved the attention, but she preferred to be on the edge of things. Not in the center. Not like that.

He pulled her around the side near where the tour buses waited for them to load up in a couple of hours.

"Wanna make out?" he asked.

This was fun. This version of Bax. This guy who pulled her behind the VIP tent.

"Pretty much whenever we're within three feet of each other." She lifted, pressing her mouth to his.

Her stomach cramped.

Not in a dairy milkshake or bacon kind of way, but like a hug that stole her breath. Not painful, but enough to catch her attention.

"Hah. Whoo." Yes, that was her making those breathy sounds.

No. She didn't love that she was making them.

"Court?" Bax held her against him as she took a deep breath.

As quick as it started, her abdomen released, and Tiny Badass gave her a solid kick in the ribs.

"I'm okay," she said, way more perky than she intended. "One of those Braxton Hicks-y things the doctor mentioned." She rubbed at her now soft belly. "I'm good."

"Where's Irina?" Bax glanced around the lot, more frantic than necessary over nothing more than a teensy-weensy contraction.

"Bax." She pulled his face to hers, so they were eye to eye. "I'm pregnant. This type of thing is going to happen. I have them all the time."

"Since when?"

"Since about three weeks ago. It's like practice labor."

That did not seem to reassure him.

His heart beat quick against her palm.

"Your public awaits." She tilted her head toward the back entrance at the edge of the tent before she rolled up on her toes to press a light kiss to his mouth.

"Shit, are you two going at it a-gain?" Knox asked, striding off his bus toward them.

"Courtney had a contraction." Bax said this like an accusation as he ran his hand through his hair. He did the hair thing when he got super stressed or she'd said something that made him particularly gnarly.

"Sweet." Knox strode forward, grinning. "Can I feel?"

"No," Courtney and Bax said at the same time.

"Where's Irina?" Courtney asked, eyeing the bus where Knox came from.

"She's inside watching more birth videos." Knox shook from head to toe. "Have you seen those things? The kid comes out nasty and covered in gunk. Talk about freaky. It's like a Freddy Krueger movie."

"You are not helping," Courtney said.

Calming Bax down to the point where he could go into the VIP tent did not involve Knox talking about the delivery room.

"Bax." She rubbed his arms with her palms. "This is the first of many changes for us. It's okay. I'm okay. I just need to sit down for a bit and hydrate. It always works."

Sonofabitch, he was right again.

"Okay." He nodded.

"I'll see you after the meet and greet."

"Okay." He nodded again.

"Okay," she said, since it was the word of the moment.

Tiny Badass thumped her in the ribs again and did a loop movement. Courtney reached for Bax's hand and held it against that part of her abdomen. Tiny Badass could be a performer like Dad because the little munchkin kicked right on command.

"See?" Courtney asked when Tiny Badass went over the top with the acrobatics. "We're good."

"Good." Bax seemed a little more like himself. He cradled her belly with his hands, and the precious movement seemed to stroke her soul.

"See you after." She pressed a kiss to his lips and headed to find Irina and sit down to drink a not-milk milkshake.

Chapter Twenty-One
COURTNEY

"I TOLD him I was going to sit down. Not *where* I was going to sit." Courtney sucked the straw of her kale-mango-carrot-ginger smoothie. A smoothie made with fucking oat milk.

Tiny Badass better understand everything she was doing to make him or her happy.

She'd elected to grab Chet and Becca and Irina and grab herself a smoothie. Hydrating and sitting. The two things she'd promised she'd do.

While she'd gone smoothie, they'd gone for milkshakes. Because none of them were pregnant with Bax's baby, who denied her every form of processed sugar and most processed carbohydrates.

Once she got to Shake Shack-A-Roo, Tiny Badass demanded vegetables.

The joint was a little hole-in-the-wall place with a smattering of glossy tables, yellow walls, and a giant cartoon cow painted on the wall.

"Technically, you are sitting. And hydrating. As your professional traveling birth guide, I approve this choice," Irina said. She'd gone cookies 'n cream. "It counts."

Butterscotch Becca didn't seem so certain. "I'm just here

because Linx would withhold bedroom time if I let anything happen to you."

"Are you ready to head back yet?" Chet had gone with mint chip. Courtney wouldn't have pegged him as a mint-chip bodyguard. He always seemed like more of a water guy. Maybe unsweetened iced tea.

Bax would be…

Bax would order…

Damn.

She did not know.

Bax's smoothie, or milkshake, order sat as a blank void in her mind.

Holy crap. They were dating. Sleeping together. Having a baby. Yet she didn't even know his milkshake preference.

"I don't know what milkshake Bax likes," she said, horror in her words. "I know a lot about him. Right? This is just a blip thing? One of those small things we don't know yet?"

"Yes." Becca reached across the table and squeezed Courtney's hand. "It's a blip thing. You've got your entire lives to ask him."

"What if he likes strawberry shrub?" That would be the worst. Could she be with someone long-term who liked a strawberry-shrub milkshake?

"What's strawberry shrub?" Irina asked.

"Strawberry ice cream with vinegar," Courtney said.

"Do they even make that?" Becca was clearly unconvinced.

"I don't know. What if they do?" Courtney's heart beat fast like Bax's had earlier when she'd experienced the one contraction. "What if they do and Bax prefers that?"

She needed to ask. Find out.

She dug through her pocket for her cell but came up short.

"I left my cell on the bus." Blah. Okay, fine. She'd ask him later. *Deep breaths. In. Out. Drink the smoothie.*

Her heart started beating at a more normal level when Becca's eyes went wide.

Irina's too.

Chet showed nothing.

"I don't think you're going to have to wait." Becca stared at the glass door of the Shake Shack-A-Roo.

"Courtney?" Bax blew through like a Dimefront tornado, with Knox, Linx, Tanner, Mach, and even Hans hurrying after him.

Behind Hans was an entire pack of paparazzi and fans.

Courtney stopped mid-suck.

One paparazzo scuttled in front of Knox, aiming his camera toward Bax. Knox caught camera guy's foot and fell right on back, taking Linx with him. Tanner hopped to one side. Mach to the other. Hans looked ready to strangle someone. Hopefully not her.

Knox and Linx recovered quickly, but the momentary distraction seemed to take the heat off of Bax and his momentum toward her.

"Thank fuck." Bax strode across the store, apparently oblivious to the gaping customers and the mess he left in his wake.

She swallowed the gulp of smoothie. "Shouldn't you be signing autographs?"

"You weren't there." His voice cracked. Damn. The guy had impressive vocal control, so his level of upset must've been extreme.

"I left a note." She had. Just in case he came back before her.

"How do you think we found you?" Linx asked. He didn't look amused either, and she knew he was privy to her milkshake routine because she often brought one back for him.

"I'm sitting down." She held up the cup. "Hydrating."

"You weren't on the bus." Bax pulled her up into a super-tight hug.

"Bax," she said against his shoulder. "I always go for milkshakes while you guys do your thing." This was not really new. "Sometimes if I can't find milkshakes, I go for cocktails." Not right now, for obvious reasons. One very obvious reason.

"How am I supposed to know that?" He held her back a little, and, well, damn, she hadn't meant to worry him.

"Because you're always there? I'm never there." At some point, she sort of figured he'd noticed her absence.

The not noticing thing made her heart hurt. Not in a pregnant heartburn way, but in an emotional he-really-didn't-care way. It stung. Ached. Actually, it freaking hurt.

"Good show, everyone." Hans clapped his hands. "Grab yourselves a milkshake on Dimefront."

"I guess it's time to go back." Becca stood.

Courtney held her hand out to Bax. He linked their fingers together.

"Uh-huh." Courtney needed to think about this. "It's time to go back."

COURTNEY HAD minimal time to process the Bax panic situation—given that social media was blowing up and Dimefront was getting loads of attention.

She was getting loads of attention.

Bax's new pregnant girl, Linx's little sister, and Bax going bananas at the Shake Shack-A-Roo apparently made her interesting.

Even Hans buying everyone ice cream hadn't quelled the curiosity, the internet chatter, or the fans' disappointment that she was the one to take Em's place.

That one sort of stung the most.

So she was now playing defense again, on her phone, curled up on the tour bus with her feet propped up on pillows.

"I'm ready to talk," Bax said, freshly showered and striding into the living area—if one could really call it that.

They hadn't spoken much since the buses left the lot. A few words here and there, but the air practically crackled with unspoken words. Starting with "What's your favorite milkshake?" and ending with "What the actual fuck?"

Speaking of—

"A pirate hat?" Courtney couldn't really believe was she was seeing. And yet? She totally could. "You want to talk about this while you wear a pirate hat?"

"No. I wants t' natter about it while we both wear pirate hats." Bax removed two folded-up cardboard paper pirate hats from Pirate Pizza Palace and placed one smack on his head.

Perhaps this was the part of pregnancy no one ever talked about—where your baby's father turned into a pirate-hat-wearing cartoon character.

"You're trying not to be angry." Also, she was not wearing that hat.

"Aye. No ship here fer us. So we'll 'ave t' do wit' a stand-in option." He handed her one of the two hats.

"Or we could just move forward." She took the hat so it didn't become a whole thing. She did not, however, put it on her head.

Bax sat, crossed his arms, then said without an ounce of pirate, "You freaked me out."

"I was totally fine. This happens all the time when you guys are touring. Every time, this is what I do. It's not like I did something that's out of the ordinary. Becca and Irina got an introduction to how I handle the crowds. That introduction involved a smoothie with kale. We brought Chet with us."

"I came back, and you weren't here."

"And that's going to happen again. Every time we stop on tour. I've got my complete plan mapped out."

"I don't like you going out alone."

"Okay." She shifted on the settee, moving her feet to the floor so he could sit closer. "I am an adult."

"And we're in this together."

"I'm an adult," she said again. "I get to decide about things that affect me. For example, if I want a smoothie, I will have one."

Surprisingly, he said nothing. Didn't argue. What the hell, she'd just keep on trucking. "I will take the precautions and bodyguards and traveling birth guides, but you can't start telling me everything I can or can't do. You don't want me to do that to you. I don't want that to be who we become."

He nodded. Pulled the hat off his head. "I got scared."

"It's gonna happen a lot when Tiny Badass comes. I'm pretty sure ninety-nine-point-nine percent of parenting is being terrified."

He nodded.

"I'm betting it's that small percentage in the middle where the good stuff happens."

Look at her sounding so sage. She should bottle this shit up and sell it in journals.

"I'm sorry," he said, his throat working. "Sorry I made a scene. Sorry I panicked."

She scooted to him so they were thigh to thigh.

"I'm pretty sure there will be many times in this thing we've got going when I make a scene and panic." Actually… "What's your favorite milkshake flavor?"

"I don't have one." He scrunched his eyebrows together. "Why?"

"What do you order when you get one?" Because *none* would be worse than strawberry shrub, and she didn't think before this moment that there was really anything worse than that.

"Whatever looks good."

"So you don't have a preference?"

"I have a preference. But it changes with the day."

"That's bizarre."

"It's not bizarre." He pulled her to him, wrapping his arm around her shoulders, and she settled in. "Like today, I would've probably gotten a smoothie like you had. That thing looked amazing."

"It was green." And not in a mint chip kind of way.

"Yum." He took the pirate hat from her and pressed a kiss to the top of her head. "I guess my favorite milkshake is a green smoothie."

"Green isn't a flavor."

"But it should be."

This wasn't awful. This camaraderie after the storm.

Well, the storm still brewed, still raged online. But with the two of them like this? There didn't seem to be anything that could actually pull them apart.

They were like two reset magnets, finally pulling in the right direction.

For good this time.

Chapter Twenty-Two
BAX

WHEN THINGS WERE GOING TOO WELL, Bax understood he should probably buckle up for the inevitable crash.

That crash hit him in the head.

On a cross street in downtown Boise no less.

There at the street corner, traffic buzzed by, horns honked, somebody yelled an obscenity at a driver.

There he was, standing and waiting, holding two breakfast burritos, when she said his name.

"Bax."

He knew intuitively the lips that spoke those syllables, and he didn't press the button for the crosswalk. Instead, he searched the sidewalk.

She stood there, almost like a mirage.

Except this wasn't a good mirage in a desert with lots of fake water when he was thirsty.

This was a bad mirage—a woman who had stolen the hope from his heart, screwed shit up on the regular, and showed up when he'd finally gotten it back.

"Em?" he asked, his throat suddenly parched, and the urge to run away intense. Find Courtney, hide, and raise Tiny Badass without the rest of the world knowing shit about anything. Those instincts fought against his urge to rant. Tell Em how badly she'd hurt his heart. How badly she'd fucked their lives.

But.

Had she?

She walked away.

He found Courtney.

He had Tiny Badass.

He reconnected with his band.

If by some chance he'd stayed with Em, he'd have had a woman who enjoyed spending her time with his Los Angeles neighbor as much as him, if not more. Probably more, given the sounds she'd made when he walked in on the two of them.

She'd either been faking it with him, or faking it with *him*.

"Hi." Em bounced on her toes like she did when she got nervous.

Why was she nervous? Fuck, why is she even here?

"Hi." Yeah, that was his voice. But it sounded foreign coming from his lips.

The best part of Boise was that the band had checked out of the tour buses and into a five-star hotel, with cushy mattresses, lots of horizontal time with Courtney, and room service.

The worst part? He'd foregone room service to head out on a morning breakfast burrito run. Without meaning to, he'd meandered his way smack into his ex-fiancée.

"Hi." He frowned, and gripped the brown sack in his hand a smidge harder than necessary.

She said nothing. Blinking at him. Waiting.

He said nothing. Blinking at her. Waiting.

This had been great, but he needed to get back to Courtney. "I've got a place to be—"

"Thank you," she said, quick, to the point, and totally knocking him off-kilter.

His heart seemed to stop beating. "For what?"

Because the last time they'd talked, there'd been yelling, then the breakup, then Hans had tossed money at her to keep her quiet.

The last time he saw her, she was selling him out for cash.

"For letting me go." She stepped forward, toward him.

He recoiled.

She had no business stepping into his space. Her presence acted like barbed wire poking his skin—not enough to cause injury, but enough to make him want to get away.

He moved back. Whether the move was intuitive for self-preservation or simply the precursor to escape, he wasn't sure.

"Sorry." She held up her hands.

The time apart had not been super kind to her. Her hair didn't look as glossy or styled as when they'd been together. Her clothes seemed to hang looser. More than that, her eyes had a sheen of sad resignation.

That was not what he'd ever wanted for her.

"Do you need money?" He reached for his wallet in his back pocket.

There wasn't a ton of cash in his billfold, but he could offer her a few hundred bucks. If she went to Hans, he'd toss her out on her ass. Likely she knew that.

"You know me." She made her crystalline blue eyes bigger in that way that had always tugged at his heart. This time, it didn't work. It only made him want to get back to the hotel more quickly, toss the cash at her feet and run. "I always need money," she finished with a flash of confidence that he didn't buy for one instant.

He pulled a handful of bills from his wallet, handing them over.

She took them.

Because she was Em.

He got that now.

She wasn't a bad person, only a product of who she'd groomed herself to be.

That might not make sense to many people, but it made a helluva lot of sense to him.

He didn't hate her—didn't think he ever could.

But he didn't like how her presence made him itchy when he could be wrapped up in the warmth of Courtney.

Courtney, who acted as a balm to the fuckups of his past.

"I didn't come for the cash." Yet, of note, she stuffed the cash in her pocket. He couldn't help but notice the irony. "I came to tell you thank you for letting me go. For not fighting for something that would've made us both miserable."

The sentiment was nice. The presentation? Questionable.

"Courtney's pregnant," he said, and dammit, the words sounded like he was in a confessional.

Why these were the words he said, he couldn't be certain. And yet—

"I know." She smiled a genuine smile. The kind that made her entire face brighten. "Congratulations, I know you wanted a family so bad. I'm glad you got that."

She totally missed the point.

The point might as well have been on Mars, and she was here on Earth. But he didn't want to spend any more time with her. No more time for arguing. No more time... for anything.

"Thanks." The breakfast burritos were getting cool, Chet was probably getting antsy for him to return, and this reunion had gone overtime by about ten minutes, even if it'd only taken five.

"Bye, Em." He pushed the button on the crosswalk, glancing both ways to see if he could make it without getting squashed.

He had a solid opening, so he stepped from the curb, even though the orange hand flashed at him.

"Bax," she called.

He stalled mid-step.

He didn't want to go back, but they had history, they had planned a future. A present and a future together were no longer part of their lives, but the past made him glance over his shoulder.

"I hope she's good to you," Em said, and she seemed to mean it.

Then she stepped forward, right into his personal space, and seemed to go in for a kiss. He turned his head, so she got his cheek instead.

You know what? He didn't care. The past could kiss his ass for all he cared, as long as Courtney was his present.

"The best," he said without missing a beat. "Courtney's the best."

Then he turned toward the hotel, and he didn't have to look back to know that Em had already disappeared.

She was good at that.

<hr>

Chapter Twenty-Three
COURTNEY

<hr>

COURTNEY SHOULD'VE BEEN SLEEPING. Sleeping made more sense.

But her phone woke her, she got news, and now she paced through the five-star suite, the cushy carpet between her toes.

To the window. Turn. Back to the wet bar.

Chewed on her fingernails.

Forced herself to stop because that was a habit she didn't want to get started up again.

Where is he?

She tugged at the hem of one of Bax's kick-ass *Rolling Stones* T-shirts she'd slept in. Bax T-shirts and Bax boxers had become her sleepwear of choice—though usually he removed them about halfway through the night.

The email that came through? It made her antsy. Made her pace the room, her hand at her lower back as a counterbalance to the baby in the front.

"Where are you, Bax?" she whispered to the empty room.

As though on cue, the keycard clunked in the door, and Bax was there.

She went to him, went straight into his arms.

He didn't ask questions, just wrapped her in his comfort, inhaling deep.

"You okay?" he asked finally.

She nodded. Looked up at him. Met his gaze head-on.

"Tiny Badass is a little girl." She choked a little on the last word.

They'd spent most of the pregnancy certain that they didn't want to know. Wanted to wait to find out.

And then…

They'd talked. Decided they wanted to know.

Courtney'd gone to get some blood work drawn for a genetic test just to be sure everything was fine. (Everything was fine.)

As a by-product of the test, they could also know the birth sex of their baby.

The lab sent that information over this morning.

Two X chromosomes meant… a little girl.

"What?" He dropped the paper sack in his grip, so it hit the ground with a thud.

"It's a girl." She did a jazz-hands ditty and lifted on her toes to graze her lips against his.

He seemed a little shell-shocked. She could totally relate, since that was her reaction too.

She didn't care whether the baby was a boy or girl, but knowing somehow made Tiny Badass more real. More tangible.

"That's amazing." He hugged her tighter, her baby belly squashed between them.

"Little Harley," she murmured.

During their little chat, they'd also agreed on names. Harley for a girl. Xander for a boy.

"She'll always be Tiny Badass to me," Bax said against Courtney's hair.

"I can't believe you dropped our burritos," she said, gripping the cotton of his shirt so he wouldn't try to pick them up yet. This was their moment to just be… them.

"Got a little distracted," he said, low and rumbly.

"I should call the moms. Let them know. Let Linx know."

"Agreed." He pulled away, picked up the sack, and motored to the kitchenette. "Are you feeling salsa or no? I had them put it on the side."

"As long as it's not too spicy." Because heartburn.

"I got the blandest I could find." He flashed a grin, and things were good.

Excellent.

"Courtney." Linx knocked on the door. He knocked again. "Courtney."

Courtney opened it, and Linx looked her over like he was waiting for her to say something.

"Hey, big brother."

Linx looked at Bax funny, like he wasn't sure what was going on.

"Everything okay?" Linx asked, cautious and with substantial side-eye at Bax.

"Better than okay. We found out Tiny Badass is a little girl." There wasn't any news that could pop that balloon of excitement.

Linx grinned. "That's fantastic. I love nieces."

"Did you need something?" Courtney asked, because she had a breakfast burrito and celebrating to get to.

"Yeah. Uh." Linx shook his head. "No."

"What are you not telling me?" Courtney's radar pinged that there was something up with him—something she wouldn't like.

"Ask Bax," Linx said, again with the side-eye toward Bax.

"Ask Bax what?" Bax asked.

"Ask Bax about Em," Linx said, and he didn't sound happy about it. Then again, whenever they talked about Em, he rarely sounded happy. "Or check your social media and see for yourself."

Bax turned pale. "Courtney—"

What had Em done now? Courtney pulled out her phone, and her notifications had blown up.

They had planned no promotions for the morning, since this was a down day. Lay low. Concert tonight and then headed to Telluride. Then back to Denver.

Swiping her thumb across the screen, she scrolled through her social media.

Linx was correct in that there were developments. Paparazzi photos.

Bax in the clothes he currently wore. The sack of burritos in his grip.

Her fingertips went cold. Numb.

Bax *with his ex.*

Courtney's hands felt heavier than usual against the screen.

Bax handing Em cash.

Courtney's tongue couldn't seem to move.

A comfortably close cheek kiss between them.

The worst part? Em wore her Bax bracelet.

That just rubbed salt on the wound that Courtney thought had already closed.

She did a quick search, and though this had just happened, the interweb had already splashed Bax and Em photo montages across their pages. The Harley excitement from moments ago was replaced with dread seeping deep in her gut.

"Bax?" His name sounded funny coming out of her mouth. "Did you forget to tell me something?" The words sounded foreign—hurt, even.

But, no, this was Bax. There was a solid explanation, and she'd hear him out.

"You saw Em?" she asked, shaking off the dread because they'd worked for more than that.

There was an explanation here, something that made sense.

Something that wasn't "Dimefront Lead Meets Up with Ex" and "Trouble in Dimefront Paradise."

He glanced at the burritos and stared at the plastic cup of sour cream.

She wasn't hungry anymore, not even the blandest of salsa held appeal.

"It's not what you think," he said, his knuckles turning white against the knife.

"I'm not thinking anything right now." She tried to give him a reassuring smile. "Linx? Do you mind giving us some space?"

Linx didn't seem to like it, but he left.

"What happened?" Courtney asked, keeping her tone neutral.

He strode to her, flipped through the photos. "Apparently, I got set up."

"That much is pretty clear."

"Nothing happened." He pointed to the screen. "That's the closest she got to me, and I didn't like it. Didn't want it. Left immediately."

"Okay." Courtney chewed her bottom lip, putting her cell away. She'd need to come up with an official response from the band, from Bax, from her. Something that said, *Hey, we're happy*, without coming right out and saying it.

Maybe a baby update announcement? That would do it.

Or maybe not? Maybe this type of clickbait didn't deserve her attention.

Perhaps...

"I don't want to hate her." Bax's fingers looped in the waistband of his jeans. "But she's making it hard." He rubbed a hand over his hair. "The thing I don't get is that she was really genuinely happy for us. She knew I wanted kids. She was on the fence. Here I am with a kid on the way. A little girl." He glanced up at Courtney, his eyes more vulnerable than she'd ever seen before.

Something about the way he said that Em knew he wanted kids. That Em was on the fence. That gem of knowledge sat sideways in Courtney's stomach.

"This is awkward," Courtney said because, well, it was. Super awkward. Weird. Odd. And not a little fun.

"It doesn't have to be," Bax assured, too quickly.

She nodded. "But it is."

"I don't want Harley to search for her parents online someday and find Em," Bax said, genuine concern in his tone. "How do we make it so that doesn't happen?"

Now that was a question Courtney could answer.

"We're both really careful and stick with Chet," Courtney said, turning the options over in her mind. "Stay away from anywhere there could be cameras that aren't contained." That would have to be the plan. "Avoid everything paparazzi."

That naked concern in his gaze hit her in the heart.

She could relate to that feeling—parenthood did that to a person.

This was the moment, she could feel it in her gut—the moment where she had to decide if she trusted Bax.

Without hesitation, she knew her answer: she trusted him.

She'd committed to trying with Bax for Tiny Badass—Harley. She still cared, appreciated what they were building.

Was that enough?

It had to be enough.

She'd make it be enough.

Chapter Twenty-Four
COURTNEY

MUSIC, mountain air, and making memories for the fans.

Courtney sighed a good sigh. The kind that mattered.

The last concert of the tour was not in a stadium. They'd selected the Telluride Town Park venue for multiple reasons, mostly because the air blew fresh and cool, and they closed off the town entrance to anyone who didn't live there or have a hot little ticket. This is what they did in Telluride. Literally closed down the town when good music showed up.

Courtney, Becca, and Irina had set up shop in the staff tent, just off the stage. On one side, they had the mountains. On the other, the band and lotsa speakers. Wow, oh wow, was it loud.

And in front? There were the fans.

"I think I need an oxygen tank," Becca gasped dramatically, dropping into the chair next to Courtney.

The extra thousands and thousands of visitors in Telluride to see Dimefront must've taken up a lot of the air because there seemed to be a substantial amount of oxygen molecules missing.

This was the mountains for them. Denver was at altitude,

but Telluride beat that altitude by a lot. This was a *Rocky Mountain* high that required a little adjustment.

"For real, where do they keep the oxygen?" Irina shook her head. "Though I think I see Oprah over there, so I'm good with the whole no-air part of the town."

Oprah and the San Juan Mountains made for an impressive background to the music. Telluride sat in a valley with the jagged mountain range surrounding. The atmosphere screamed Pabst Blue Ribbon, laid-back with a dash of diamonds.

They'd even taken the gondola up to Mountain Village to walk around and play a game of gigantic checkers.

The only thing better than a pirate ship was a gigantic outdoor checkerboard.

She'd already decided that was what she'd be getting Bax for his birthday this year.

Look at her making plans for their future together.

Who would've thought?

"No complaining about the oxygen saturation until you're breathing for two," Courtney said, shifting in the metal folding chair while she picked at her oatmeal for dinner because it was the only thing that sounded good. She'd planted her ass in one chair and her feet on another—elevating her ankles so maybe the swelling would reduce.

Along with low oxygen levels came swollen ankles.

"Do you mind if I… uh…" Irina tilted her head toward where she apparently saw Oprah.

"Go do your thing." Courtney grinned, even as she gave up on the oatmeal and set it aside.

As the pregnancy progressed, she'd found fewer and fewer foods appealing, which made no sense because she should eat for two, not pick at oatmeal for two. Even carrots had lost a lot of their appeal, and yesterday's breakfast burrito was a total bust—not only because of the Em thing. Even bland salsa couldn't make it palatable for her.

The last stroke of a guitar from the opening band rico-cheted through the park, probably sucking up even more of the scarce oxygen. But it was worth it because the opening act—Badger Dream—was fantastic.

Well on their way to giving Dimefront a run for their money.

Not tonight, but someday.

Tonight, Dimefront was ready for the stage, and it didn't matter that the air was so thin, because it still sparked electric. A palpable sizzle. No actual way to describe it except that it was as though Mother Earth had blissed out at the idea of a rock concert and created the perfect atmosphere for music.

Courtney loved this feeling.

Not the nothing-tastes-good problem or the no-oxygen situation, but the collective energy of the fans, the content-ment of the completion of a tour, paired with the enjoyment of the last concert before they headed back to the studio.

Work done, she could relax and enjoy the music. Atmosphere. The way everything had come together. The role she'd played in that.

Linx entered the stage first. Mach and Tanner with him. Then Knox. Finally, Bax—wearing a T-Rex head.

While he'd done it for her, he embraced it for the fans. They ate it up.

Touring agreed with him. He crashed hard, sure, but rose ready to get to it the next day. The tour lifestyle agreed with him.

This career was perfect for him.

The guys played the first bars of their most popular song ever, their first hit to go platinum, Bax ditched the dinosaur head, and the crowd went more than a little nuts.

She could be content. The outside world was the outside world. Right here, witnessing Bax take the stage, was enough. Maybe even falling for him a bit more every time they were in the same space.

Wow, things have changed.

Harley kicked Courtney in the kidney to punctuate that point. Even that internal discomfort couldn't ruin the vibe of good music. An outdoor venue, her best friend probably meeting Oprah, and… Bax.

"I wrote a little fucking something!" Bax shouted into the microphone. "Something new. Think you'll dig it."

The crowd went bananas. Being the first crowd to witness a new Dimefront song was an extra kind of special, but—

"What's he talking about?" Courtney sat up, kicking her feet down from the chair where she'd had them elevated.

Because she would've appreciated a little time to prepare the social media team for the influx that was about to converge.

"Prepare to lose your fucking minds." Bax tilted his chin up at Linx, and he played a new song Courtney'd never heard.

Lots of drums and bass. Sad but pissed.

The fans screamed.

Cameras flashed.

Bax bathed in the spotlight.

Then he launched into the lyrics of the new song. A song that was beautiful. Heartfelt. Gripping. Painful.

And 100 percent about his ex.

Courtney's stomach soured, and not because she'd only picked at the oatmeal. Her stomach turned over as though she'd chugged a whole vat of bacon grease, because reality was hitting her upside the head. Knocking her over. Drowning her.

Bax's lyrics were about Em.

They were sad. Angry. But worst of all… they were hopeful. They were gorgeous.

They were for a love story that shouldn't have ended.

Everything he'd said to Courtney yesterday seemed to dissolve with the force of his art and she could see clearly that he wasn't over Em. He could say it, he could promise, but some part of him—a part big enough to write Em a song—wasn't over her.

And how could he be? The asshole lens of clarity seemed to slap her. He'd loved Em, had only been apart from her for less than 24 hours when they'd hooked-up in the shower and their lives linked together forever.

He hadn't had time to mourn the loss of that relationship and all that it promised.

She felt a little dizzy at the realization that he loved Em, and it wasn't entirely past tense. That kind of commitment and promise and love… it didn't just go away overnight.

Even when you made a baby with the wrong woman.

"Shit," she whispered, pressing her palm against her chest where it ached. At the same time as she felt that pain, she couldn't seem to feel anything else.

"He's really going there, huh?" Becca asked, her hand coming to Courtney's back and rubbing the spot between her shoulder blades. "You know this isn't about you."

Oh, she knew. This was not about her. None of this was about her. That was the problem.

It always was.

Harley kicked, fluttered, and moved at the sound of Bax's voice. This song.

Courtney swallowed back any residual emotion and did her best to just be there in the moment. Not think about what this meant or why he felt the need to write a heartfelt song about the woman he loved leaving him for a guy in wing tips.

The raw ache in his voice as he sang the lyrics was eerily similar to the way her heart felt at that moment. For entirely different reasons.

Or perhaps—and this was the part that really hurt—for the same reason.

She shouldn't have expected any different. Expectations bred resentment. She knew this. She understood this.

At some point, she'd closed her eyes to it. Pretended everything was A-okay, and that they were hunky-dory as a little makeshift family.

He'd done the same thing.

But she just woke up from the dream.

Damn.

"Let's go," Becca said. "We can head back to the buses. We don't have to stay here."

"I think I'm supposed to hear this." Courtney regained control over the tears that threatened—the problem with pregnancy and the way it jacked with her hormones was that she had a much looser rein on her ability to control her feelings. Which sucked, because that was what made it easier to function in life on the road. Life with Bax. Life in general.

Irina took up the other side opposite Becca, draping her arm over Courtney's shoulders. "Hey, chickadee."

"Did you find Oprah?" Courtney asked, willing herself to stay strong until she was in a place where she could fall apart with no one witnessing.

"Yeah, actually." Irina nodded, leaning her head against the side of Courtney's. "But then Bax dropped his megaton bomb on the tour, so I figured I should do my job and ensure you're drinking water and not poisoning the father of your kid."

"I don't think she's gone arsenic yet." Becca's gaze met Irina's, and something passed between them. Courtney wasn't exactly sure what, and she didn't care, because just as the song seemed to be ending, Bax really let it all hang out when he finished with *"Never could stop with the love part. Even at the end."*

The way he sang the words was not pretty. Oh no, it was grit and ice and pain.

"Maybe now we've hit arsenic levels." Irina squeezed Courtney into her. "Let's go. Why don't we hit up Mach and Tanner's bus, since they have the best snacks?"

Courtney shook her head. "No."

She wasn't sure what she was saying no to. It didn't really matter. The word just fit the moment.

"Maybe you heard I'm gonna be a papa!" Bax shouted into the mic. "Only a few months left."

Courtney's breath caught in her throat.

"Well, now he's just making a mess for no reason." Irina crossed her arms and stared laser beams at Bax.

He was too far in the zone to realize he'd pissed off the three women who had the power to pull the spark plugs on his bus.

"Wrote this for the munchkin," he said, smirking at the crowd in that panty-dropping way of his.

That made the women scream louder.

He started the song. This one was sweet and not gritty. The lyrics that couples would play at their weddings for years to come. But not her.

He wrote the song for their baby.

Em got a song.

Baby got a song.

Courtney didn't even get a bracelet. She didn't get the rock star.

Somehow she had to figure out how to be okay with that.

Unfortunately for her, in the past ten minutes, she'd become certain that she'd have to do that part alone.

Chapter Twenty-Five
BAX

HE FUCKING LOVED THIS GIG. Couldn't even fathom how a few months ago he'd considered walking away from it.

The rush. The joy. The pulsing energy of the crowd that enveloped him and the rest of the guys.

When he hopped off the stage, Hans was there. Like, right there. And he didn't look thrilled.

"Fucking brilliant." Bax gave Hans a light, friendly shove.

Hans was a brick wall to that playful nudge.

"What crawled up your ass?" Bax asked. Because there was nothing that would put a damper on this day. Nothing.

"Your little song?"

"Which one?" Because there were two, and the crowd loved them both. Ate them up. These could be the next Dimefront hits, and they'd have his name all over that byline.

"Your breakup song, specifically." Hans shuffled Bax to the side while the other guys tromped off the stage next. Everyone gave back slaps on their way past.

The whole groove they'd carved for this concert translated into epic shit.

"They loved it." Bax couldn't have asked for more.

"Did you forget that Courtney was here?"

"Why would I forget that? She's my girl."

"And yet you stood on a stage and crooned a song of lost love to clearly your ex-fiancée. A fiancée you were recently seen in an embrace with?"

What? No. That was not what he'd done.

He'd sang a breakup song that came to him. Linx had helped with the arrangement, and he had said nothing.

"That's not what it was." Bax shook his head. It wasn't.

Was it?

Fuck.

"Oh my God." The groovy vibe? Totally gone. "Where's Courtney?"

"Becca took her back to the buses." Hans pursed his lips. "Take care of that so you can get to the VIP meet and greet."

Of everything important to Bax in that moment, the meet and greet was not one of them.

The other guys could handle that.

It looked like he'd be cleaning up a mess he hadn't realized he was making.

"She loves you," Hans said. "Probably doesn't realize it yet, but she does. Probably has since before you two got pregnant."

Bax did not understand what the hell gibberish Hans was spewing.

"You need to handle that heart with care." Hans stared at the ground before looking back up. "I think you probably love her too."

Maybe he already loved her. He hadn't spent too much time thinking about it, because things had been good. He didn't find a need to focus on labels or brand things into little boxes.

"Before you can love her, you've got to let Em go," Hans said, stabbing Bax right in the heart.

"I let Em go." Bax's blood beat a ticked-off race from his

heart. "Let her go and moved on, and am with a new woman who I adore…"

"Then why'd you write a whole song about her?" Hans lifted his eyebrows, and it took everything in Bax not to continue arguing with him.

Now wasn't the time. If Courtney was hurting, he needed to get to her. Explain things. Make it clear that Em was in the past. Courtney was the present.

He turned to jog back to the buses.

It wasn't like he couldn't honor what he'd once built with Em. Just like he savored what he'd built with Courtney.

He didn't love Em anymore.

His jog slowed as his heart hurt.

Fuck.

Did he still love Em?

He stopped completely.

No, he didn't love Em. Didn't want to love Em. Didn't like the feeling of the hurt that came with loving Em.

Who would've thought there would ever be a time when Courtney was the simple choice?

Yet…

Here he was. She was it.

The idea of life without Em still ached a little, but not in the same way it had. The idea of life without Courtney? He couldn't breathe.

This was a ridiculous train of thought because he had Courtney. Had what he wanted with her.

Chet stood guard at their bus.

"She in there?" Bax asked.

Chet nodded.

"How pissed is she?"

Chet rolled his teeth over his bottom lip. "Not my place to say."

That was remarkably unhelpful.

Bax hurried up the stairs, let himself in, and drew up

short because she was right there. Sitting by herself, holding Tiny Badass with her arms around her belly, and looking wrecked.

"Courtney." He pushed the door closed behind him.

"I just need a minute," she said, and dammit, she sounded strong even with a broken expression on her face.

"I fucked up." Best to just own up to that shit.

She shook her head. "No. You didn't."

"Yeah, I did." And he didn't want a hall pass for it either. He needed to own it so they could get through it.

"I fucked up, Bax." She patted the seat beside her, but something told him he probably shouldn't sit, because the result of this conversation was not one he'd enjoy.

"You didn't."

"The songs you wrote were truth. I needed to hear that." She nodded while she spoke, as though that would make the words true. "I needed to know where we stand. Where *I* stand."

"That's jacked." He reached for her hand, and thank fuck she let him, but she didn't squeeze his hand in return. Didn't even truly acknowledge the touch.

"When we started this whole thing in the shower…" She paused. Her throat worked. "It wasn't supposed to mean anything."

This felt like goodbye. He didn't want goodbye. There was too much future for them to have a goodbye.

"Courtney…"

"Just hear me for a second, Brennan."

That brought him up short. He was ready to listen. Hear whatever she needed to say, as long as it wasn't goodbye.

"It meant something," she continued. "That day in the shower. It meant a lot, actually. I didn't realize it before. What I mean is… it meant more than just Harley." She stopped. Pulled her hand from his. Laid it against her stomach. "I guess I was in a little deeper earlier than I'd realized until today. And then the baby. Moving to Denver. And you being so awesome to me."

He wasn't sure how to forgive himself when just being a good guy to her was a notable change.

"I didn't even get a bracelet, Bax." She paused. Swallowed. "Even Em got a bracelet."

He clenched his jaw because "You're not the kind of woman a guy gives a bracelet to."

She wasn't the kind of girl he could hand some jewelry and send on her way.

"Ouch. That smarts, doesn't it?" She sighed, and again she looked wrecked.

Fuck, he so was making a mess of this. "I'm making a mess of this."

"You've got work. They'll need you in the VIP tent."

"You'll grab a milkshake or a smoothie or whatever, and then I'll meet you here?"

Her subtle headshake was like a pinprick deflating his balloon of hope. "I think I need to go home."

Unfortunately, he didn't know which home she was referring to just then.

"Talk to me, Courtney," he said through gritted teeth.

"It's Harley," Courtney said. "You always wanted Harley."

"Of course I wanted Harley. We both wanted Harley." That was the one thing they agreed on in the beginning.

"But you got me too," she said.

Why did she say this like it was a bad thing? This was the best thing. They were a package deal, the best buy one, get one he'd ever been offered. "Because you're her mother."

"Right." Courtney pursed her lips.

He wanted to move to her, but understood that wasn't what she needed or wanted, so he didn't. "You're not making any sense."

"There wouldn't be an us if there wasn't a baby." She tossed that out like a grenade.

"Courtney, she brought us together. She's the glue—"

"I would want you without her." Courtney whispered the words like they caused her great pain.

The muscles around his mouth didn't seem to work anymore. Didn't hold his lips closed. Did nothing.

"I cannot think about life without her," Courtney said. "But if I'm being honest with everyone in this room, I wanted you long before I knew there was a baby. I just hadn't put that together yet. Hating you was so much easier than considering the possibility that I could want you."

This time he did step toward her. "I think Em's gotten in your head. She does that. It's her thing. Don't let her in your head."

Courtney didn't look wrecked, she just looked sad. "If there wasn't a Harley, I'm pretty sure you'd be back with Em."

"Going down the path of what-if will only make a person miserable. That's what you said, and I believe you. It's the truth."

She said nothing.

His heart seemed to break as she continued with her nothing.

"Don't do this." He reached for her, but she dodged, so he stopped. "Don't turn this into something it's not."

"Bax." Her hair brushed against her shoulders as she shook her head. "I think we need to step back from each other."

"No, that's not what we need." Not what he wanted or was able to give.

"You need time to process everything that happened with Em." She spoke like this was distant and not right in front of them, not their present. "You never got time for that. You *need* time to mourn that relationship ending before we can even give *us* a shot."

"I don't need that." He didn't. Didn't want it. Didn't need it.

"I need you to do that," she said, the words so quiet he almost didn't hear them.

"What if we don't find our way back to each other?" he asked, unwilling to even think of that as a possibility, but fear gripping his entire body because it could happen. This was like watching one of Knox's horror movies where the killer was living among them the whole time and no one realized it —not even the audience. When the big reveal happened, it wasn't a big in-your-face scream fest, but the kind of betrayal that dug in deep because it'd been there the whole time, oozing into everything.

"Then we'll be the best parents who ever co-parented *ever*," Courtney assured. "It'll be an opportunity to figure that out. An opportunity to do it whole and complete and not holding on to a heap of history."

The knock on the door came loud and long, but he didn't break the link between their gazes.

"VIP's waiting," Hans said through the door.

"Go," she whispered.

He wasn't entirely certain if she was telling him goodbye or see you later.

To be honest with himself, he was pretty sure it was the former.

And the walls were closing in, he couldn't breathe, and he was stupid as hell… so he left.

In the moment, walking out the door seemed like the worst thing he could've done. Seemed like his gut screamed at him to stop, but his feet kept right on moving.

"What happened to you?" Linx asked when Bax arrived at the photo-op area. The fans would be streaming through any second, and all he wanted to do was hit something.

"I…" Bax looked at the guy he'd betrayed by falling into the shower with his sister and then falling in love with her. "I can't lose Courtney."

The hard expression Bax had become used to with Linx softened.

"What'd we miss?" Knox asked, hopping on his toes and scooting right between them, Tanner and Mach in tow. "Looks intense."

"I love Courtney," Bax said.

"Cool." Knox nodded. "We ready to take some pictures?"

"No." Bax shook his head. Then he stopped.

Turned.

Began walking back in the direction he had come from. Back toward Courtney. Toward his family. Toward his future.

Mach and Tanner stood in the way with goofy grins on their mugs.

"I think he finally gets it." Tanner held a fist up to bump with Mach. "I was beginning to worry."

Mach fist-bumped Tanner, and Bax walked right past them. Jogged. Sprinted.

He opened the door to the bus, saying, "You're not a woman a guy like me gives a bracelet to, because you're the kind of woman who deserves a ring. When you get jewelry, that's what it needs to be."

He'd been thinking about that a lot lately. Maybe they weren't there yet. When they were ready, if she decided that was what she was up for, he'd be ready. First, he needed to be sure she didn't feel the pressure of motherhood pushing her down the aisle.

"I don't want to be with you only because you can't be away from our daughter," Courtney said. "I don't know that I could forgive you for that."

"I want to be with *you* because I can't be away from *you*." He tilted her chin, stroking the soft skin there beneath her jaw. "It's always been you. I can't be me without you."

"Brennan, let's be honest here. I'm not the girl who gets the rock star."

Fuck him, she'd held onto that.

"You always saw right through me, and that pissed me off so bad." He dropped his hand and paced the length of the small room. "I didn't enjoy being vulnerable. I preferred to be Bax. Bax doesn't care if you hate him. If anyone hates him."

"I never saw through you," she said. "You convinced me you're a total asshat."

"But deep down? Deep under it, you saw I was still Brennan?"

"Honestly?"

"We're doing the honest thing, so yeah." He put his hands on his waist. They had a baby, and they had each other, and they had honesty.

"No. I thought you liked who you'd become. Convinced myself. You're exceptionally good at convincing people," she said, the shock of her words hitting him in the solar plexus.

"What do I do, Court?"

"Bax is who you've become, but he's not only who you are. I can see now that you're still Brennan. And you're still Bax. It's time to be both."

"You're right. And I was right. You don't get the rock star because you get the man. The man isn't the rock star. That's the illusion. That's what Em got." He took the deepest breath he'd ever had. "Maybe the reason we were always at odds was because we didn't turn the magnets the right way. Make them see that they can't live without the other. The pull becomes unstoppable." Hell, it made sense to him anyway.

"You really can't live without me?" she asked, as though she didn't really buy it.

"Courtney, I can't even catch a breath without you," he said, totally serious, through clenched teeth. "Em got Bax for a little while, yeah, but *you* get everything. Brennan, Bax, whoever I am tomorrow and day after."

Something in her shifted, he saw it. Caught the moment she believed him.

"What comes next?" she asked.

"I'm thinking forever." Forever sounded pretty damn good.

"It can't be that simple."

Nothing about what they'd been through was simple. "We've had years of hard. I think we deserve a little simplicity."

She didn't seem convinced.

"When the future stares you in the eye, you don't tell it to wait," Bax said, meaning every word. "I don't need any more time to mourn what I had, because you're not the consolation prize. You're the grand prize. What I had with Em? That was the consolation prize… I just never realized it."

"Are you still going to give me shit?" Courtney asked. "After this revelation of yours?"

"Yes." He nodded. "It's who I am."

"Good. Then we can move forward with this. This thing between us." She stood. Moved toward him.

"That's what I'm asking for." He opened his arms so she could fit right in there.

"It's a big ask," she said against his chest.

He pressed his cheek against her hair. "The biggest."

"You sure you're ready for this?" She pulled back, but stroked his biceps with her fingertips.

"I've been waiting my whole life for my future to show up." That future had been there the whole time. Surprise!

"Bax—"

"There's a place here—Butcher and Baker—they have kick-ass carrot cake," he said, nuzzling his nose against hers.

"I don't know what that has to do with anything."

"That'll be our thing." Why did he feel like he was hyperventilating? "When you're feeling a sweet tooth, we get extra icing. When you're not, we go muffin. I think you can even make it into a milkshake. The point is, we'll do it together."

That made no fucking sense, but he hoped like hell that she understood what he meant.

"You said you were going to figure things out." Her lips were right there next to his, sharing the same air. "Take some time to sort through everything."

Uh-huh. That was the plan. "Yeah. I did."

"You barely left," she said, low and from deep in her throat.

The panic disappeared because he knew exactly where he should be and who he should be with. "Sometimes that's all it takes."

He went in for a kiss, and then he could breathe.

"Bax…"

He continued kissing her as he said, "I wrote a song about Em. I didn't know that's what I was doing, but I was saying goodbye to her. Because we had something, or at least I thought we did." His lips continued to find Courtney's. Nip at her skin, shower her with emotion. "And now it's over, and I've got something better. Some*one* better. Maybe I started seeing you different because you're carrying my kid—I'll give you that." His hand pressed along the side of her belly. "But now I just see you. It's like"—the residual energy from the concert seemed to make an appearance because he couldn't hold still, couldn't stop kissing her—"you were there, but in the periphery. I didn't want to see you, because I knew you saw me. Now you're close-up, and dammit, I want that. I want you. I want the entire package. When it's just us at the end of this road, when the kid goes wherever kids go when they grow up, it'll be enough."

Fuck. She was crying.

"Don't cry, Court." He caught the tears with his thumbs.

She nodded. "Okay."

"You're still crying." He kept swiping, unable to keep up.

"No. I mean, okay. If you're in a place to move forward, I'm there too. Let's move together." She squeezed him to her.

He wanted to give a massive fist pump with a screamed, *Hell yeah!* What he did instead? He kissed her again.

He didn't ravage her mouth or try to take it further. He held her face between his hands like she was precious, and let the kiss be what it was, what it was going to be… like them. No pressure, no expectations, just the two of them.

"This is what falling in love feels like," he said against the side of her mouth.

"Then I think I really like being in love with you."

"Yeah? Think so?" He pulled back, not a lot, only a little. "Do you *like* like being in love with me?"

"I love you, Brennan."

"Thank you." He winked at her.

She chucked him on the arm. "Really?"

He moved in closer, peppering kisses along her nose and cheeks. "I love you, Courtney. I want this. I want us."

She pulled her bottom lip in with her teeth. "That's good, 'cause you're stuck with me."

Oh, hell yeah. This was going to be good.

Chapter Twenty-Six
BAX

Three Months Later

"YOU'RE sure she won't be pissed?" Bax asked, taking in the Brek's Bar transformation.

"She won't be pissed," Irina assured. "I'm her best friend, I know what pisses her off."

"Maybe a little pissed?" Linx asked. "She's not really the surprise type."

"What are you talking about? She loves surprises." Irina paused where she fluffed one of the black tablecloths.

"In what century?" Linx sort of snorted and made an attempt at fluffing another cloth. He failed, but he tried.

"All right, boys, here's the deal—she's gonna love this because I made her a baby shower that looks like Club Pew in LA. Got it?" Irina used a tone that brokered no questions.

"Ve are here." An elderly woman with a strong Russian accent trotted through the door with about six other retirement home–aged women behind her. "Let the party begin."

"Sorry," Bax said. "Who are you?" And how did they get past Chet and his crew?

"I am Nadzieja. This is Etta." She went through the rest of the names, but they didn't mean anything to Bax.

"They're with me." Tanner emerged from the kitchen with a huge grin, and a death wish, because Courtney didn't care for surprises, and she probably didn't want a bunch of people she didn't know attending her baby shower.

"The place looks fantastic." Nadzieja wandered through the room. "So gorgeous."

Irina had gone overboard turning the dive bar into a swanky club for Courtney's surprise baby shower. Not only was Irina a birth coach who had become Courtney's best friend, but she had party planning skills that rivaled the moms.

Irina took charge of the decor and the menu, while the moms handled the guest list.

"Did you run this addition past the moms?" Bax asked Tanner.

Tanner nodded. "I mentioned it. They're my friends, they're cool."

Tanner was friends with the elderly crowd? Huh. There was probably a story there.

"Ve brought gifts," Nadzieja said, snapping her fingers as Chet balanced a crapload of presents on the bar.

Courtney liked gifts, so maybe that would even out the whole "Surprise, and also, there are people here you don't know!"

"You are Dad?" Nadzieja sized him up, then down, then up again.

Why did he feel like he'd just had a whole-body MRI and an uncomfortable cavity search?

"I'm the dad-to-be." He nodded and crossed his arms because, seriously, he hadn't felt that exposed in forever.

They were creeping up on the expected arrival date for baby Harley, and Bax was attempting to give Courtney a little something that she could enjoy while also making the moms and Irina and everyone else happy.

The Club Pew makeover? That was for Courtney.

The baby shower? For the moms, and Courtney. Mostly, the moms.

The craft beer? For the band.

The elderly brigade? Apparently, that was for Tanner.

The cake? That was for Linx.

While some might not think taking a due-to-deliver-any-day woman to a sort of swanky dive bar turned Denver club was a good idea, they knew nothing about Courtney.

"Bax?" Courtney called from the doorway.

Crap, she wasn't supposed to be here until later.

"What did you do?" she asked, platform strappy heels in her hand and bare feet on the floor.

"Sorry, man." Mach strode up right next to her. "I sort of told her what was going on. In my defense, she asked."

Bax stared at him a beat. "You're fired."

Mach seemed cool with that. "From the baby shower duties, right? Not the band?"

Bax shook his head. No, they couldn't fire Mach, he'd become a fan favorite. "Go help out in the kitchen."

Mach did as he was told, and Bax went to his Courtney.

"Surprise." He sang the word so maybe she would get all melty and forget that she didn't like surprises.

"You did this for me?" she asked, and there was no anger or annoyance in her tone, just a whole heap of adoration.

This was so much better than fighting with each other.

"I had help," he said, because he'd been the maestro, but everyone had pitched in—mostly the moms and Irina.

"When is my surprise baby shower starting?" she asked, doing the thing where she never moved her gaze from his. He loved this between them, the ability to just be the two of them in a room full of… elderly women and Tanner.

"Now?" he asked.

"Then I guess I need my shoes." She held them up, and he grinned. He was sort of going to miss when she could buckle her own shoes again.

So he knelt before her, helped slip them on her feet, pulled the straps up over her ankles, and let his fingers trace circles over her skin there. Once they were buckled, he pressed a kiss to her shin.

She shivered.

Yeah, he dug that, and wished like hell they were home so he could take her to their bedroom and take off everything but the shoes.

"I have brought you gifts." Nadzieja practically shoved him aside, and pressed a crocheted yellow blanket in Courtney's hands.

"Thank you." Courtney studied the stitching, then looked back at the elderly woman. "Who are you?"

"I am Nadzieja. You call me Babushka." She held her hands together. "I have made you gift."

Rolling her bottom lip under her tongue, Courtney held up the blanket, which in hand-crocheted detail read, *Welcome, Harvey*.

"Oh," Courtney said, sliding her gaze to Bax. "I love it. So much." That was remarkably unconvincing.

"Vhat is vrong?" Babushka asked. "You do not love this."

"Nothing. It's perfection." Courtney held it to her chest. "I love it. Thank you."

"I know lies vhen I hear them." Babushka did the MRI thing to Courtney, and this time Courtney shivered for an entirely different reason.

"It's just that her name is Harley." Courtney squeezed the blanket in her grip. "Not Harvey."

"I tell Tanner that Harvey is not good name, but he says it's vhat you pick. Zat boy." Babushka scowled.

"Yeah. No. But I still love it." Courtney did sound convincing there.

Bax reached for the blanket, but Babushka snatched it back and huffed, scuttling toward Tanner.

This was the start of what seemed to become a knitting circle where all the elderly women were tearing out stiches and restitching the correct name onto the blankets, hats, and even crocheted diapers—diapers that he would like to point out had lots of holes for seepage. He wasn't an expert, but it seemed like that might be a bad idea.

By the time the shower was in full swing, the bar was dark, except for some laser lights and spotlights on platforms throughout the room. Women dressed in Denver Broncos cheerleading outfits go-go danced to the music on the risers. Some of the elderly women took time away from their crocheting to hop on a riser or two and boogie. Frankly, he was worried someone would break a hip and he'd be liable.

Meanwhile, an entire **LED** wall along one side lit the room while a woman hung upside down from a trapeze in front of it, contorting her body into all kinds of pretzel shapes. Thankfully, none of the elderly women had tried to do *that*. Yet. The night was still young.

"Having a good time?" he asked Courtney, even though he knew the answer.

Courtney'd been laughing like he hadn't heard in weeks. Mostly because she'd gone all Knox on him when the pregnancy stopped being comfortable. At least when she complained, she was cute, he gave her that.

Knox? Not so much.

She nodded. "Just getting tired. I have a headache."

"We can stay, or we can go. Your call." Seemingly of its own accord, his fingertip reached up to trace her collarbone.

"Funny how the things you want change, huh?" she asked, shifting her gaze longingly around the room.

Looking at her, he could relate. "Yeah, funny."

"You think it'll ever be like it was before?" she asked. "Having energy and not feeling like a hot-air balloon?"

He hated that she didn't have energy, but she could be carrying twins and two-hot air balloons, and he'd still be attracted to her, still want her like that.

"When Harley comes, we'll find a new normal that gives you all kinds of energy. Then you can eat all the sugared cereal you want, dance on the risers with the retirement home crew, and we'll hire a sitter and come clubbing whenever the mood strikes."

She rubbed at her stomach. "I feel like I fell off a cliff."

"Then hang on tight, we'll go down together." He pulled her in for a side hug.

She squeezed her eyebrows together, glancing up at him. "I'm not sure that sounds as romantic as you were hoping."

"Want me to sing it instead?" In his experience, that could make anything romantic.

"You're being silly." She settled against his side.

And then he sang, gravelly and low. "*Hang on tight. We'll go down. We'll go down together. Because down is up. Up is heaven with my girl.*"

"I think I know what that means." She grinned up at him, still letting him hold her weight.

"Yeah?"

"Yeah."

He moved his hand to her belly, where Harley moved around.

"She's lucky you're her dad and you love her so much," Courtney said.

"Ah. So you *don't* get it." He repositioned her so they were face-to-face because this was important. "I mean *you*."

The way her expression turned tender and her eyes watered? Maybe he'd finally gotten through. She was plenty to him. The baby was the bonus, not her.

"Go play with your friends." He pressed a kiss to her mouth, and then watched her as she moved to the table with Irina and Becca.

Then he grabbed a cherry seltzer and chatted with Babushka about how Harvey and Harley were not the best names for their little girl and maybe he and Courtney should consider something more Russian—like Nadzieja.

"Bax?" Linx called on his first slug of cherry seltzer. "Courtney needs you."

He scanned the VIP area and found her with Knox and Becca near the booth they'd reserved. Her expression? Not good.

Yeah, the horrified expression on her face had him leaving the seltzer on the bar and heading right toward her.

"Shit," she said as he approached.

"What's wrong?" He was ready to pick her up and fire-fighter carry her out the door.

"I just got dizzy. No biggie." Her pale skin and the little beads of sweat on her forehead said differently.

"Your head still hurts?" Bax asked, ready to take her home and away from all the lights.

She nodded. "Let's get out of here."

"How long has your head hurt?" Knox stood up from the booth with an authority that Bax seriously questioned.

"A couple of days… Why?" She eyed him cautiously.

"Any spots in your vision? How's your blood pressure? Swelling?" Knox started a new game of twenty questions.

Courtney licked her lips and looked at Bax. "Yes, to the spots—just when I stand up. I don't know about the other. And I'm pregnant, so yes, I'm swelling."

Knox pulled a duffle bag from the booth and dug through it, removing a stethoscope and a blood pressure cuff, because he was Knox and he'd taken his duties toward this pregnancy seriously. He immediately went to work, and for some reason, Courtney let him.

He frowned as he released the pressure from the cuff, chewing on the inside of his lips.

"What's wrong?" Bax asked, not liking the expression of concern on Knox's mug.

"Nothing's wrong," Courtney assured. "Pregnancy is totally normal."

"I'm going to need a urine sample to be sure." Knox rubbed the back of his neck. "Let me go grab a cup from the bar."

"Hah. No." Courtney started to heave herself up. "I'm not peeing in a bar glass."

Knox glanced at Bax, and the way he looked? Bax would've given him his own urine to sample.

"What do you think is wrong?" Bax asked, not digging that there was an answer coming he probably wouldn't like.

"Nothing to panic about." Knox held up his hands. "This happens to a lot of women in the last trimester."

"What happens?" Bax asked, trying to cut out the menacing tone but failing.

Courtney grabbed his arm. "He's not a doctor, let's not get too—"

"Patient reports cephalgia, which indicates neurological or cerebral manifestations. Test shows hypertension, possible albuminuria… I'm thinking she could have a little toxemia, also called preeclampsia. Best to go get that checked."

Everyone stared at Knox like he'd just announced he was going to play the accordion and bagpipes solo.

"I don't have whatever that is he's talking about." Courtney waved him off.

"The thing is"—Knox gnawed at his lip—"you should go get checked out by your doctor because it can be common, and it's dangerous if you don't rule it out. Preeclampsia becomes eclampsia, and it's a big deal."

It's dangerous… It's dangerous… It's a big deal… The lines ran on repeat in Bax's head.

"Where's Irina?" he asked, glancing around. "She'll know what to do."

"I'll find her." Becca took off toward the bar.

"Uh." Courtney slid her gaze to Bax. Then to Linx. Back to Knox. "I think we should go find a doctor or someone with an actual medical background."

"Where do we go?" Bax asked, because his brain seemed to have shut itself off when Knox used words that were really big and scary.

"Let's call a car so we can get to a hospital." Knox clapped his hands together like he was in charge and ready to roll.

"I'll call for the car," Linx suggested when Bax made no move to do anything because he was frozen in place.

Good call, since they couldn't walk all the way there.

"Courtney, do you think you might be in labor?" Knox asked. "It'll make everything easier if you are already in labor when we arrive."

Courtney stared at him like he'd lost his mind. "I don't know what labor feels like, so I don't know."

"Are you feeling any pressure? Do you need me to check for the head?" Knox asked, serious as fuck.

"You're not checking my anything." Courtney pushed his face away from her like she would've done with Linx, total palm-to-face shove backward.

Knox glanced at Bax and said out of the side of his mouth, "It's totally normal for laboring women to get testy. Nothing to worry about."

"I'm not testy, and you're not sticking your hand up…" She made a face. "Yeah. No. Bax, can you help?"

"No." Bax shook his head.

Wait. That wasn't the right answer.

"Yes. I'll help. No one sticks their hand up Courtney unless they're me or a doctor." Well, damn, that didn't sound quite like what he'd wanted it to.

Irina headed their way, chugging her martini as she speed walked.

That seemed like a bad idea, given that they were headed to have a baby.

"What do we do?" he asked, relief filling him cleanup. She was here, and this is why she was there—so he could hand the reins to her.

"Uh." Irina glanced at Knox like he'd know better what to do, but that was ridiculous because so far his suggestions had been medical gibberish. Except for the getting a car and going to the hospital part.

"Here's the thing." Irina wobbled as she leaned forward conspiratorially. "I'm actually not a traveling birth guide," she said in a stage whisper. "I mean, I am because I did the job. But I'd never done the job before. Everything I know is from YouTube." She held her hand out to him. "I'm actually Courtney's best friend. You know that part. Honorary aunt to your child. You know that part, too." She frowned. Then apparently remembered. "And a classically trained actress." She bowed. Like she was onstage.

He stared at her, unsure what to do or say or think or be. "But I saw you in doctor clothes on Courtney's wall."

"Huh?" Irina slurred. Then a light seemed to dawn. Her eyes got wide as she said, "Oh, that was from an audition. I didn't get that job." She shook her head. "I don't get a lot of the jobs."

"Don't discount yourself." Knox came up behind her and squeezed her shoulders.

What the hell was going on?

Irina jerked her thumb toward Knox. "He also learned everything he knows on YouTube, so don't let him catch the baby."

That wasn't even in the consideration box.

"Bax." Courtney tore his attention away from the current house of cards crumbling in front of him. "Contraction. Maybe this is labor?"

"You cannot be in labor," Babushka said. "I am not finished vith the blanket."

"I don't think the baby waits for that," Bax said, because… contractions didn't wait for crochet.

"Car's here," Linx said, gesturing toward the exit at the back where Chet waited.

Great. Car.

Baby. Coming.

"Let's go," he said.

Chapter Twenty-Seven
COURTNEY

"OH, HEY. EVERYONE'S HERE," Courtney said, walking through the door into the waiting room of the hospital with no baby in her arms and Bax at her side.

She'd decided to forgo a hospital gown and wore some super-comfy pajamas instead, but the admission band on her wrist and the IV stand she had to wheel around all screamed, *I'm a patient!*

Linx. Becca. Her parents. His parents. Knox. Mach. Tanner. Irina. They had set up a board game—the Game of Life—in the middle of the room.

Mom eyed Courtney's still very pregnant belly.

"So, I have preeclampsia and had a few contractions," Courtney said, way more cheerfully than she felt. "Yay! We're having a baby tonight."

"I'll let Babushka know we're gonna need the blanket." Tanner stood and headed toward the hallway.

"If you're having the baby, why are you here instead of having the baby?" Mom asked.

"We're just… they told us to go for a walk to see if we can get the contractions to speed up," Bax said, and looked at Knox where he sat by Irina.

Bax hadn't been super thrilled when Courtney had fessed up to the Irina situation after Irina totally blew her cover.

Four martinis and Irina was not good CIA agent material. Apparently, she'd tell anyone anything.

"Knox…" Courtney slid her gaze to Bax and then gestured to Knox with her chin, because Knox had saved her bacon tonight. And Harley's bacon too. "Where did you get scrubs?"

"I found 'em. Dr. Knox reporting for duty." He saluted.

She was pretty sure if he was pretending to be a doctor in an actual hospital, that was probably not legal.

"You were right," Bax said, crossing his arms. "Courtney had the preeclampsia stuff, and we needed to induce. Had you not said something…"

"It could've been bad." She moved to sit beside Knox because she actually had something important she wanted to ask him.

Knox did a fist pump. "Cha-ching. All that YouTube wasn't for nothin'."

"Bax and I talked," Courtney said, pulling the IV stand a little closer. "We decided that since you saved the day, you can be in the birthing room to welcome Harley."

Knox's jaw fell like she'd told him he was the father. "For real?"

"For real," Courtney said.

"Can I break your water?" Knox asked, like an overexcited puppy.

"Absolutely not," Bax said.

"Fine." Knox held out his hand to shake. "I accept your terms."

Bax shook it. Then he turned to the room as a whole, and, oh yeah, Courtney knew where this was going.

"Who knew about Irina?" Bax asked, and he seemed to war with how to approach the topic. "Because that's the part I want to discuss."

"A damn talented actress. You gotta give her that," Knox said, not helping the situation one bit. "Unless she gets too drunk on martinis. Then she's"—he whispered the next part —"not that good."

"I don't know whether to be pissed. To be worried." Bax looked at Courtney. "Or to be proud."

"Go with the last one," Linx suggested. "It's the easiest on Courtney."

Also, it didn't require wearing a paper pirate hat, which Courtney seriously appreciated.

"Courtney, why don't you go walk in your room far away from... everyone?" Becca used a tone she probably only used when she was in a therapy session because Courtney hadn't ever heard her pull it out before.

Also, she didn't feel an incredible need to argue with her when she used that tone. Even if she put on a pirate hat.

"Go with proud, Bax," Courtney said as she sauntered toward their room. "Go with proud."

Then Bax was behind her, his hand at her back, as they headed back to their room to meet their little girl.

Chapter Twenty-Eight
BAX

"YOU'RE DOING GREAT," Bax whispered, keeping his eyes on Courtney's, helping her breathe.

The epidural had kicked in, and she was handling everything way better than him. He was a sweaty mess of soon-to-be dad.

"Make sure it's not Dr. Pepper," Courtney said, in between deep breaths.

"You don't like Dr. Pepper?" Knox asked, sorting through the cabinets of the room.

"Quit it," Bax hissed. "They might need that stuff."

Knox held up a box of condoms. "Why do they have condoms in here?"

"You don't want to know," Bax replied, turning his focus back to Courtney as she munched on ice chips. "Even I don't want to know, and I know."

"Who do I have to sleep with to get a soda around here?" Knox asked, finally sticking his head under the faucet and lapping up a stream of water like he really was a puppy. "They need a filter on that water."

"Maybe this was a bad idea," Courtney said, gritting her

teeth and making a deep guttural noise that Bax had never heard before. It didn't sound entirely human.

"She's pushing." Knox hopped over the stool and a birthing ball to push the call button near Courtney's hand. "You need to stop doing that," Knox said, as he relayed the information to the nurse who took the call, finishing with "Do not bring any Dr. Pepper, but I'd kill for a Sprite. Not 7-Up, but a Mountain Dew would work."

Things happened pretty quickly after that. Courtney was ready to push, Knox tried to glove up, and Bax banished him to the birthing ball in the corner where he couldn't break anything, touch anything, or say anything.

And then Courtney was a rock star in her own right as she brought their daughter into the world.

When it was all said and done, Brennan sent Knox to tell everyone that Harley was home. Then he climbed onto the bed and held his girls, pressing a kiss to Courtney's temple in a move that had become nothing out of the ordinary for them.

That was what made it even more extraordinary.

Happily ever after was not overrated, not one bit.

Epilogue
COURTNEY

"ARE YOU GUYS FOR REAL?" Courtney asked as Bax meandered toward her with infant Harley strapped to his chest.

Linx moseyed beside him with leather-jacket clad Gibson in a front pack as well.

Tanner had adopted an adorably goofy rottweiler named Lacey who was scared of her own shadow, and Mach walked alone like the badass rock star he was becoming.

Tanner had an issue talking to women—he always froze up. Mach? Not so much. That was why Mach had become nearly as popular as Bax used to be with the ladies, and that was saying a whole helluva lot.

"Are they always this goofy?" Irina asked, moving to stand beside Courtney at the end of Knox's front drive.

She and Becca and Courtney were helping Knox pick out new carpet colors. He'd really wanted to go with black, but Irina was working on gray. Courtney liked white, and Becca preferred whatever everyone could agree on.

Bax and Linx took the kid and the cat and the new rock stars for a walk with their dog, while everyone else argued.

"Is your guy sniffing your daughter's head?" Irina asked,

250

because Bax was, in fact, holding a thread to Courtney's gaze, while he inhaled Harley's baby scent.

He was addicted to their daughter.

Courtney was cool with this, because he was also addicted to her.

Funny, Courtney used to want a Mustang and the life that came along with it, but now she preferred the life she had.

Aside from Brennan and the baby and the pirate ship house, they'd finally scraped themselves clear of Em. She'd tied herself to the drummer for Blue Night. Poor guy, he had no idea what he was in for as her new rock star ATM.

"Brennan," Courtney said, sauntering toward him and reaching to push his sunglasses onto his head. "My Brennan."

He grinned at that—all rock star magic holding their baby.

"Courtney," he said, leaning in to brush his lips against hers. "My Courtney."

"I need everyone's attention." Knox clapped his hands, loud, from the door. "We have a major issue."

"Issues are opportunities," Courtney said, still staring into Bax's eyes as she spoke.

"I'm the asshole," Knox announced.

Okay, wha?

Courtney turned toward him, and he was not happy.

"We all already agreed on that," Bax said.

"No, the media says I'm the asshole because you two yahoos decided to fall in love and start making plans for families and shit. Tanner and Mach are the new generation—congrats, boys—and I'm the asshole who doesn't have a cat or a kid or a serious relationship. How are we going to fix this?"

Courtney glanced from Bax to Harley and then settled her gaze on Irina.

What if…

No, that was a ridiculous idea. But it could work…

"Irina, you're still searching for that big break?" she confirmed.

Irina had been flying to Denver between auditions to spend time with Courtney and Harley, but she also spent a good deal of time with Knox and Mach and Tanner.

"Always in search of that elusive break." Irina nodded.

"And in this industry, connections matter," Courtney continued, musing on her own thoughts.

Irina nodded again. "Bax posting photos of me on Instagram has been huge for my audition numbers, *and* I got the cat food commercial because of Linx."

"Hold up." Bax held up his hand. "I'm posting photos of you on social media?"

"I am." Courtney brushed off his question because none of the boys ran their own social media accounts—she did. "It's okay. All appropriate."

"What brand of cat food?" Linx asked. "Is it better than what I'm feeding Gibson now?"

Courtney shook her head and pursed her lips. "Everybody focus. I'm trying to craft a plan here."

"I just want the best for Gibson, you know?" Linx continued, like Courtney hadn't spoken. "If this food is better, I wanna know."

Courtney totally ignored her brother. "Irina, you don't hate Knox."

They actually got along pretty well, since they'd bonded over labor and delivery.

"No, but I do not like your tone right now." Irina squinted at Courtney. "You're cooking up an idea I'm not entirely sure will end with a cat food commercial."

"I am." Courtney nibbled on her bottom lip. "And it won't be a commercial—it'll end with a blockbuster."

"Oh." Irina's eyes got huge, and she clapped her hands softy in front of her face. "I like this idea already."

Probably because she hadn't heard it yet.

"I thought we were figuring out how to make me *not* the tabloid asshole?" Knox asked, elbowing his way into the semi-circle. "Because it's seriously stupid and untrue. I mean, I am an asshole, but not like that." Knox nearly stomped his foot. "Linx had perma-groupies in every city, and now he's great because he found Becca. Bax gave out bracelets to half the country, and he's fabulous because he's got you and a kid. Me? I'm a good boy with no worldwide groupie attachments, and I've never had to mark women with jewelry. Yet here I am... the asshole."

"How bad does this asshole thing bug you?" Courtney asked.

"What's your angle?" Knox asked carefully.

"You two get married." Courtney glanced between them. "Preempt all of us and our good publicity. Boom. Make Mach the new asshole." She gestured to Mach.

"I'm down with that." Mach nodded. "Can I get bracelets?"

"I could marry a rock star." Irina shrugged a shoulder. "As long as he has gray carpet in his foyer."

"Hah," Knox said. "Marry Tanner, then, because I'm going with the black carpet."

"Okay." Irina looked at Tanner. "You in on this? Knox'll still be the asshole, but it could work out for both of us?"

Tanner nodded and opened his mouth to say—

"Hold up." Knox slung his arm over Irina's shoulder. "I can make gray carpet work. But I'm doing black carpet in my bedroom."

"Fair enough, I have no plans to be in your bedroom." Irina smiled.

Was Courtney seeing things or did Knox frown at that?

Huh. That could be an interesting twist.

"Marriages of convenience have been used by publicists for generations in Hollywood. This isn't anything new," Courtney said, though she'd never coordinated one before.

"How are you going to propose?" Irina asked, eyeing Knox and crossing her arms.

"You're going to have to wait and find out." Knox turned on his heel and stomped up the stairs to his house.

"Am I still the new asshole?" Mach asked, more than a little excited.

Courtney nodded because it looked like things were about to get even more interesting for Dimefront.

Bax moved his face right up next to Courtney's, and with Harley strapped to his chest, he kissed her. "Do you want to preempt their marriage with one of your own?"

"Did you just propose to me?" Courtney tilted her head to the side.

Bax responded by singing her a song. If she were to guess, the title was "My Courtney" because that's how each refrain began. He told their love story in song and her heart swelled with love for this man of hers.

"You orchestrated this, didn't you?" Tanner stared at Courtney when the song was done. "The whole damn thing… You're like an evil savant who gets what she wants."

Well, she hadn't orchestrated the *whole* thing. The Harley-creation shower could never have been planned, but she'd sort of figured if Knox decided to get engaged, then it might give Bax a little incentive.

He dropped to his knee in the middle of the drive and pulled a massive diamond from his pocket. With Harley strapped to his chest, he was down on one knee, and butter-flies stormed her chest.

"Marry me?" he asked, holding the ring to her hand and already slipping it on her finger before she could even comprehend what had just happened.

"I'll always marry you, Brennan," she said as he stood, and she breathed in the scent of him and their daughter. The scent of happiness.

Tanner pointed at Courtney. "I think you're a witch."

"It's likely," she agreed, staring into Bax's eyes.

He pulled her to his side and held her there, pressing a kiss to the crown of her head. "But she's my witch."

"Always," she said, smiling up at him, over the moon with the man who had become her everything, and safe in the knowledge that she'd become that for him too.

There's more Courtney & Bax!

A special bonus scene Christina created especially for newsletter subscribers!

Claim the bonus scene at:
ChristinaHovland.com/knockedup-bonus

Acknowledgments

My kids and my husband are always supportive of my writing time. I am so grateful to them for understanding that doing what I love sometimes means I need to retreat into my stories.

Mom and Seren, as always, you are my rock star supporters. I love you both.

Thank you to my critique team and beta readers: Tara Wine-Queen, Serena Bell, A.Y. Chao, Dylann Crush, Patricia Dane, C.R. Grissom, Jody Holford, Diane Holiday, Deb Smolha, Renee Ann Miller, and Becky Wesnidge.

Thanks always to the fantabulous Dr. Victoria for always seeing to the medical needs of my fictional characters.

Emily Sylvan Kim and the team at Prospect Agency make my job a dream.

Holly Ingraham, I just adore you. Thank you for sticking with me.

Tiffany, thank you for the awesome copy edits!

Shasta Schafer, thank you for always being here for me and my characters.

Courtney, Dallas, Leeann, Lindsay, Sarah—thank you for being you.

Karie, thank you for being my best friend.

Kiele, thank you for being my person and the voice of reason I need in my life.

Denise Allen—my friend and supporter. Thank you so much for always seeing the best in me.

Thanks to the team at Audibly Addicted for the fantastic

narration and audiobook production. Kim, Mo, Rose Dioro and Jason Clarke—you are true rock stars.

And thank *you*, yes YOU, for reading my stories.

Also by Christina Hovland

The Mile High Matched Series

Rock Hard Cowboy, Mile High Matched, Book .5

Going Down on One Knee, Mile High Matched, Book 1

Blow Me Away, Mile High Matched, Book 2

Take It Off the Menu, Mile High Matched, Book 3

Do Me a Favor, Mile High Matched, Book 4

Ball Sacked, Mile High Matched, Book 4.5

The Mile High Rocked Series

Played by the Rockstar, Mile High Rocked, Book 1

Knocked Up by the Rockstar, Mile High Rocked, Book 2

Married to the Rockstar, Mile High Rocked, Book 3

From Entangled Publishing

The Honeymoon Trap

The Mommy Wars Series

Rachel, Out of Office

There's Something About Molly

April May Fall

Everything's Fine, Emmaline

About the Author

Christina Hovland lives her own version of a fairy tale—an artisan chocolatier by day and romance writer by night. Born in Colorado, Christina received a degree in journalism from Colorado State University. Before opening her chocolate company, Christina's career spanned from the television newsroom to managing an award-winning public relations firm. She's a recovering overachiever and perfectionist with a love of cupcakes and dinner she doesn't have to cook herself. A 2017 Golden Heart® finalist, she lives in Colorado with her first-boyfriend-turned-husband, four children, and the sweetest dogs around.

ChristinaHovland.com
  Twitter.com/HovlandWrites
  Facebook.com/HovlandWrites
  Instagram.com/HovlandWrites
  Goodreads.com/HovlandWrites
  bookbub.com/profile/christina-hovland

Enjoyed the Story?

**Turn the page for chapter one of
Played by the Rockstar!**

**He's a rock star.
She's a waitress.
He's about to rock her world.**

Certified behavioral counselor (and former band groupie) Becca Forrester needs a break. Taking a leave of absence from her job, she moves into the apartment over her parents' garage, and clinches a gig waitressing at a dive bar known for bringing in big name musicians.

Cedric "Linx" Lincoln is a certified rock star. Bassist for the hugely popular rock band, Dimefront, he's in Denver while the band is on hiatus a-freaking-gain. He's looking for something—anything—to keep him occupied until they can all get back to making music. When he saunters into his friend's bar, he finds the perfect diversion.

Becca's presence is a breath of fresh air. The sizzle she ignites in him is precisely what he needs. Bonus: no-stress, no-strings hookups are his specialty. But when things between them tip toward serious, his band implodes, and Becca's leave of absence ends, they're forced to decide what their "real" lives should look like. Maybe there's room for an encore...

Chapter 1

Becca

NEON BEER SIGNS totally signaled a new beginning. Sure, a girl might not think it possible, but Rebecca—Becca—Forrester was out to prove they could. The scent of hops and bourbon paired with the blast of music through the speakers and constant hum of life in the background at Brek's Bar in Denver, Colorado. Outside, the snow had turned to a slushy mess. Inside, the bar warmed her like she'd taken a shot of top-shelf whiskey.

Oh yes, this joint was the perfect place for a fresh start that did not involve anyone else or the baggage they dragged along with them.

"Why do you want to wait tables here?" Brek asked, giving a dose of emphasis on *here*. "I'd have thought you'd prefer some place with tablecloths."

Becca laughed. Brek was as biker as biker got—long hair, leather, and an abundance of tattoos. His wife was...not. She was a financial planner, and Becca's friend.

Becca shook her head. She definitely didn't want to wait

tables anywhere else. "I'm looking for the diviest dive I can find."

The idea to wait tables was a complete one-eighty from her recent past as a certified behavioral counselor, but she wouldn't go back. Not yet. Especially not when she was having a perfectly lovely time at the local go-to spot for great music in Denver, hanging with her friends, and harassing Brek into hiring her as a part-time waitress while she took a life break.

"Diviest dive? Well, I guess this is your place." Brek flashed her a smile.

"Exactly." Becca tucked a lock of her thick, brown hair behind her ear, where it belonged but never stayed. "Until I figure out what comes next for me."

"You can live the dream right here with me." Brek patted the bar top like it was a living, breathing thing. Something he adored.

Sigh. Someday she wanted someone to look at her like Brek looked at his wife and his bar top.

Not now. She was on a break from all of that—the relationships, the responsibility, everything—but, someday, the adoration thing would be fun to have, too.

He'd created the perfect dive bar atmosphere—neon lights on the dark wood over the bar with his name lit up in blue. The wood paneling covering the walls was new enough to make the place look well-kept but beat up enough that it didn't look like he had tried too hard. Aesthetically, nothing matched. Yet everything still worked together. The place was definitely Instagram-worthy.

The darkened room hopped in preparation for the band to take the stage. A vibe she loved pulsed through the air. That feeling right before music blasts and the lights come to life. Yep. This was exactly what she wanted for her present life: loud music and the familiar faces of the bar's regulars, with no further obligation for the mental or physical well-being for those around her.

Also, the best bands played at Brek's Bar. Sometimes, because he had the connections, Brek brought in huge names. Like *huuuge*. Waiting tables here was perfect for a recovering groupie on hiatus from life.

"You can start next weekend?" Brek asked.

"Next weekend would be perfection." Becca glanced at her friends, mingling across the room.

Then *Linx* entered Brek's Bar. Becca choked on nothing but air.

Linx. Walked. Through. The. Door.

Bassist for Dimefront. Hot as all hell. Heartbreak in leather pants when he took the stage.

She, on the other hand, was only hot when she wore a sweater. Definitely not heartbreak in any kind of clothing. Unless… Could a woman be heartbreak in yoga pants? She was sure that wasn't possible. She shook the thought from her head as he moved her direction.

Her mouth didn't just go dry; her entire body froze in time.

Tonight, he'd ditched the leather and wore shredded blue jeans instead. Lanky, with ridiculously long dark hair, stubble that was a half day away from being a full beard, and all the charisma of a man who could get tens of thousands of screaming fans on their feet with one chord on his guitar. He scanned the room like he owned the joint.

Brek may have owned the bar, but Linx owned the room.

"Looks like my current assignment is here," Brek said, offhand with a touch of growl.

"Linx is your assignment?" Okay, she tried to resist sliding her gaze back to Linx, but she failed. Every woman in the house got the Linx grin as he continued his slow saunter through the room.

"I'm his babysitter…" Brek said, glowering in Linx's general direction.

Crumpet crap-ola. Her blood seemed a whole lot thicker and her skin a whole lot thinner when he sauntered toward Brek… and her. The blue neon halo was a nice touch. Well done, universe. Well done, indeed.

She sighed because…. Linx.

All eyes were on him. Every woman in the room got a solid eye canoodle as he strutted right up to where she stood across from Brek. His eye canoodle could likely get a girl pregnant. She sucked in a breath and braced for her turn.

Linx moved less than an arms-length away, and her heart stuttered like he'd asked her to remove her panties. Surely, he wouldn't recognize her. It'd been years since they partied in the same circles.

She held her breath because she couldn't take the risk of his scent. Not because she had any special superpowers that involved scented rock stars—that she was aware of—but she knew he smelled amazing. Rock star heaven and concerts and something musky, like oak trees in the rain.

"Do you want me to wait for the drinks, or do you want to send them over when they're done?" Becca asked Brek, ignoring the fact that Linx was right-freaking-there doing some kind of intense handshake thing with him.

"You should definitely wait," Linx said, blasting her out of her knickers with that smile of his.

Yes, she often thought in British slang that she'd picked up one summer on a European Dimefront tour. She really took to their language choices. Refined, but still rather raunchy.

Like her. Rather, who she wanted to be.

She slid her gaze up the length of Linx—long and lithe. Not beefcake, but definitely built. He had more of a runner's build. Muscle and sinew, but not overdone.

He leaned against the bar top, a look of pure happiness on his face. This wasn't a cat's-got-his-cream smile. This was a cat's-about-to-play-with-his-dinner-before-devouring grin.

"Becca, this is Cedric," Brek said, slinging drinks like a pro.

Cedric?

Right. Sure, yes, she knew that was his given name. Cedric Sebastian, wasn't it? Last name was Lincoln, and all the original members of the band took a nickname that had an x at the end. Together, they made a triple-x, which they found hysterical, as pointed out in multiple Rolling Stone articles.

"Becca," Linx—er, *Cedric*—stretched her name across his tongue and played it like an instrument.

He held his hand out to her. *What to do? What to do?*

She could touch him. She should touch him. He was expecting her to touch him.

Do something already, Becca.

She was overthinking this way too much. So she gave him a solid handshake.

The way he squeezed her palm was nearly erotic. For no good reason, either. It was just a handshake. He didn't make any lewd gestures or anything.

Still, the bar seemed to zip to a pinprick and focus on Linx.

"Becca is a friend of Velma's." Brek tossed Linx a look like her dad used to give her when he thought she was going to use very poor decision-making skills.

Becca extracted her hand from Linx's grasp. She noted how he kept the touch for as long as she'd allow.

"I like Velma." Linx grabbed a pretzel from the bowl on the bar and flipped it into his mouth.

"I do, too." Brek continued working. "That's why I'm making it clear to you that *Becca* is a friend of *Velma's*. Which means stop looking at her like that."

"Like what?" Linx held up his hands.

"Like you want to make her Denver," Brek said with a growl.

What the heck did that mean?

Linx popped another pretzel into his mouth. Somehow, he chewed, smirked, and smoldered, all at the same time.

"She's not Denver. Denver is Denver. Becca is Becca."

Brek crossed his arms. "You and I need to discuss what you're allowed to do and not do while you're visiting."

Linx held his palm to his heart and wobbled dramatically. "I am offended."

For the record, he didn't sound offended.

"It's not visiting if I bought a house. That makes it my home," Linx said to Brek.

He bought a house in Denver? Huh.

Perhaps Becca wasn't the only one in the midst of reconsidering life choices.

"You *bought* a house in Denver?" Brek asked. "I thought it was a vacation rental."

"It was," Linx said with a shrug.

"The landlord was being a total dick about Gibson, so I made him an offer." Linx did the pretzel thing again.

"Who's Gibson?" Becca asked.

Not that she had any real reason to be part of the conversation, but Linx hadn't asked her to leave.

"His cat," Brek said, arms still crossed.

"He's more than a cat." Now Linx crossed his arms. "So what if I bought one little house so he has a place to live?"

Brek shook his head. "Whatever, man. You do you."

"That's my plan." Linx slid his gaze to Becca. "Unless Becca wants to sit here and have a drink with me? Then we can see what happens."

Linx gave her a charisma-soaked smile.

Ah. There it was, her eye canoodle. She felt that stare deep down in her soul.

Yeah. Total player.

A player who went through sex partners like they were potato chips. This was according to his bandmate, Bax, and general female knowledge when meeting a player of his magnitude.

Back when she'd followed Dimefront concerts she'd had her eye on Linx. Something about him was like a magnet, pulling her in his direction. She had wanted him. Full. Stop.

But Linx was bad news for her. He rocked a total love 'em and leave 'em vibe. The kind that made a girl like Becca—someone who tended to see only the good in people and, therefore, fall for the wrong men—step away. He had just the right amount of baggage for her to want to unpack. And he was exactly the type of guy to pick up those suitcases and leave town right after she committed to the unpacking.

So she kept far away from his wandering gaze, preferring to observe him in his natural rock star habitat, and not let her heart, or body, get involved.

Brek handed a bottle of Coors to Linx.

"I've actually…" Becca jerked her head toward her group of friends. "Got to get back."

"That's a drag." Linx shrugged and gave Becca an extra-long, excessively thorough glance.

She shouldn't have done it. But she did. Yes, she totally canoodled him back.

"Becca?" Brek's voice cut through whatever the heck was going on between the two of them.

Brek had, of course, known Becca during her groupie days. Back then, he'd managed Dimefront and she'd been a Ten, the pet name they called their groupies. The Grateful Dead had Deadheads, Justin Bieber had his Beliebers, and Dimefront had their Tens. She'd spent a summer being Queen of the Tens.

This was not something she shared regularly. With anyone. No one else in her real life knew. Not even her best friends. That summer had been her first attempt at a life vacation. And it'd worked. Lucky for her, Brek didn't, and she was quoting here, "Broadcast shit that wasn't his to tell."

She let out a long breath and turned to Brek. He glanced pointedly to the order he'd prepared.

"Thanks." She snatched the remaining drinks and—and this was the hard part—she walked away without looking back at Linx and his neon halo.

Enjoyed the sample?
Played by the Rockstar is Available Now!

Played by the Rockstar
Copyright © 2021 Christina Hovland
All rights reserved.